"Delightful . . . Honorable canines, good-hearted people, a serious discussion of current financial woes, and top-notch narration make for a surprisingly winning mix."

—*Publishers Weekly*

"Appealing . . . [and] expressive . . . the various plot lines, sub-plots, interrelated characters and unsolved murders will hold your interest."

—Bookreporter.com

Praise for
A Nose for Justice

"As is her wont, [Rita Mae] Brown creates well-drawn characters (human and quadruped), fashions a nifty plot and mixes in enough local color and history to make the read as educational as it is entertaining."

—*Richmond Times-Dispatch*

"[A] born storyteller . . . that rivals Agatha Christie or Isaac Asimov in sheer numbers of books and sustained quality—[Brown] just never wastes your time. This is a mystery novel that also illuminates a large social and political issue. . . . Good fun and good value, as always."

—*The Sullivan County Democrat*

"A hotbed of mystery and suspense . . . a humor-filled story that is loaded with quirky but loveable characters."
—Wichita Falls *Times Record News*

"The human and canine cast is strong and the whodunit exciting."
—*The Mystery Gazette*

"Strong-willed older women abound in Rita Mae Brown's novels. Now Brown . . . has created yet another character with a similar stamp in *A Nose for Justice* . . . [which] ends with a twist."
—*The Fredericksburg Free Lance–Star*

"*A Nose for Justice* is timely and thoughtful with characters expressing a variety of political and social opinions on a gamut of current issues . . . An entertaining read."
—Bookreporter.com

"Jeep, Mags, and their two dogs—King, a shepherd mix, and Baxter, a white-haired dachshund—also discover a really cold corpse and, among the bones, a nineteenth-century Russian 'Star of Guard' ring buried in Jeep's barn. . . . [T]he search for the skeleton's identity will keep most readers turning the pages."
—*Publishers Weekly*

MURDER
UNLEASHED

A Novel

RITA MAE BROWN

Illustrated by
Laura Hartman Maestro

BALLANTINE BOOKS • NEW YORK

Murder Unleashed is a work of fiction. Names, characters, places, and incidents either are the product of the author's imagination or are used fictitiously. Any resemblance to actual persons, living or dead, or locales is entirely coincidental.

2012 Ballantine Books Mass Market Edition

Illustrations © 2011 by Laura Hartman Maestro
Copyright © 2011 by American Artists, Inc.
Excerpt of *Fox Tracks* copyright © 2012 by American Artists, Inc.

Published in the United States by Ballantine Books, an imprint of The Random House Publishing Group, a division of Random House, Inc., New York.

BALLANTINE and colophon are registered trademarks of Random House, Inc.

Originally published in hardcover in the United States by Ballantine Books, an imprint of The Random House Publishing Group, a division of Random House, Inc., in 2011.

ISBN 978-0-345-51184-3
eISBN 978-0-345-53017-2

This book contains an excerpt from *Fox Tracks* by Rita Mae Brown. This excerpt has been set for this edition only and may not reflect the final content of the forthcoming edition.

Cover art: Jamie Warren-Youll

Printed in the United States of America

www.ballantinebooks.com

Ballantine mass market edition: October 2012

In memory of Doughboy, an American foxhound,
who brought wonderful, generous
Anne Fortune Henderson into my life

CAST OF CHARACTERS

Magdalena Reed, **"Jeep"**—Born into poverty in 1924, she's now one of the wealthiest women in Nevada. Always a trailblazer and a high-spirited lover of life, Jeep was a WASP (Women Airforce Service Pilot) in World War II. A lifetime of smarts, hard work, and a little luck has yielded her a comfortable life on her sprawling Wings Ranch, but dust doesn't settle on this octogenarian: when someone needs help, she's ready, willing, and able.

Magdalena Rogers, **"Mags"**—After the death of her parents, she was raised by her great-aunt Jeep and taught the importance of honest labor and common sense. Despite this, Mags toiled for years on Wall Street until her career as a stockbroker went down in flames. Far from being a freeloader, after returning impoverished to Wings Ranch at age thirty-two she's hard at work blazing a new path; it may be that her passion for revving car engines and a certain cop will help Mags find the fulfillment she seeks.

Deputy Peter Meadows, **"Pete"**—Reno police detective with a strong pitching arm and a good nose (for a human) for detecting the truth. Divorced from local TV reporter Lorraine Matthews, this tall drink of water has caught the eye of Mags, who thinks he's something special. A razor-sharp mind, a dogged devotion, and a rugged jaw are among Pete's notable qualities.

Officer Lonnie Parrish—Pete's twentysomething partner on the Reno PD, Lonnie is eager to learn the art of detection from Pete, though he's easily distracted by bacon cheeseburgers and beautiful women. Still, it's sometimes surprising what the kid picks up.

Barbara Gallagher, "Babs"—In her late forties and impeccably coiffed, she's the owner and chief broker of Benjamin Realty. Boldness, intelligence, and a "can-do" attitude have brought her business success and many admirers. Though hardly a political person, a heart of gold and a strong social conscience lead Babs to come up with innovative strategies to help her ailing community.

Howie Norris—Ex-v.p. of Reno National Bank, chairman emeritus of the city's annual Bus Expo, irascible Howie takes justifiable pride in the annual convention's rollicking, utterly eccentric bus parade. Howie's ranch is just four miles from Jeep's and the two go way back (and that means *way back*). A man with few enemies, it's hard to figure why anyone would sneak up behind him with a rock.

Donald Veigh—Unable to earn a working wage to pay for a roof over his head, he squats in an abandoned foreclosed house on Reno's Spring Street. The young man keeps an eye on his neighbors—both defensively and protectively. It's tragic to see a smart young person unable to get a job, yet Donald refuses to give up.

Michelle Speransky—The gorgeous and successful senior loan portfolio manager at Reno Sagebrush United, it may be that she understands the ongoing housing crisis better than anyone in Reno. Many seek Michelle's guidance, and Mags looks up to her.

Bunny Matthews—A fortyish hardworking employee of Silver States Resource Management (SSRM), Bunny has a sharp mind and great skills with a wrench, though he'd do well to keep his temper under control and his mouth shut. It just might be that the love of a kind woman could sand down those sharp edges.

Twinkie Bosum—Two years older than Bunny and his partner at SSRM, "there ain't nothing Twinkie can't fix," though it's no easy task keeping Bunny out of hot water.

Patrick Wentworth—You know the type: A local politico running for Congress, this blowhard's undisguised ambition and misguided crusades rub a whole lot of folks the wrong way.

Teton Benson—A disgraced rich boy, ex-thief, and ex-drug addict, he's got a penchant for bestowing lavish gifts on big-busted, inattentive strippers. When the going gets tough, Teton heads for the hills.

Lark XX—A hardworking employee at Reno's Black Box, she's kind to lovestruck Teton, but has plans to escape the topless life. Appearances deceive, as she knows, and if anyone fails to see the brains behind her more obvious assets—well, their mistake.

Tu'Lia—Most strippers are in it for the money, but Lark's best friend, the gregarious and ever optimistic Tu'Lia, craves the attention. Unfortunately, such an ardent desire for the spotlight can land a person in deep trouble.

The Deceased (or some of them)

Robert Dalrymple, "Bob"—Smart, but not smart enough, this ex-gambler and ex-banker was in his mid-thirties when a love of money led him to the wrong side of the tracks and a spectacularly bloody end.

Dorothy Jocham, "Dot"—With an exquisite eye and a great passion for art, Dot exposed Jeep to the finer things in life, artistic and otherwise. Jeep's greatly cherished life partner, Dot didn't live into the twenty-first century, though her loving presence and keen wit are dearly missed every single day.

Daniel Marks—An ex-fighter pilot, Jeep's other life partner died in 2001. A rough-hewn man who helped build a business empire with Jeep. Until the day he died this remarkable man revered Jeep and her huge capacity to love. When big-hearted people meet big-hearted people, amazing things can happen, and do.

The Saviors

King—A somewhat arrogant shepherd mix who thinks he knows best—as he often does. Handsome, strong, and frequently baffled by the foibles of humans, if Jeep would only let King sleep on her bed more often, life would be perfect.

Baxter—A Manhattan transplant to the Nevada desert, this pint-sized, wire-haired dachshund has managed to win King's respect after some not-insignificant friction. Unflaggingly loyal and brave, size doesn't matter—or so he tells himself.

Ruff—Hard to trust a coyote, but it turns out he's a fairly straightforward canine—as long as one steers clear of his bones. Also, Ruff's in possession of a valuable secret that a good many others would love to know.

Toothpick—You'd be timid and jittery, too, if you were homeless and starving. After tragedy strikes, the skinny Manchester Terrier is hoping for a miracle to save him, and hope's a powerful thing—for dogs, humans, and all animals.

CHAPTER ONE

Waiting for spring in Reno, Nevada, is like playing weather roulette. Just when you think the ball will drop on your lucky number, the winds pick up, the mercury plunges, and the odds turn against you one more time.

Tuesday, March 15 dawned promising, but that promise was soon dashed as low clouds rolled over the Peterson Mountains. Babs Gallagher—late forties, owner and chief broker of Benjamin Realty—drove past the Aces baseball park toward one of Reno's modest working-class neighborhoods. She noticed the darkening skies, flicked on the SUV's radio for a weather report, and instead heard an ad for a used-car dealer.

Like many other real estate agents, Babs had computer files chock-full of old, possibly expired listings. She had printed some out, and decided today to visit a neighborhood especially rife with them. As she was the listing agent, she wanted to see firsthand if there remained any hope of future sales. She could have sent out another agent from Benjamin Realty, but one of the reasons Babs had succeeded over the years was that she did her own homework.

Street after street of abandoned homes signaled the hard economic times assaulting her state. Nevada led the nation in foreclosures and unemployment, although sometimes it shared the dubious distinction of the highest unemployment statistics with other benighted states, such as Michigan.

While not a political partisan, Babs kept up with newsworthy events. Unlike the government in Washington, D.C., the state government of Nevada couldn't print more money. Nevada would need to be resourceful and make unpopular, unpleasant decisions if it was to crawl out of this economic morass.

She pulled over on Spring Street. Keeping her motor running to ward off the cold, she propped her folder onto the steering wheel and flipped it open to the first page: 267 Spring Street. There were a number of expired listings on this one block alone.

Buttoning her coat, and taking her folder of listings, she stepped outside into the chilly air. Walking up the sidewalk to the front door of 267, she noted that the real estate office's lockbox was missing. Gingerly, Babs tried the doorknob. The door opened.

Stepping inside, she was surprised. Even with the busted door, the interior remained in good shape. As she went room to room, she noted on her sheet that the appliances were missing. Other than that, nothing was destroyed. She flicked a light switch. Nothing. Tried a faucet. The water had been cut off.

Making a few more notes, she left, walking down the street to another expired listing. She passed empty house after empty house. Some were boarded up. No "For Sale" signs in what was left of these front yards. Other sellers and real estate agents had given up.

As she opened the door to 232—lockbox also missing from the doorknob—Babs heard someone in the kitchen.

"Hello," Babs called out, voice friendly.

A young man, perhaps twenty, stuck his head around the door then stepped into the living room. "Are you the owner? I haven't taken anything."

"No. I'm the real estate agent."

"Oh." Sandy-haired and slight, the young man wore only a sweater, inadequate against the cold.

"You have no heat?"

"No. There's no heat, electricity, or water. But it's better than sleeping on the street. Are you gonna throw me out?"

"No," she answered, unsure what to do. "How do you keep warm?"

He pointed to a small ceramic chimenea, an outdoor stove that he'd placed in the living-room fireplace. Focusing only on him, she hadn't noticed it before.

"At night I put wood in. Most everyone down here has something like this that they light up once the police patrols pass by. They don't usually come back after nine. So we start fires. It helps."

"Wouldn't it be easier to just put wood in the fireplace?"

"The ceramic holds the heat better." He smiled.

"Light?"

"An oil lantern. Smells a little."

"I see." She looked him in the eye. He looked like a decent enough guy. "How did you come to this?"

He shrugged. "I was working my way through UNR, lost my job and had to drop out. I couldn't get another job and I don't yet have my degree."

"I'm not sure it would help in these times." She held out her hand. "Babs Gallagher. I own Benjamin Realty."

"You're not throwing me out? Are you going to report me? The cops don't like squatters."

"Actually, I'd rather have someone inside the house who isn't destructive than for it to be empty. Here's my card."

"Thanks."

"How many people are living in the neighborhood?"

"I don't know. A lot of houses have somebody in them. Some have whole families." He paused. "If you go three blocks east it's full of crack dealers, meth dealers. I hope they don't move into our neighborhood. It's the end when they do."

"Yes." She hesitated. "Your name?"

"Donald Veigh."

She headed for the door. "I promise not to tell."

Once back in her SUV—a good vehicle in which to haul clients, especially if they were tall—she sat for a moment. Then she started the motor, turned the vehicle around, and drove to 141 Spring.

Again, the lockbox had been removed. Opening the door, Babs surprised a little girl, who was bundled up and riding a pink tricycle around the living room. The chill in this house was sharper than that in Donald Veigh's.

Smiling, Babs asked, "Where's your mommy?"

"Out. Who are you?"

"I'm Mrs. Gallagher. That's a nice tricycle."

"Uncle Bob bought it for me. I have lots of uncles. Do you?"

"I did." Babs's voice sounded soothing. "Are you here alone?"

"Mommy told me never to answer that."

"I see. Do you have any idea where Mommy is?"

"She's next door. She works there and I have to stay here while she works."

"I see." Babs walked into the kitchen. The child followed, nearly running her over.

The kitchen counter held bottled water neatly lined up, canned food, and a small camp stove. A skillet rested on the one burner.

A cooler was on the floor.

"Honey, when was the last time you ate?"

The little girl shrugged.

Babs then asked, "Are you hungry?"

The child, not fearfully but forcefully, replied, "Mommy told me never to take food from anyone."

"Your mommy told you some important things. I'll go next door and talk to her."

"She'll get mad."

With that warning in her ears, Babs left the little girl to her tricycle and walked across the denuded front lawn to the next house, which wasn't her listing. She noticed a few cars parked farther down the street.

She was going to knock on the door but then she thought better of it. Carefully, she opened the door. It was warmer in this house. Unlike Donald Veigh, whoever lived here wasn't worried about smoke. Perhaps they had made some sort of deal with the police.

Babs listened. The unmistakable sounds of sex filtered down the stairs.

Sighing, she let herself out. Maybe crack dealers hadn't moved in yet but other dysfunctions had.

She thought about the child in 141 and wondered if she should wait until her mother finished up and joined the little girl. She thought better of it. The child seemed fine, knew her mother was next door, and Babs had nothing to offer the little girl. Even if she'd bought food, the kid would not have eaten it. She seemed clear about her mother's orders.

Back in her car, she removed her coat and turned on the ignition. The heat was welcome.

If she reported these people, they'd be thrown out—and they'd go where? The shelters were jammed. They might be turned away, banished to the cold.

As numerous courses of action ran through her mind, she noticed several children coming home from school. She watched as they entered various abandoned homes. Opening a front door, a haggard mother hugged a boy with a heavy backpack.

How did these people survive? No water. No heat. No electricity. How did they bathe?

Donald Veigh had no furniture that she'd seen. Perhaps some of these people slept in beds, sat at kitchen tables.

How had it come to this? Who knew about this hidden segment of society, and more to the point, who cared?

For professional reasons, Babs worked hard to cultivate good relationships with bankers. She always tried to steer her clients toward the responsible banks but people, being who they are, jumped at low rates and low down payments without considering the fine print. Babs called those kinds of loans "Liar's Loans," because the loan officials making these offers invariably knew that sooner or later the mortgagee wouldn't be able to make their payment. Three missed payments and you're out.

What the banks had never foreseen was these same people, disenfranchised by these upside-down mortgages, simply walking into the bank and handing back the keys. There was no longer enough value in those homes to fight for ownership.

Still sitting in her SUV, Babs spotted the woman she assumed to be the tricycle child's mother in her rearview mirror. The woman left her place of employment and headed to 141. Of medium build, in her late twenties, she was raven-haired and attractive.

About to pull away from the curb, Babs stopped when a Silver State Resource Management truck rolled down the road. She put the car in gear and followed.

The truck stopped in front of a house with a blue door. The SSRM driver, Twinkie Bosum, got out.

She came up alongside and put down her passenger window.

"Twinkie."

"Babs. What are you doing out here?"

"Checking old listings."

"Hell, Babs, you can't even give these houses away."

Bunny Matthews, Twinkie's partner, got out and came over to Babs's window. "Hey, girl."

"Fellas, what are you doing here? I thought you'd be out in the county fixing things."

Twinkie took in a breath. "SSRM's let a lot of people go. We're all doing double duty now."

"Yeah, we do repairs like always but today we're down here cutting off water," Bunny grumbled.

"Guys, there are squatters with children in these places."

"Yeah, I know. Sucks." Twinkie spat on the ground.

"What would happen if you left the water on in a few houses?"

"We'd get fired," Bunny answered.

"Well, what if you turned on the water in a few houses, came back tomorrow and turned it off, then did the same at a few other houses? People could at least wash up."

"Babs, once that meter's running, SSRM knows where it is and how much water is being used," Twinkie said.

"Sorry to put you on the spot." She meant it.

"We don't like doing this. We don't care about cutting service in Cracktown." Bunny referred to the bad part of town. "But a lot of people in this neighborhood are just down on their luck."

"Whole nation's down on its luck." Twinkie sighed.

"You got that right, brother," agreed Babs. "My business is nowhere. Thank God, I put a little away, and you know what? I don't know when the good times are coming back." Babs shook her head. "Know one thing, though."

"What's that?" Twinkie leaned his arms on her windowsill along with Bunny.

"If this gets fixed, it will be because we fix it. Don't wait on Washington."

"I wish I had a solution." Twinkie smiled at Babs.

"Well, I'm getting one little idea and it's that I want to help these people get back on their feet and I want to restore value to these homes. That might be a good start."

"Let me know when you're ready." Twinkie reached over and touched her hand. "I'll help."

"Thanks. I'll keep you posted."

As Babs drove off, her emotions roiled. She truly did want to do something about this problem. If she didn't, who would?

The person who would have the best ideas, who very well might come up with a good plan, was Jeep Reed.

You could always depend on Jeep.

CHAPTER TWO

Legs crossed under her, Jeep watched the flames jump in Howie Norris's river-stone fireplace.

King, a German shepherd mix, stretched out at Jeep's feet. Zippy, a dark chestnut-colored Australian kelpie, sat next to Howie in his deep club chair.

Outside, a light snow fell. The sun had set a half hour ago, the dark sky deepening with the passing minutes.

Howie's house had been built about the same time as Jeep's, back in the early 1880s. Over the years both houses had expanded, a room here, a porch there, creating a wonderful lived-in feeling. Sometimes Jeep felt she heard those early voices whispering, but she kept the prospect of ghosts to herself.

Knowing each other since the fifties, Jeep and Howie had remained close. With Ronnie, Howie's wife, having passed away two years ago, Jeep made a point of weekly visits to see how he was, to check the place out, and to make sure all was well. If a big job needed doing she'd send her ranch crew over to do it, despite Howie's protests.

They talked on and on, laughing as only two people who adore each other can. What richness there was in a friendship nudging six decades. Jeep's memories of Howie harkened back to when she was trying to make a go of it after World War II. He was young and finding his way also.

"Is he buying any?" Howie, a cattleman like Jeep, asked about her adopted son's trip to Sheridan, Wyoming, to look at the red Angus.

"He is. Enrique's buying twenty-five head to start. You know me, I love my Herefords. I know the horns are a problem. People always tell me I need Polled Herefords but I love the true old Hereford, have since I was a kid. They are the sweetest cattle, I love being around them. 'Course you have Baldies—good, good cattle." She complimented his choice.

Baldies were Angus crossed with Polled Herefords. They were popular across the United States, bringing good prices at auction.

Jeep didn't like black cattle in hot climates. She was out of step with most of the country on this. Even in the American South people thought black cattle were better. She didn't understand why.

The heat kept the meat-to-bone ratio down, plus it was harder to keep fat on them. It's fat that makes meat taste delicious and makes all those uptight dietitians self-righteous—they're all for low fat.

"He's a good hand with cattle, your boy."

"Dot and I sent him to college thinking he might go into medicine or law. He was bright enough. He majored in agriculture and he's doing what he loves. I don't think Enrique could sit behind a desk any more than I could. You know, Howie, if more people worked at what they loved we'd have far fewer problems."

He lifted his shoulders slightly. "But they can't. Our economy is geared toward sedentary jobs. I hardly think most young men and women want to park their butts in front of a computer in a cubicle in a bland office in a city. How can you be young and alive and want that? I sure as hell didn't. When I got back from Korea, I just wanted to run cattle. But Ronnie said I'd learned so much as a quartermaster, about finding supplies, delivering them, locating quarters, that I should go into banking. Ronnie figured if I could do all that, banking would be easy. She'd run the cattle and I could ride with her after work and on weekends. She was right. I did pretty good at Reno National, though I was glad to get out. I always felt most alive, happiest, in the saddle, moving the herd or cutting one out. I'd be a richer man if I'd stayed in banking every time we merged, but Jeep, I hated it. If I sat in a bank meeting today and talked about the character of a loan applicant I'd be laughed out of the room. I prefer ranching."

"Me, too. Well, ranching and flying. I dream about the cockpit, those big Flying Fortresses. I'm always on my way to the airbase in Montana to leave the bombers for the Russians. Isn't it funny the tricks your mind plays on you when you sleep?"

He laughed. "Mine does it even while I'm awake." He sat up straighter, animated. "You know what I can't get out of my mind these days?"

"Couldn't say." She grinned at him.

"The Garthwaite treasure."

She touched her silver hair for a moment with her right hand. "I believe it exists. In fact, I have no doubt. It's written about in the Fords' scrapbooks."

"The Garthwaites stole from the Fords, from everyone, I reckon," he said.

The Ford brothers had built the house Jeep lived in. The original ranch spanned three thousand acres. Jeep bought it, renamed it Wings Ranch, and added onto the original holding. It now covered a glorious ten thousand acres.

"The Fords were certain Hank and Bertie Garthwaite had stolen a payroll saddlebag. That would have been greenbacks. But the Fords couldn't prove it."

"Well, we know for sure that those Garthwaites killed the president of Sunrise Mine, walked off with what was in that vault, and lifted a bag of gold and silver ingots, as well," said Howie. "Then they went to my old bank, Reno National. Given that Winston Froling, the president of the bank, and his assistant were still counting deposits, no one really knows how much they got away with. Killed the assistant, too. Three men shot to death."

"I always thought they might have hid it in an abandoned mine around here," Jeep said.

"But there're no abandoned mines on Peterson Ranch." Howie's ranch was named for the Peterson range in full view.

"Not that you know of," Jeep answered.

"I know every inch of this ranch." Howie puffed out his chest. "And so did Ronnie. We never found anything that looked like a mine shaft. They captured Hank in San Francisco, living high on the hog. He wouldn't tell where he and his brother had hidden the money, raw silver and silver bars, too, except he never denied hiding out at Peterson Ranch. He killed himself in prison. They never found Bertie. Hank said Bertie took some of the loot and took off for Brazil."

"I've got all those old newspaper articles," Jeep said. "Like so many things, it's a fascinating mystery. Like the skeleton we found in the old barn. Eventually we found out he worked for Buffalo Bill."

"You still wear his ring."

"I do. Brings me luck, I think."

Jeep held up her left hand, on which was the ring from the St. Nicholas School of Cavalry, St. Petersburg, Russia. Jeep smiled and said, " 'Course if it is found, part of it may belong to me. A saddlebag full of money."

"Well, depends on which saddlebag," said Howie. "Some will be the banks' and some will be the Fords'."

"If that treasure's found, I'll bet you one good heifer that the Ford saddlebags have their brands on them." Jeep's expression suggested she was quite sure about this.

"It's a bet." He smiled.

As he walked her to the front door, she said wistfully, "I worry about you, Howie. I've got Enrique, Carlotta, and now Mags, but you're here all alone."

"I've got Zippy."

"I'm good company." The medium-sized dog wagged her tail.

"Zippy's a wonderful friend." Jeep smiled. "I think love is the wild card of existence. Don't rule it out. Old as we are, it may still get thrown on the table."

He smiled back. "Could be, could be, but with you, I don't know if it would be a king or a queen."

She laughed. "I never did care. I think of the body as an envelope for love. Well, Howie, the odds may be against us, but you never know."

"It's better that way." He kissed her cheek as she stepped out onto the porch with King at her side, snow-flakes swirling.

Three blocks away, in what Bunny Matthews dubbed Cracktown, Deputy Pete Meadows and his partner, Lonnie Parrish, pulled up to an abandoned house: 93356 Yolanda Street. Unlike Spring Street's abandoned houses, these homes bore testimony to hard use.

An anonymous call had brought them here. All that the muffled voice had said to the person at HQ was, "You'll find blood at 93356 Yolanda Street."

The street bore no signs of life. No cars were parked by the sidewalk. The Washoe County sheriff's men parked, pulled their pistols, and approached the cedar-lined house.

Pete turned to nod at Lonnie, who stood behind him, as he knocked on the door.

"Sheriff's Department," Pete announced. He stood to the side of the door in case anyone tried to shoot through it.

No reply.

Cautiously, Pete swung open the door, again flattening himself against the outside wall.

No bullets. No sound.

The two men, senses razor sharp, crossed the threshold—Pete first, Lonnie behind.

A small entry hall led to a living room, where the two young police officers saw a man's body: hands tied at the wrist behind his back. Feet tied also. He'd been gagged, his throat slit. A giant pool of blood had soaked the cheap wall-to-wall carpet.

They bypassed the corpse, checking the rest of the house for anyone else, dead or alive. Garbage littered the floors but the place bore no signs of recent inhabitation.

Once each room and all the closets were checked, they opened the back door and surveilled the yard. Again, no one.

Slipping guns back into their holsters, they returned to the body. The blood was still congealing. He hadn't been dead too long.

"Guess they killed him here." Lonnie checked for ID.

"Looks that way." Pete knelt down, slipping a bit in the blood.

"Whoever slit his throat found out it's more difficult than you think." Lonnie observed the ragged cut.

"No sound. A gunshot might have drawn attention," Pete noted.

"Well, somebody knew what was going down or we wouldn't have gotten the call," Lonnie said. "Think this is the start of another drug war?"

"I hope not. He's in his midthirties. So if it is a drug beef, he's way above being a runner." Pete stood up and called HQ on his cell.

"Deputy Meadows and Officer Parrish. We answered a call for 93356 Yolanda Street. Victim is white, male, midthirties, dead for perhaps two hours, if that. Send in the team."

After a few more words with the dispatcher, he cut off his cell.

"There's no sign of drugs."

"Well, they wouldn't be stupid enough to kill him where they do business. No smell." He inhaled deeply. "I can sometimes smell the stuff."

"Yeah. Meth kind of bites your nose." Lonnie stood

up. "Wonder if they can trace the call that came in from the tipster."

"I doubt it. Probably when we check it out it will be one of those cheap cellphones people buy and throw away. Whoever called this in has their own agenda."

"Right." Lonnie shivered. "Cold in here."

"Sometimes I think spring will never come." Pete smiled. "But I'll play baseball even if it snows."

"You guys start practice already?"

"Next week. I've been running, though. Three miles a day plus my gym workouts." Pete's head turned as he heard backup arrive out front.

Lonnie opened the front door and tried to sound like the voice-over for a documentary. "The crime team has arrived at the scene of the murder."

"I'm guessing he doesn't have drugs in his system," Pete said. "The smart ones never take it."

"He can't be that smart. He's dead."

CHAPTER FOUR

The glow from the fireplace in Jeep Reed's living room cast soft light on the beautiful paintings throughout. Jeep could take no credit for acquiring them. Her late partner, Dorothy Jocham, wisely acquired Remingtons and Charles Russells while everyone else was buying up Impressionists for a lot more money. Dot had also turned what looked like a barracks into a home.

Jeep, a flier for the Women Airforce Service Pilots, lacked any sense of domesticity. She lacked little else. Born dirt-poor in 1924, she made a fortune in mining after World War II, still holding a thirty percent interest in that first mine. She made another fortune in salvage with her male lover, Danny Marks, who'd flown P-47s in the war.

Jeep had juggled two lovers, a big career, and a lively interest in protecting Nevada's harsh but fragile environment. Never one for convention, she acted as Danny's best man when he finally married, ultimately understanding that Jeep could be a lover but not a wife. It all worked out just fine. But now only Jeep was left with the memories and a resolve to continue to live in a way both Dot and Danny would admire. She never forgot her friends, dead or alive.

Babs Gallagher grew up knowing Jeep, who had been a good friend to her parents. Sitting on the sofa with the fit old lady was Magdalena Rogers—her great-niece, called Mags—as well as King, the shepherd mix, and Baxter, Mags's wire-haired dachshund.

The three women spanning two centuries and three generations sipped tea, coffee, and nibbled at cookies while Babs told Jeep and Mags what she'd seen.

"A child alone and a mother turning tricks in the next house." Jeep exhaled forcefully. "That's a hell of a way to grow up."

"She was a tough little chick." Babs smiled.

"She'd have to be." Mags, a beautiful woman of thirty-four, smiled, too.

"If I call child services, they'll take the kid away from the mother. While there was no electricity, heat, or water, she seemed well cared for, under the circumstances. And Jeep, there are more children in those homes. I just hope all their mothers aren't turning tricks."

"It's so odd to me that prostitution is legal in Nevada but illegal in Washoe County," commented Mags. She'd come to stay with her great-aunt after her career bottomed out on Wall Street.

"Not so odd." Jeep reached for a chocolate chip cookie. "Some states have wet and dry counties. Leave it to the locals. In fact, it's a good idea for so many issues." She looked up at Babs, sitting in a leather chair, the frame of which was made out of longhorns from cattle.

Dot had just about died when Jeep bought those chairs, but she had wisely shut up. Jeep had taken only a sporadic interest in the interior of the house, which Dot said she always wanted.

With her frosted blonde hair impeccably coiffed, Babs measured her words. "You taught me, along with my parents, to create situations where divergent and competing interests can have singular beneficial interests."

"Thank you, Babs."

"So I've tried to come up with something along those lines. Clearly, having children in a cold house without services is not in the best interest of those children or of Washoe County. I would think that's obvious."

"I agree." Jeep nodded as King put his head on her lap and closed his eyes.

"Okay, here's what I think. It's a raw idea and will need tweaking. I'd like to approach SSRM, the power company, and the bottled gas companies to restore services to those homes. If they hired some of these people, say in warehouse jobs, that's another step. We can start a campaign to hire the adults, provide some kind of care for the toddlers—the bigger kids are in school—and as the people begin to earn wages the banks who now own these properties could grant low-interest mortgages. That would bring a little bit of revenue to the county since the homes are occupied and it's better than banks being in the real estate business. They know nothing about real estate"—she paused—"obviously."

"Well"—Jeep considered this—"that's the truth. The hardest part, I think, will be convincing the water company, the power company, and the gas company to turn services back on."

Mags had a good head for business, even if she had been sidetracked by the bad dealings of the leadership in her huge brokerage house. "Unfortunately, we can't ask them to put these services back on at a lower rate. Everybody will scream about that. They'll want a lower rate, as well."

"Can't blame them." Jeep was intrigued by this problem.

"But we can possibly get them food for less." Mags, green eyes enlivened, was also being drawn in.

"My acres won't be productive until fall harvest and the first harvest often isn't that good." Jeep was irrigating one thousand acres of her contiguous ten thousand acres to be used to grow food that would be sold cheap, locally, removing the middleman. This was her new pet project.

"The churches could help with food," Babs offered.

"And so can the casinos. But here we have another problem to circumvent. Regulation. So much good food is wasted, both in those casino refrigerators and at the supermarkets. Somehow we have to get those foods that are near their sell-by date to the people. This will take some thought." Jeep was not a woman to be deterred by regulations she thought foolish, and she thought most of them were.

"Where do we start?" Babs threw up her hands.

"Actually, Babs, we start on Spring Street. You, myself, and Mags need to talk to people there. I expect they'll be reluctant. Why should they trust us? We could be part of some government agency, all that crap."

"We take the dogs." Mags smiled.

Baxter sat up. *"I can convince them you're okay."*

King opened one brown eye. *"Ha. You look like a fuzzy muffler pipe."*

Baxter refrained from a comeback. No point starting a fight when there's company.

"Well, why not? Children love dogs and I have yet to see any government official paying calls with dachshunds." Babs smiled. "Mags, I am so glad you left Manhattan."

"I'm glad to be home with Aunt Jeep," Mags diplomatically replied, for she still sometimes missed the excitement of New York City. "She took me in and gave me a second chance."

"Tosh." Jeep waved her hand. "I raised you since you were in ninth grade. This is home." Then she looked at Babs. "Mags didn't trust her instincts. That's a lesson we all learn sooner or later. I want you to know she gets food and shelter, but she has to make it on her own. No point in crippling initiative."

"You never have." Babs smiled and while she thought Jeep right she also thought perhaps a bit of coddling might not be out of order.

Babs then addressed Mags. "I could pay you for your time."

"Never," Mags quickly responded. "Aunt Jeep gave me her old Chevy 454 truck. I have a part-time job Tuesdays and Thursdays. And I hope to start school in the summer. I'll be a plus, not a minus."

"I have no doubt," Babs sincerely replied.

Jeep held up her forefinger. "I'll speak to my priest at Trinity Episcopal. You speak to yours. A shot of church people delivering cartons of food will help, too, if we can get the media interested. We've got a lot to do. When do you want to go to the houses?"

"How about this weekend when the children will be home? The dogs will be more effective then."

"*Yes,*" Baxter said enthusiastically.

As they walked her to the front door, Babs smiled. "Thank you for taking the time, Jeep. It's wonderful to see you, to be back at the ranch. This place has so many happy memories for me. You, Dot, Mom, and Dad sitting on the porch. Enrique and me riding the horses. Weren't those lovely days?"

"They were. They were. Let's make some new memories."

"Indeed." Babs leaned down and kissed Jeep on the cheek.

"I'll encourage you with what I used to tell my copilot, Laura, when we'd crawl into the cockpit: 'Tits to the wind!' "

CHAPTER FIVE

On Saturday, March 19, Jeep, Mags, King, and Baxter met Babs at 232 Spring Street. Clear, crisp, light winds washed over Reno.

The three women disembarked from two vehicles, the two dogs on leashes.

"All things being equal, it doesn't look too run-down," Jeep observed.

"Not yet, which is exactly why I still have some hope for this area." Snug in an Austrian boiled-wool jacket and a long wool skirt, Babs led them to the door.

She knocked. "Mr. Veigh, it's Babs Gallagher."

They heard footsteps, the door opened a crack.

Donald Veigh couldn't imagine what three women and two dogs wanted from him but as one of the women was quite beautiful he invited them in.

"Hello." Baxter waved his tail.

Donald bent over to pat his head.

"No food smells," King noted.

"Ladies, I don't have anywhere for you to sit."

"That's fine. This is Jeep Reed and Mags, her great-niece. We've stopped by to let you know we're hoping to get services restored and see if we can't interest some companies in hiring."

This surprised him. "I can't pay for anything and I don't think anyone else can, either."

"We know that." Jeep smiled. "We think if some em-

ployment can be found, those utilities will work out
something along with the banks, so you all don't lose
your shelter."

Bowled over by their generosity, he asked, "What can
I do?"

"Do you have a cellphone?" Babs asked.

"I do."

"If you give me your number I can call you and keep
you informed. This isn't going to happen overnight but
the three of us will push hard."

As Donald looked at this unlikely trio, Mags gave
a megawatt smile. "Never underestimate the power of a
woman."

He smiled back. "Not me."

"We know the people in these houses won't trust us.
We're going to knock on doors and try to talk to them.
Do they know you?" Babs asked.

"Some do."

"Would you take us to them?" Jeep asked.

"All right. Let me get my coat." He disappeared into
the kitchen and returned wearing an old flannel-lined
barn jacket.

Together the four of them walked house to house.
Mostly women answered the doors, and when children
saw the dogs they rushed forward despite their mothers'
entreaties. Many of the houses' occupants had either lost
their money gambling or worked in the casinos and lost
their jobs in the severe economic downturn—gambling
had been hard hit. Most people don't gamble if they're
broke or close to it.

As they worked their way down Spring Street, the
women began to understand how very many people had
sought shelter in these homes.

One place had two brothers living there, their ages
hard to tell—somewhere between forty-five and sixty.
They did not appear to be in the best of health. Fearful

and highly suspicious, the only reason the women managed to get into their house was that King opened the door, which had a handle lock.

"These are my people!" A medium-sized keeshond faced off the two dogs and three women.

"We're here to visit," the imposing King said.

"Tookie, that's enough," commanded Mike, who was swathed in layers of old sweaters.

Tookie sat down, shut up, and cast a baleful eye at King and Baxter.

"Who the hell are you?" asked skinny Milton, the elder brother, his face covered with gray stubble.

"I could ask the same of you." Jeep fired right back.

The two dogs stood on either side of Jeep, just in case.

"We're here to see if we can get work for people on Spring Street," Babs said smoothly.

"I live here, too," Donald added. "Just up the block."

"Oh." The shorter brother, Mike, grunted. "Don't recognize you."

" 'Cause you don't have your glasses on Mike," Milton said.

Unrolled sleeping bags lay in front of the fireplace. A couple of wooden crates passed for chairs. That was it.

"Our jobs program may well take us some time but if you have special skills, please tell us," Mags chipped in.

"Welders. We used to be welders," Mike said with pride. "We could weld in our sleep. We worked with Aaron Wentworth. His kid's the one making all the noise about"—Mike shrugged—"stuff."

Milton added, "Aaron's a good guy. Least that's how I remember him."

Warming up to the dogs, Tookie piped up, *"Mike has epilepsy. I tell him and Milton when he's going to have an attack."*

"That's important." Baxter praised Tookie.

"Sometimes they don't eat but they always feed me. I'd give them my food but they wouldn't eat it."

"Humans are so fussy," King said, recognizing how much the two old men loved Tookie.

The brothers' reticence wore off. They rarely talked to women, but soon the stories poured out. With effort, the foursome left, but not before Jeep gave them fifty dollars, since it sounded like Mike had bronchitis.

"For meds," was all she said.

House after house bore the same story: cold, sparse furniture, camp stoves, and firewood.

The dogs worked their magic.

Not everyone was friendly. At some houses, people ran out the back doors. Jeep figured those were illegal immigrants. She had no answer for this problem, but she didn't think anyone should go cold and hungry, no matter where they came from.

Finally they reached 141 Spring Street.

The little tricycle girl recognized Babs. "Doggies!" she exclaimed after opening the front door.

Her mother hurried out from the kitchen.

"Tomato soup." King inhaled.

"I met your daughter a few days ago." Babs held out her hand and the pretty young woman shook it. She introduced herself as Irene.

Once again, they repeated why they were there and Donald, who didn't know this block very well, told Irene where he lived.

Nobody mentioned how Irene, she gave no last name, was making ends meet—literally.

A fleeting look of hope passed over the young woman's face at the prospect of employment. She said she could read and write and she had worked as a greeter in a casino but had gotten laid off. As a single mother she couldn't take work without help for CeCe, the little girl. Jeep, again, gave money.

Finally, after they'd canvassed three blocks, Babs drove Donald back to his house, thanking him and paying him for his time.

He gratefully accepted the money.

Afterward, Babs met up with Jeep and Mags in a small parking lot on Sixth Street.

"What do you think?" Babs asked Jeep and Mags.

"We should start small," Jeep said. "Stick to the three blocks we've canvassed. The first thing is to feed them. Then what we've got to do is get those services turned back on. This won't be easy."

"Between us and our friends, we can work on food," said Babs. "The utilities will take combined effort and not a small amount of pressure. It will take time. I hate to think of those people still cold."

"After seeing what I've just seen, I understand why you couldn't walk away from this," Jeep said. "Now I can't, either."

"Or me," Mags echoed.

"*I go wherever you go,*" Baxter added.

"*Me, too.*" King's deep voice rumbled.

For the rest of the day Jeep and Mags called on people they thought might help. They were gratified at the response of the various priests, pastors, and preachers. None of them were sure as to how to best approach the utilities, but all promised to deliver food cartons.

As they drove under the entrance to Wings Ranch, the crossbar at the top of the high entrance gate bearing the propeller of a P-47 and a small sprig of evergreen, Jeep, Mags, and the dogs were exhausted.

Once inside, Mags warmed up the casserole that Carlotta, Jeep's daughter-in-law, had left for them. Jeep fed the dogs.

"I don't know why I'm so tired," Jeep complained.

"I am, too. Talking to so many people wears you out."

"But you had to talk to people when you worked on

Wall Street." Jeep poured warm broth on King's kibble and then Baxter's, the two dishes placed at opposite ends of the large kitchen.

"Phone or email. I preferred the phone, though. Got a better sense of the person on the other end of the line. But this, in and out of the truck, driving from church to church . . . Lucky we have cellphones so you could call ahead." Mags inhaled Carlotta's cooking. "Smells good."

"Carlotta is just the best cook, I wonder that I'm not fat as a tick."

"You never sit still." Mags set the table.

"Better to wear out than rust out. You know, Saturday is the best day to visit the clergy because they're working on their sermons."

"Never thought of that." Mags folded a linen napkin. "I can't imagine giving a speech a week."

"If you follow the ecclesiastical calendar you won't run out of topics. The big question is whether they can deliver a sermon without being boring."

"Ever notice how preachers and politicians get this singsong cadence to their voices? Most seem so fake," Mags noted shrewdly.

"I turn right off when I hear that." Jeep changed the subject. "Here we are about to eat a wonderful meal and I keep thinking about those people who don't have enough to eat. I bet half the time they do eat the food isn't even hot."

Mags dished out the chicken casserole and sat down. "I know. I feel bad and I shouldn't. I didn't do it."

"In a way, we did. We've allowed individual responsibility to be subsumed by government. I mean, I hate it, but that's the way things have drifted since the thirties, I guess. Those people on Spring Street lost their jobs. I doubt many of them are well educated. Most Americans don't even see what you and I saw today, except maybe on TV. But things seem far away on TV. Maybe that's another reason that personal responsibility has eroded."

Mags savored Carlotta's dish. "I feel guilty eating this, but what good does it do for me to go hungry?"

"Doesn't. You have to keep your strength up. The war taught me that. Remember when you first came back here right after Thanksgiving and I told you I wanted to cultivate some of my land, grow food, and sell locally? If you're well fed, you can think, you have energy and hope. What are the basics of life? Food, water, clothing, and shelter. No one in our country should be denied those things, but I don't think it's the government's job to provide it. Therein I differ from many. It's our job! The churches, the businesses, we can take care of our own. Just think, if every church pledged to feed even one hundred people in its parish, or district, wouldn't that go a long way? Every time you rely on government, the money sticks to hands as it's passed along."

"I'd like not to believe you but I don't know anymore. The sight of those children, some of them didn't have enough clothes but they were as clean as possible. I can't imagine how those mothers struggle."

"We'll do what we can. Anything is better than nothing."

Mags changed the subject. "How about the red Angus cattle Enrique is looking at in Wyoming?"

"He loves them." Jeep smiled.

They chatted, finished up, washed the dishes, and retired to the living room to watch the news.

Patrick Wentworth, a local politician running for Congress, was being interviewed by a reporter. Behind him, Cracktown looked desolate and dangerous.

"There was a murder here on Wednesday. The police haven't one suspect. This is intolerable. Reno deserves better." Patrick's voice vibrated with righteous wrath.

"Dammit to hell." Jeep cursed.

"The authorities believe it may be a gangland murder," the TV reporter said.

"Where's the suspect?" said Patrick. "This is about drugs. Drugs fuel violence. Look at Mexico. Will Reno turn into another Juárez?"

"Now there's a big leap of reason." Mags tucked her feet up under her. Baxter jumped onto the sofa.

Patrick Wentworth roared on until the three-minute segment was over.

"Boy, they sure gave him a free pass," Jeep said.

"I hope this doesn't hurt Pete. He and Lonnie were called to that scene."

"I remember, you told me. What worries me, apart from the fact that I hope Mr. Clean doesn't name the officers, is that Cracktown isn't all that far from Spring Street."

"Violence?" Mags's eyebrows arched upward at the question.

"That, and how long before this lame-brained politico starts pointing the finger at all abandoned areas? You get the idea?"

"I do."

"It's endless campaigning. Have you noticed? If this bozo gets elected to Congress, he has two years. He'll pretty much get his office established and he'll be running for the next two years. It's destructive to all of us."

"Raising the money alone for a campaign is exhausting."

"How come you aren't out with Pete tonight, to shift gears?"

"He had to work today. We're going to dinner tomorrow. Sometimes I think about all the terrible stuff he sees. I couldn't do it."

"That reminds me of something Danny said after the war. He felt no guilt because he was a fighter pilot. The fellows I knew who were infantrymen or on destroyers felt no guilt, but the bombers felt guilt. Danny would mention that sometimes. He always said he was glad he didn't have to drop bombs. He saw his enemy. The thought of killing civilians upset him. Pete sees a different kind of destruction. It appears individual but it's always tied to larger issues. At least Pete isn't killing large numbers of people."

"He just has to find the bodies that others have killed," Mags replied.

CHAPTER SIX

Running cleared her mind and awakened all her senses. Mags had gotten into the habit back in Manhattan, running at five or five-thirty in the morning with Baxter. Then at night after work, walking the little guy two more miles kept both their minds and bodies sharp.

Gliding along Dixie Lane on a Sunday morning, heading south, the creek to her left, she breathed in the frigid air at 31°F. Baxter and King loped along, little puffs of steam coming from their mouths.

Thanks to the snow this winter, the creek was running higher. Its banks were almost vertically sloped in some places, four feet deep at the most. In other spots, the grade was gradual. Mags didn't know the land as well as she might have. Aunt Jeep had taken her in, and her sister Catherine, after their parents were killed in a car wreck. As soon as Mags graduated high school, she hastened away to college. Her sister, two years older, also left Nevada. Catherine's progress was quite different from her younger sister's. She wound up in porn films where she made a lot of money before burning out on drugs. Mags, a hot trader in commodities, went down in flames with many others when the market crashed. Both sisters had succeeded and failed quite spectacularly.

Mags was putting herself back together. Catherine still believed she could be a legitimate movie star. Unfortunately, she couldn't act with her clothes on. Worse, she'd tried to break Jeep's will so Enrique wouldn't inherit as much of the estate. This had so enraged Jeep that she threw Catherine out of her will and out of her life. The estate would now pass to Enrique and Mags, not that Mags counted on that. She'd make her own money her own way, and when the time came she hoped that Enrique and she could, together, wisely manage her great-aunt's vast resources.

Looking up, she noticed snow swirls on top of the Peterson range. Spring didn't come to Reno any faster than it did to New York, but still the sight of more snow coming their way on March 20 was depressing.

The unpaved, hardpacked road proved easier on her legs than macadam or asphalt. The two dogs preferred this surface, too. Sometimes asphalt got slippery. The dogs dug in with their claws and then later had to pick the black bits out. Tasted awful. Dirt was better.

Mags turned, heading back toward Wings Ranch. Traffic was a rarity on Dixie Lane. Even once out on Red Rock Road, twisty in parts, one could run in relative peace. The road clogged up for the morning and evening commute, as Reno was eleven to twenty miles south depending upon how far out one lived, but still it was pleasant enough.

A wet snowflake landed on her nose. Then another. Within minutes, visibility diminished.

"Remember, she can't smell the snow, can't retrace what scent we've left to get back home," Baxter reminded King.

The bigger dog replied, *"Good eyes. Humans can see through this. It's not that bad yet."*

Mags's long stride came up on the gateway within ten minutes. She looked up to see the evergreen sprig behind the P-47 propeller. When spring finally arrived, her aunt would have the propeller taken down, cleaned, put back up, and a new evergreen sprig placed behind it. Another thing that she claimed brought her luck. Given her long life and talent for making money, she might be on to something with her superstitions.

Mags sprinted toward the porch, a half mile down the road. She could hold it together for a quarter of a mile but a half mile tested her. For the dogs, this was effortless but people were terribly slow.

She reached the porch steps, stopped, and bent over to catch her breath. Then she put her foot on the lowest step, slipping a bit. She grabbed the railing and quickly got up under the roof overhang. The wraparound porch offered extra protection to the house, which faced west, plus it was perfect to sit on when the weather was better than this.

Opening the door and entering, she wiped her feet on the heavy rug as the dogs walked over it, then left perfect wet paw prints as they proceeded down the hall.

Jeep, in the kitchen, called out, "Good run?"

Mags walked back. "Yes, but it's snowing hard."

"I can see that."

"When does spring really arrive?"

"When the snow has melted from the top of Peavine Mountain." Jeep named a mountain just north of Reno that still had vast fields of peavines in many spots. Originally, it had been covered with the rose-purple flowers, but then the land became overgrazed.

"Well, I guess I'd better keep my eye on Peavine." Mags unzipped her close-fitting running pullover.

"By May first it's usually clear, and then you can plant."

"Seems far away."

"Six weeks give or take. Coffee?"

"I'll take a fast shower, then join you."

"I'll be here. You know I'm not going out for a jog." Jeep laughed.

The old lady had had a hip replacement. She could move around pretty well, but she never was one for running and she wasn't about to start.

Jeep fed the dogs, then sat down for her second cup of coffee.

Mags soon joined her. "Is this one of your special blends?"

"Kona. Carlotta buys all these different types. It's fun to taste them."

"We're going to church, right?"

"Unless you want a big breakfast, we can make the early service."

"That's perfect."

After the service at Trinity Episcopal, light snow still falling, Jeep and Mags lingered briefly outside to talk to their friends, as well as other congregants who had agreed to deliver food. Given the hardship the families on Spring Street endured, a number of folks had promised to deliver food that afternoon.

Babs, a Methodist, also had people from her church on board for today's delivery. Blankets, scarves, and other warm things had also been gathered.

It was a start, thanks especially to Babs. After seeing the weather report Friday, she kept after all those with whom she'd spoken at the various churches, to work for Sunday delivery. Jeep had done the same.

Jeep and Mags returned home, as Jeep didn't want to walk in the snow. She was pretty tough, but if she fell it would do her more damage than someone younger.

That evening, Pete took Mags to dinner, then she asked him to drive her along Spring Street. She told him what they'd done and what they hoped to do.

Little curls of smoke rose from some of the chimneys but the weather flattened the gray plumes.

"I hope it works." Pete smiled. "There's not much danger that the sheriff will ask us to throw people out. We've got other things right now to concentrate on."

"Like that murder in Cracktown?"

"Candidate Wentworth is sure pounding on the department, at least to the media. This makes my boss nervous. Remember, in Washoe County the sheriff is elected."

"He's a good sheriff."

"Yes, he is, but it only takes one person to throw mud, to create doubt by giving out half of the facts. You've seen it done."

"It seems like that's all politics is anymore. One big smear campaign. Whatever happened to the common good?"

"Couldn't say, but the truth is, we do have a problem. We have so many homeless. We have the usual types: alcoholics, drug addicts, the mentally impaired, but we also have able-bodied gambling addicts. Add to that an endless flow of people escaping California, some bringing what money they salvaged and others broke, fleeing a sinking ship. Reno has a lot of unique problems." His brow furrowed momentarily before continuing. "The best we can hope for is that what you, Aunt Jeep, and Babs Gallagher are doing will encourage others to help. But if these people you're trying to help don't get jobs, the problem will just worsen."

"I can see that." Mags loved the sound of his deep voice.

"The real reason the Reno police department hasn't been sent down here to clear those people out is there's nowhere else for them to go."

"Kind of a brutal reality, isn't it?"

"It's when people lose hope that you have to worry,"

Pete said, a thoughtful expression on his strong mascu-
line face.

"Because then they feel they have nothing to lose.
Yeah. I get that."

Pete headed back toward Red Rock. They chatted
away, two people in tune with each other. They'd been
dating since shortly before Christmas and were steadily
growing closer. They'd both been hurt in the past; each
wanted to enjoy the relationship's progression without
rushing into things or creating unnecessary pressures.

Pete walked Mags to the door. Baxter waited on the
other side.

"Come on in. I'll make you a nightcap."

Pete stayed the night for the first time. Mags's room
was at the other end of the long upstairs hall.

In the morning Jeep was probably as happy as Mags.
Jeep loved having a man in the house. She loved a man's
voice, his scent, his laughter. Enrique lived in a smaller
house on the ranch. She loved having her son around,
too.

Jeep kept her nose out of her great-niece's romantic
life, but she adored Pete. She'd known him since he was
a child. He was a good man and plenty handsome,
which never hurt.

The day started with warmth, laughter, and still more
stray snowflakes. This pleasant interlude wouldn't last.
As with many things that go wrong, it started with
something out of the blue.

CHAPTER SEVEN

Every city in America, even if no bigger than a minute, has its seedy side wherein the residents are not rendered tedious by respectability. No exception to this rule, Reno proved creative in this direction.

Fourth Street was festooned with tattoo parlors and exotic dance clubs, where dubious antique furniture was displayed while the real merchandise—sex toys—was found in the back. A topless bar had a painted black front and recessed door with a bouncer of biblical proportions. The Black Box was a hub of activity, especially a few hours after sunset. The seasons did not affect the clientele, always there to admire nature's bounty.

Washoe County outlawed prostitution. The legality of this oldest moneymaker was decided county by county. In reality, laws on the books meant nothing on the street, especially where physical pleasure was concerned. The young women dancing inside the Black Box weren't hookers, though this didn't mean a girl in need might not service a customer after hours and far away from the bar. Still, mostly the stripping working girls held themselves above the oldest profession. Some had boyfriends, some had girlfriends, some even cared about them. Many were young, filled with Hollywood hopes. Unfortunately, they were forty-watt bulbs in one-hundred-watt sockets. They all liked a good time, clearly being extroverts.

Like any bar, the Black Box had regulars. One, Teton Benson, from a leading Reno family, haunted the bar-stools. Teton, who'd changed his first name, was estranged from his family thanks to a long struggle with drink and drugs. There wasn't a substance he hadn't inhaled or ingested. Initially, when he was in college, the family paid for two hideously expensive rehabs. They didn't work. They often don't, which is no comment on the rehabilitation centers, more of a comment on the person who relapsed.

While he wished no contact with his family, he also didn't want to embarrass them further. His sister, Lolly Johnson, kept in erratic touch with him. As her husband was president of SSRM, Darryl Johnson, and Darryl had shelled out his own money to help Teton during one of his forty-thousand-dollar, twenty-eight-day stays in a clinic, the situation was fraught with difficulty. Darryl didn't hate his brother-in-law, but he disregarded him, had written him off as a hopeless, self-centered nonentity.

And he was. After stealing a car, Teton had saved himself a jail term by squealing what he knew about a scam. But he still worried sometimes, usually at three in the morning when he especially wanted a drink, that there may have been silent partners in that scam. He prayed to sweet Jesus there weren't.

His rehabilitation had come through love. Lark, the star of the Black Box, had grown to like him. He pursued her quietly, with lovely presents, usually jewelry. Lark was fond of display. The customers were fond of Lark, though not so much for the jewelry—which looked wonderful on her for she was naturally pretty—but for her rack. You could put a dinner setting on it.

Tu'Lia, Lark's best friend, could have held up a full dessert plate.

The girls, each of them having paid good money for them, proudly paraded their distinguishing features. Those patrons at the table enjoyed it when the girls, bringing drinks, leaned over to serve them.

Breasts raise spirits and the temperature, hence the bouncer.

Congressional candidate Patrick Wentworth, along with a small video team, trolled Fourth Street this Saturday night. They'd banked shots of storefronts, dim colored lights inside, men in old coats leaning against buildings smoking skinny cigarettes. Other reprobates drank from bottles wrapped in paper bags. One urinated publicly, against city code. As he faced the camera, evidence in hand, Patrick realized the shot would be useless.

"We need to get someone who at least has the decency to turn his back," said Reggie Wilcox, the cameraman.

"If he had decency, he wouldn't pee in public." Patrick sniffed.

"Hey, sometimes you can't get to a head," said Reggie. "You need to spend money to pee in America. There are no public urinals. If you can't find a gas station, you pee wherever you can."

"Are you on my team or not?" Patrick growled.

Reggie's reply was clever. "I'm only throwing at you what your opponents will throw at you. Keeping you on your toes."

"Anson Sorenson writes me off, thinks I'm not on the political radar screen. Believe you me, my name will be fixed in the public's mind, come election time." Merely voicing the incumbent's name, the man who had paid no attention to his challenger, infuriated Patrick.

A candidate needed a focus as well as personal appeal. Patrick had focus: Clean up Reno. His appeal was visceral. He was good-looking, young but stiff, censorious.

With his camera steadied on the sill, Reggie shot out of the open window in the backseat of an SUV. In the seat directly in front of him, Patrick drove.

"Okay, now we've got both sides of the street for half a mile." Patrick turned the SUV around.

"Not too many people out on the street in this cold," Reggie said.

"Let's see if we can get inside one of these dumps."

"I'm the one who will be hit, not you," Reggie complained.

"I'll go first. All you have to do is shoot over my shoulder. Get a few pole dancers, get some sound from the audience if you can. Catcalls show them up for the vulgarians they are." Patrick said this with relish.

Parking the SUV on the Black Box block, the one with the most shops, they first ducked into a storefront advertising antiques. The antiques happened to be statuary of an erotic nature. The shop owner, a man of Arab descent and quite fat, managed to get on his feet, waved his arms, and finally shooed them out.

"All he needed was a fez." Reggie laughed because he knew they'd use that film.

Next they shot through the window of a tattoo parlor. A young woman was having an elaborate tattoo of interlocking roses done on the small of her back. Reggie shot a close-up. The interior of the shop was clean, he swung the camera to get the needles in their sterile, hot tray. The tattoo artist never looked up from his canvas nor did the canvas.

They moved on to a pole-dancing bar. No sooner did they get through the door than the bouncer, a wiry, quick man with a long, ragged scar on his left cheek, sprang for them.

All they got was a long shot of one woman, leg wrapped around the pole, and a red-faced middle-aged man pounding on the table in a group of middle-aged men. He was shouting, but the audio didn't record cleanly.

As they were shoved out, Patrick said to Reggie, "I couldn't make out what that geezer was shouting."

"Show us the baloney sandwich."

"How revolting." Patrick's upper lip curled.

Reggie thought genitals, male or female, were pretty much like any other body part. Some people were better-looking than others. Best not to dwell on it because that was one area plastic surgery couldn't much help.

As it wasn't yet peak hour, and it was cold outside, the bouncer at the Black Box happened to be at the bar sipping a Perrier with lime. He wasn't a drinker. In his capacity, he couldn't be.

The door opened and it took him a moment to grasp the situation.

The girls did before he did.

"Hey, get out of here!" Lark growled.

Teton leapt from his barstool about the same time the bouncer did.

Reggie ran backward.

Tu'Lia defiantly shook her breasts at Reggie, even following him out onto the pavement.

Seeing the shock on Patrick's face emboldened her. "Hey, pervert, you want a look but you don't want to pay? This is your lucky night."

She held out her arms lengthwise and shook her glories for all they were worth. Quickly, she realized that exposing her assets to potential frostbite was unwise. She turned tail with a shiver.

"Boss, we've got some good stuff here," boasted Reggie.

"Let's go back to HQ, go over it together, and I'll start writing a script."

"Don't you want more footage of you on the street?"

"Not here. We'll shoot in Cracktown for the next series of ads."

Reggie never asked where all the campaign funds came from. So long as he was paid in full and on time he didn't care. Still, he did wonder.

CHAPTER EIGHT

There's eighty miles an hour, driving fast, and eighty years old, which comes on fast.

Howie Norris never could figure out how he got that old. Ranching four miles north of Jeep as the crow flies, he'd always run cattle, even when he was vice president of Reno National. Over the years the local bank had been gobbled up by bigger banks. Howie hated it because the policy decisions were made wherever corporate headquarters happened to be. After the first buyout, headquarters were in Salt Lake. The second, in Denver. By the time he retired at sixty-five, a huge outfit from Los Angeles had taken over. Against all odds, ownership, a few years ago, had shifted to Las Vegas. Best to keep decisions about Nevadans' money in Nevada. A good banker knows the community, knows people's characters, and is, most important, part of the community. The lack of this, as much as complicated duplicitous financial instruments and loose federal banking guidelines, had provoked the nation's current crisis. How could a vice president of a bank, headquartered in L.A., make a good call on a borrower from Sparks, Nevada?

Howie Norris loved Washoe County. He had loved building it. As Jeep's neighbor, the two of them had often cooked up ideas together, one of them being the now-famous school bus convention.

Funeral directors have a national convention wherein hearses are displayed by auto companies. Years ago, Howie had asked: Why not a convention for the purchase of state educational needs like transportation? Even after the idea took off, Howie stayed on as chairman emeritus. This year the convention was set for April 29 to May 1.

Highlights in his life since his wife Ronnie had passed away a few years ago included upgrading his herd of cattle and riding in the new school buses during their annual parade. When Howie was the vice president at Reno National he'd realized that Reno, with all its casino hotel rooms, could host all manner of conventions more easily than, say, Cleveland. He'd been a driving force in publicizing his beloved city. Anything bringing in clean money was a huge plus.

This last month, the cold and the continuing snowfalls had slowed Howie down a bit. He knocked out all his chores, but they took longer. And when he came back inside, it took longer to warm his bones.

He owned stock in Reno Sagebrush United, the latest version of his old bank. Meticulously he pored over his portfolio reports, as well as the bank's annual statements. It made him so angry it helped him warm up after coming in from outside.

This afternoon, he called Asa Chartris, vice president of Reno Sagebrush United. Howie unleashed a fulsome barrage about what he considered, at best, accounting errors, and at worse, misappropriation of funds.

Accustomed to the old man's outbursts, Asa promised to look into it. Howie had helped him in the beginning of his career. Asa owed it to him to listen but he also liked him. Most everyone liked Howie.

Slamming down the phone, Howie told Zippy, "Goddamned liars and idiots in Las Vegas. I used to run a bank, Zippy. You can't tell me the numbers in this report are legit." He jabbed the glossy, heavy paper with his forefinger, which made a little thud. "I know better, Zip. I think they're overvaluing their assets."

"*I believe you, Poppy.*" Zippy's golden eyes registered deep faith.

"Know what I should do? I ought to commandeer one of those school buses in May and drive it right through their goddamned front door!" He let out a whoop.

"*I'll sit with you, Poppy. I can navigate. Your eyes are going.*"

Fortunately, Howie only heard a murmur. If he'd known what his best friend was telling him, he'd have taken offense.

CHAPTER NINE

Twinkie, mouth clamped shut, stood in front of his new supervisor, John Morris.

Bunny lurched toward the SSRM supervisor. "One day. One fucking day!"

"You cost this company money," John spat.

"One day." Bunny repeated himself.

"You know the rules. Now get out."

Bunny moved around the desk, yanking John off his chair.

Twinkie grabbed Bunny. "Come on, bro, he's not worth it."

"I'll kill the fucker. I swear I will."

John, on all fours on the floor, finally stood. "Get out."

Twinkie dragged a shouting Bunny from the office. In shock, SSRM employees watched the two men. No one knew what had happened.

Down in the company garage, some of Bunny's fury evaporated. "Now what am I going to do?"

"Nothing. For now. Let me think about it."

"That shithead will get me for assault and battery."

"I'll talk to George W."

George W. Ball, former director of Internal Resources, and their old boss, had been promoted to vice president because of an excellent record. George W. could handle the men in the field.

After two years of college in engineering, George W. had been hired twenty-three years ago. He studied new technologies for bringing water up from the aquifers, as well as new technologies for conserving water. He started repairing equipment, proved farsighted and resourceful, and won promotion after promotion. His suggestions on which new technologies to purchase had proven sound. Thanks to years of fieldwork, he knew more than the people who had their degrees.

"I got you fired, too. I'm sorry." Bunny felt awful.

Twinkie shrugged. "Don't know how much longer I could have worked for that bastard anyway."

Leaning against the company truck, Bunny folded his arms across his chest. "I went back there. I saw that little girl. I figured what's one day. One friggin' day. So I turned the water back on and told the mother. You know, she cried." Bunny looked up at his workmate and friend. "Tears me to pieces when a woman cries."

"Me, too." Twinkie nodded.

"Then I went back the next day like I told her I would and I turned the water off. What's that bastard do, read every meter in town?"

"All he has to do is look at his computer screen. He was checking the units we turned off. Reckon he saw 141 Spring Street."

"I should have lied. Told him something had gone wrong with the meter."

"Bunny, you did the right thing. I wish I'd had the guts to do it. People shouldn't have to live like that."

Bunny slapped Twinkie's hand in thanks. "Well, let's get our shit out of this truck."

Twenty minutes later, they'd cleaned out their personal tools, spent Frosty cups, paper bags, and a couple of cigarette butts. Bunny had tried to quit, but stress would eat at him and he'd light up.

"Fellas."

They turned to see George W. bearing down on them.

"George, I fucked up," Bunny admitted forthrightly, then smiled. "I just knocked John out of his chair. I should have knocked his teeth down his throat."

George W. smiled, having no special love for John. "Feel that way sometimes myself. He's not going to press charges. Give him credit for that." George put his big hand on Bunny's back. "Lay low for a week. Okay? Let me work on this. You're the best damn team we've got. No one can break down a pump or fix a ruptured main line as fast or as good as you all. You're SSRM's number one team and don't think I don't know that you've had to perform chores that aren't in your job description. I appreciate that and so does Darryl."

"We don't mind so much but it's hard to turn off people's water when they're in the houses." Twinkie spoke for both himself and Bunny.

"I know, boys. I know. These are hard times. One of the reasons you're doing some of this work."

"John said squatters have no rights. Maybe that's so, but George W., there are children living down there."

"Yes, I brought that up and John's reply, which I confess is difficult to argue against is, 'If you have children it's your responsibility to care for them, not other people's.' Cold, but he's on Darryl's good list. He's already saved SSRM more money than Oliver Hitchens." Oliver was the deceased head of equipment purchasing.

"Never thought I'd miss Oliver." Bunny shook his head. "I'm sorry, George W., I've made trouble. I got Twinkie fired, too, but I couldn't help it."

He told George why he'd done it.

George W., a compassionate man and a father, listened intently, then a sly twinkle brightened his eye. "Now, Bunny, was the mother good-looking?"

Bunny paused, then grinned. "A peach."

All three men laughed.

"Give me a week. I'll get back to you and I'll try to put a lid on this, too. Who saw you come out of John's office?"

"We didn't really notice. There were some people gawking. For sure, some folks heard me yelling," Bunny said softly.

"All right." He exhaled. "I don't know what to do about the squatters. Like I said, these are hard times and it's been a long, damn cold winter. Every now and then I'll drive through on my way home. I know there are families in those abandoned homes. No heat." He shook his head. "I pray every night that this economy will turn around. SSRM's profits are down, which is part of the problem. The Johns of this world think you cut people off right and left. Me, I don't know. I keep looking for some middle ground. 'Course, it all depends on Darryl and he doesn't know neither. I can tell you one thing, boys, no man wants to be president of a company that's losing money."

"SSRM can't be losing money. It's the only game in town," Twinkie asserted.

"You got that right," George W. agreed. "But SSRM's known nothing but big profits. The readjustment will take some time. We're still making money, but less of it. We can't expect the same growth rate we've had in the past." He checked his watch. "All right. You hear me? Lay low."

The two partners watched the large, powerfully built man head toward the elevators.

"Think he can save our asses?" Bunny whispered.

"If anyone can, George W. can."

Driving back to his place, Bunny couldn't help himself. He stopped at 141 Spring Street.

He knocked on the door. Irene peeked through the window, then opened the door.

"Mr. Matthews."

"Irene. Say, I don't know your last name."

"Sapolito."

"Well, ma'am, I'm sorry I had to turn the water back off."

"Please come in."

He stepped inside the cold room. "Like I said, I'm sorry. And I know it was cold but still it was running."

"Thanks. We appreciated it." Irene reached down for CeCe, who was leaning on her leg.

"I know this is last-minute but I was hoping you and CeCe might come to dinner with me."

The biggest smile crossed Irene's lips. "Yes."

Bunny felt like a hero.

He got more enjoyment watching little CeCe eat a hot meal than he did from eating it himself. At thirty-eight, a little overweight, losing hair, he wasn't such a good-looking man but he wasn't bad-looking, either. Married young, he divorced in his thirties, tired of being told he was a failure. Why wasn't he in the front office of SSRM? Tired of being told he was a lousy lover, too. He gave his ex-wife the house, the furniture, the car. It was worth it all just to be rid of her. He'd kept to himself after that. Bitterness faded to emptiness.

After dinner, CeCe wrapped her hand around his as they walked to his 2004 F-250. He lifted her onto her mother's lap, but before he could close the big pickup's door CeCe reached out, her mother holding her steady, and wrapped her arms around Bunny's neck. She kissed him on the cheek.

CHAPTER TEN

Like most U.S. cities, Reno grew outward from the old town, which hugged the Truckee River. Some high-rises towered over the downtown area. A few attractive older residential neighborhoods provided an architectural contrast to the big ugly blocks. Apart from the huge casinos, businesses moved toward the east, and along the 395 north–south corridor. Spur roads off the four-lane 395 created ideal locations for shopping centers, car dealerships, and all manner of pleasant offices.

Lawyers, doctors, real estate firms, and brokerage houses favored these small commercial developments near the upscale shopping centers. Usually these were strips, but attractively landscaped nonetheless, the buildings perhaps two stories, painted ochre, peach, taupe, gray, or white. They often had shutters painted an attractive contrasting color. Many of these commercial places had been built in the last twenty-five years. Reno had boomed—thanks to Nevada's lack of state tax and Reno's business-friendly practices. A well-run business, most any business, could flourish here—although air-conditioning could be a surprisingly big expense for a company relocating from the Northwest or Midwest.

The airport, able to handle large jets and a fair amount of traffic, made it easy to ship goods in or out, as well as people.

Added to that was the road system, for Reno, unlike

Boston or Richmond, truly developed after the dawn of the automobile age. Driving was easy, the roads were wide for the most part, and traffic moved apace.

These advantages impressed themselves on Mags when she returned to her aunt's ranch.

She had only to look across the border into California, with thirty-six point ninety-six million legal residents to witness an even greater economic disaster. Too many people wanted too much for too little. In the eighties and nineties when people began to head here from California, pushed by overpopulation and increasing regulation, they arrived with money and set up establishments. They lacked old Nevada ways, being a far cry from the self-reliant rancher of yore, but some entrepreneurs possessed energy, drive, and vision. Many were also generous. Charities benefited, the University of Nevada at Reno benefited, but then one would have to be a total idiot not to realize that having a good university in a town is always a plus.

Mags had arrived before Yuletide with the shirt on her back, her career in tatters, and her ego badly bruised. However, the cycle of physical labor, working with her uncle and great-aunt, had helped restore her spirits. It also helped that her aunt believed falling on your face always led to something better—that is, if you pick yourself up and don't whine about it. The other thing that somewhat mitigated the disastrous situation she'd left behind was that Mags had warned her bosses at the Wall Street brokerage house about the impending implosion. Her reward was derision. She was being criticized for being a woman, meaning she wasn't the big-balled risk taker her bosses were. She should have walked out then and there. Hindsight makes us all highly intelligent. Mags looked back and it was all so clear.

Two of her ex-bosses were now serving prison terms. A once-proud investment firm with over one hundred years of history had died an ugly public death. Mags and many others lost their jobs, often their own investments, while the big bosses looked on and lied. Some investors lost everything.

Mags's immediate boss, Carl Dobbins, stood by her. Both escaped with their reputations intact but not their bank accounts. Carl left the business to start a hydroponic farm in New Mexico. His wife's savings staked them. He kept in touch with Mags and suggested she interview at Davidson and Fletcher, a Reno brokerage house. He said he'd put in a good word for her.

Alfred Norcross, the third generation to run Davidson and Fletcher, hired her part-time. Three generations is a long time in Reno. It gave the firm luster and prestige. Mags worked Tuesdays and Thursdays; her initial task was research, at which she excelled.

Living off Jeep tormented the young woman. Even though her great-aunt loved having her under her roof, Mags knew she had to contribute money, pay for food, and do many little things that required cash. She didn't want to go back into the business world, but it was what she knew best and she had a gift for it. Perhaps her greatest gift was not following the herd. Also, Mags didn't need to show off.

She still wanted to learn to repair old cars, cars built before computer chips, and she was looking at local night schools. But for now, she was happy to bring in a little money.

Good as Davidson and Fletcher was, the attrition rate had been high. One senior partner died of a heart attack, apparently natural, and three of the young Turks had recently left. They'd made money for the firm while there, but when this year's bonus pool looked shallow, they jumped ship. There was room for Mags.

Her task was investigating banks, rating them as to their investment potential. Untying this Gordian knot took immense research skills and contacts in New York and Washington, some of which she had, as well as an instinct for uncovering unexpected results, good and bad. After her experiences in New York, Mags knew where to look for those surprises in the books, especially the ones involving corruption.

At the moment she was poring over the numbers of a local bank buyout. Reno Sagebrush United had bought Truckee Amalgamated, an institution that made a habit of bad loans to anyone who could breathe.

She called Carl Dobbins, who answered on his cell. "Mags."

"Carl, are you out there in the cold?"

"No, I'm in the greenhouse. You know, I wish I'd done this when I turned forty, but hey, I'm doing it now. How do you like Davidson and Fletcher?"

"A lot. Good people. Solid. Yes, clients' portfolios have lost value but not nearly as much as the market, and a few have grown. That impresses the hell out of me."

"Well, I went to Cornell with Buck Davidson. He was solid then, although a party animal on the weekends. 'Course, so was I." Carl laughed. "What can I do for you?"

"Think. Let me throw some stuff at you and you don't need to answer. Just think about it. I'm researching bank buyouts and trying to untangle the massive foreclosure mess."

A brief silence followed.

"People have lost their homes. The bad lenders got a slap on the wrist. The banks absorbing those bad lenders get money from the government and money again when the homes sell, while the original mortgage holders lose everything," Carl said after a moment of thought.

"I see you haven't totally left the business?" Her voice lifted.

"Oh, yes, I have. I'm alert. I read. I think, but I know no matter what I do I can't fight City Hall. And I'm not going to squander what's left of my life trying. The hell with all of them."

Mags sighed. "I understand."

"On top of all of this, Mags, home ownership is falling. In 2004, sixty-nine-point-two percent of Americans owned their homes. Now it's sixty-six-point-nine percent and it will continue to fall, and new construction will keep falling with it."

"Read those statistics, too."

"The other thing, beautiful, is the government is not about to leave mortgaging to the private sector. They are every bit as responsible for this mess as the lenders but, oh, how very useful to pass the buck, literally. They will continue to hide behind the failed banks, continue to use the big banks for political purposes. As for Fannie Mae and Freddie Mac, I can't even discuss them without recourse to extreme profanity."

"Carl, whenever someone passes the buck, some of it sticks. You know? I do find buyouts fascinating though."

His voice lowered. "Mags, be as fascinated as you like but be careful. Once again a few people will cream billions off the top. Billions. It's one thing if they do that with money earned, but this is under-the-table government money, your money. It's a different ball game, more cynical, with political careers at stake, as well as the careers of bankers on top. Mags, people have killed for less."

"I'll be careful."

"Come on out and visit me sometime. Charlotte and I just love it here. We're like a couple of kids. She's even got me riding with her."

"I will." Mags liked Carl's wife.

After hanging up, she sat for a time, then returned to her computer to look in the *Congressional Record* and read what Nevada's congressman and two senators had said on the floor of Congress regarding the foreclosure crisis in the state.

CHAPTER ELEVEN

"It's incredible what people steal." Pete shook his head as he climbed back into the squad car.

"They were expensive tires."

Pete smiled. "I guess he didn't take more than he needed. Four."

A thief had broken into Reno Tires, an immaculate large building filled with product.

It had been determined that four Goodyear Eagle F1s had been taken. These were high-performance tires hardly suited to the current weather conditions. Someone was already planning for warm weather.

"Close to one thousand dollars for a set of tires is a lot of money." Lonnie was scribbling in his notebook. "Forgot to tell you, Amelia says hi."

"Hi back at her." Pete pulled the squad car out into traffic.

Amelia Owen, a high school classmate of Pete's, was dating Lonnie. She was eight years older than Lonnie, which meant they both experienced a bit of teasing.

As it was near the end of their shift, the two men were headed back to headquarters. Neither Pete nor Lonnie much enjoyed sitting at a desk but sometimes one had to.

Just as Pete sat down to check his emails, a desk officer, Fergie, came by. "The ID came in on that fellow you found over in Cracktown. Name's Robert Dalrymple.

Thirty-five. Unemployed. He worked at Truckee Amalgamated until they went under. That's it."

"It's a long way from Truckee Amalgamated to Cracktown."

"He wouldn't be the first guy to turn to drugs to forget his troubles." Fergie shrugged.

"Report back yet on what was in his system?"

"No."

"Something doesn't compute." Pete rubbed his brow.

"The manner of the murder was brutal, like a warning. That's consistent with the way drug lords leave messages. Also, the department was tipped off, that's also part of the M.O., although not always. I don't know why I can't quite buy it." He exhaled, then looked at Fergie. "You have a point, people do stupid things to forget their troubles. Losing your money is big trouble."

At his desk, Lonnie looked up. "I thought people jumped out of windows when they lost their money or when banks went bust."

"Amalgamated's only two stories high." Fergie laughed.

"Well, he could fling himself off a curbstone," Lonnie thought out loud.

"Instead he got murdered." A warning light went off in Pete's head. "Let's hope this isn't the beginning of a trend."

CHAPTER TWELVE

"I feel responsible for this." Babs spoke to Jeep on the phone in her office.

"I can understand how you'd feel that way but Bunny did the right thing." Jeep, also in her office, enjoyed the glow and aroma of the fire blazing in the simple fireplace. "I doubt it would do any good for me to talk to Darryl Johnson."

"I wonder if news coverage will help," Babs said. "The tough part will be getting some people on Spring Street to talk. They'll be scared. The attention could backfire, I suppose. It could draw the immigration people there as well as men from the Sheriff's Department."

"I expect immigration will be the biggest problem. You know, Babs, let's rethink this news story idea. I'm not saying we shouldn't do it, but we'd better be prepared for unintended consequences. Everything is a political football today."

"Patrick Wentworth will somehow make the most of this," Babs grumbled.

"What an ambitious little asshole he is." Jeep didn't mince words.

"He'd lump everyone down in that neighborhood with drug dealers, illegal immigrants, maybe even the national debt."

Jeep sat up straighter in her chair. "He's clever, though. His focus is on urban decay, crime, and the need to clean up before, as I believe he said, 'the contagion spreads.' He's also building a war chest."

"Somebody is good at fund-raising."

Jeep laughed. "That's a nice way to put it. Listen, don't worry about Bunny and Twinkie just right now. I'll call Darryl. The worst he can say is no. Those two good men shouldn't be fired because one made a mistake. Now, to switch gears, let's talk about our deliveries. We can box up food from the casinos and supermarkets that are dry goods near their sell-by date—cereals, cookies, stuff like that. Where we run into trouble is with meats, vegetables, and fruits—exactly what they need most down there. Mags has been checking into the laws. The only way we could deliver that kind of food is if we do it on the sell-by date, and the supermarkets aren't going to give it to us then. They're hoping to sell it. And we can't take anything like that from the casinos since they aren't food purveyors. In other words, tons of good food goes to waste every day in Reno and no one benefits."

"It's all so contradictory, wasteful, and stupid." Babs felt her face flush.

A long, long silence followed. "Let me think this through, Babs. You're right. It is wasteful and stupid. I know we're pushing a stone up the hill facing off against the utilities and now the food laws. We need more time to dig out facts, lean on people. Sometimes in order to do the right thing, you have to ignore the law. Know what I mean?"

"Like Nelson turning a blind eye at Trafalgar," Babs reasoned to Jeep's great delight.

After talking to Babs, Jeep called Darryl Johnson. Of course he took her call, everyone did.

She took responsibility even though she hadn't been the one to talk to Bunny and Twinkie. "Darryl, Babs Gallagher and I made an unwise suggestion to Twinkie and Bunny, moved by the plight of people on Spring Street."

"I didn't know that, Jeep. I just knew that they'd been fired for disregarding a company policy. Our new head of that department is a trifle overzealous and he probably wanted to prove he was boss."

"May I prevail upon you to hire them back? I really feel responsible. They are good men and you won't find any better in the field. But Darryl, if you could go down there and see what's happening, you'd know why we behaved as we did."

"Jeep, I'll take care of it. George W. is pretty upset, too. We'll bring them back in a way that saves John Morris's face."

"That's the new guy?"

"Right."

"I appreciate you hearing me out. I know this is a small matter."

"Jeep, anything in which you become involved is rarely a small matter."

"I don't know about that but I do thank you. And give that beautiful Lolly my best."

After hanging up on the call, Jeep allowed herself the glow of triumph. Lolly Johnson would be the one to get down to Spring Street. She'd need to wait a bit on that but it wasn't a bad idea. If Lolly got on board, getting water service to Spring Street might be easier.

The back door swung open. King stood up but didn't bark.

Within seconds, Baxter was scrambling down the hall, the long carpet runner bunching up behind him.

"Strange cattle tore through our fences!" Baxter announced his great news.

King, ruff up, hurried to the back door.

"Wait a minute, big boy." Mags, who'd just come in, met him in the kitchen. "Aunt Jeep!" she called out.

"In my office."

Coat still on, Mags reached the open office door. "Cattle all over the place and they aren't ours. Enrique is in town at the tractor supply."

"Maybe we can round them up with the ATVs."

"It's cold."

"Be colder on the ATV." Jeep pulled on her work-boots, threw a coat on, and wrapped a scarf around her neck. "Come on. We'll do the best we can."

Within minutes, they'd fired up the ATVs in the shed and were roaring across the frozen ground, dodging rocks and sagebrush. Good cattle, Baldies, were scattered in with Jeep's Herefords. She cut her motor.

The dogs stayed with the humans.

"These belong to Howie Norris. It's going to take more than the two of us to round them up and drive them back. They aren't going to tear up the barns. We can leave them." Jeep decided.

Huge rolls of hay dotted the grazing areas. Good pasture only existed in Nevada if one irrigated. Jeep irrigated two thousand acres of pasture. If she needed to give those irrigated pastures a rest, she turned out the cattle in the rougher parts putting out plenty of hay. Since winter hung on seemingly forever the cattle needed hay. Howie's cattle were tearing away at the huge hay rolls.

"Want me to call Enrique and tell him to hurry back?"

"Well, call him but he doesn't need to hurry. So long as we have enough daylight left we can do the job. But let's go back in. I'll call Howie."

Back in the house, Mags didn't have time to remove her coat. Jeep came back into the kitchen.

"No answer. Better drive over."

They had to drive on the roads to Howie's as opposed to making a straight shot, which made it six and a half miles. As they pulled in to the ranch, from the passenger seat Jeep noticed that the gates had been left open.

Mags parked the truck near the front door of the cozy old home.

They got out. It seemed colder at Howie's. He was a bit closer to the base of the Peterson range.

Knocking on the door, Jeep called out, "It's your neighboring goddess."

No answer.

"He might be out looking for his cattle," Mags suggested.

"Bet you're right."

The two women walked around to the back where big run-in sheds for the cattle had been built sixty years ago. Solid, they stood despite the winds and snowfalls.

Having heard the truck motor, Zippy ran up from over a small hill. King and Baxter ran toward him, and the dogs disappeared over a slight swell in the ground. Jeep and Mags soon heard them barking.

"Hurry," Zippy called to the two dogs.

Mags ran ahead, Jeep more or less hopped behind.

Zippy led King and Baxter to Howie, who was face-down on the ground.

"He's hurt," Baxter called to Mags.

Zippy was licking the old man's face, blood trickling down his temple.

Mags reached him quickly, knelt down, took his pulse. He still had one. She called out to Jeep, "Do you have your cell?"

Jeep reached into her coat, pulled it out, and punched in 911.

When she caught up with Mags, she knelt down. "Christ!"

"His pulse is strong but he feels cool."

"He could have been lying out here for hours. Dammit to hell." Jeep took off her coat to lay it over him.

"Aunt Jeep, put that back on. Let me do that. I've got a heavy sweater on. I'll go back to the truck and bring another coat."

The dogs stayed with Howie and Jeep.

The running warmed Mags. The old coat, which was stuffed under the seat, would work just fine. Before she pulled it on, a sheriff's squad car came down the drive.

"You okay?" Pete's voice was concerned.

Lonnie got out of the vehicle. "We picked up the distress call and were a lot closer than the rescue squad."

"Come with me," Mags said.

The three of them took off running, reaching Howie and Jeep in about five minutes.

Jeep stood up. "I can't revive him, but he still has a strong pulse."

Pete knelt down, then very carefully turned Howie over. The blood was from a gash on his head. The frozen ground was splattered with blood.

Ears pricked, the three dogs heard the ambulance.

"Someone's coming," King announced.

Lonnie said, "I'll go back. They might need a hand."

By the time they had Howie on the stretcher, another twenty minutes had passed. The rescue squad was extra careful, so it took more time.

After they drove off, Jeep, Mags, Pete, and Lonnie stood in front of the old ranch house.

Zippy spoke to King and Baxter, *"There's an old heifer who's a fence walker. We went out to check her and sure enough she'd just torn down part of the fence. I heard a shot. I turned around and he was facedown. The other cattle all ran out, too. I hurried back and licked his face but he didn't wake up."*

Wearing a serious expression, Baxter said, *"Could you smell anyone?"*

"Wind's blowing in the wrong direction. I heard a car

pull out but I was too worried about Poppy to pay much attention."

"Why shoot Howie? All he has to steal are cattle," Baxter sharply replied.

"He'll be okay." King nuzzled Zippy.

Jeep bent over, putting her hand on Zippy's glossy head. "You're coming home with us for a visit until Howie's back on his feet."

CHAPTER THIRTEEN

Sitting in the hospital room, holding Howie's hand, Jeep thought about their young days. Where did the time go? People had asked that question for millennia and no one had found the answer. All Jeep knew was it sure flew by fast.

He'd suffered a slight concussion from when his hard head hit the frozen ground. He'd lain out there long enough to suffer slight hypothermia, as well.

The doctors and nurses fixed him up and cleaned off the blood.

Jeep had been sitting beside him since she'd arrived after leaving Mags and Zippy back at Wings Ranch. With Howie's wife, Ronnie, gone, Jeep wanted an old friend to be there when he awoke. It's upsetting to find yourself in a hospital room not knowing why you're there.

Eyelids fluttered, then opened. His pale blue eyes stared at the ceiling, then he felt Jeep squeeze his hand. Howie looked at his childhood friend.

"Jeepy," he whispered.

"Howie, thank God you're okay."

He struggled, trying to recollect what wouldn't come. "What happened?" He thought more. "I heard a shot."

"You've got a crease in your head but no real damage. It's a bullet wound."

"It hurts like hell."

"Plus, you got cold. You're in great shape other than that."

"All the people who wanted me dead are dead themselves." He smiled weakly.

"Zippy is with me. Don't worry about a thing."

He sat up slightly, so Jeep plumped pillows behind him.

"Couldn't live without my Zippy."

"She led us to you."

"Zippy?"

"Yes, she did. She loves her daddy."

Tears rolled down Howie's cheeks at the thought of his dog. "My baby."

"If you don't feel like it, we don't have to talk."

"My head hurts but I can see. I remember one time playing football years and years ago. I took a pop and I saw a lot more men on the field than the normal number. Made me sick to my stomach, too."

"And you didn't leave the field, did you?"

"Hell, no. Nobody did back then."

"Well, blessed are the cross-eyed for they shall see God twice."

He smiled, reached for her hand again. "I owe you."

"You'd do the same for me. You don't owe me a thing." She took a breath, smelling the hospital disinfectant. "Your cattle showed up at my ranch. All of them. I called you. No answer, so Mags and I drove over. Couldn't reach you on the phone so I figured you were outside."

"I was. I've got a heifer that's a fence walker. She gets bored and just plows through the barbed wire. Anyway, I was checking the line and then I don't remember anything."

"Well, don't worry about your cattle. I'll keep them until you're back on your feet. Don't hurry. A little rest will do you good."

"I could get out of here now."

"Don't even think about it. Give yourself a day, then I'll pick you up."

He nestled back onto the pillows again. "Damn place is about falling down around my ears. I need new fences. After Ronnie died I couldn't get in gear, you know."

"That's all over now."

"It is and I thank you and your boys for coming over and fixing stuff up as a Christmas present. I went out and worked with them and realized I needed to work. That and Zippy brought me back." He touched his bandaged head. "I'm lucky whoever did this wasn't a better shot."

"It couldn't have been an accident, you know, target practice on your property."

He rubbed his chin, the white stubble rough on his palm. "I've been missing a steer or a heifer now and then. I chalked it up to someone needing food. Never found any bones so I know it wasn't the coyotes. That, and the carcass is so big one coyote can't drag it off too far, so I figured it was a rustler."

"Why didn't you tell me?"

"I wanted to make sure. And you have lots of folks around. Anyone'd be a damned fool to mess with your herd. But someone knows I'm alone. It's not that hard to cut a cow out in the middle of the night, especially if they're up in the back. Even Zippy won't hear them. I've been out checking every day. Maybe someone was going to rustle more than one heifer."

"It's rough territory." She leaned closer to him. "They'd have a hell of a time cutting cattle out of the herd, driving them to a safe place without leaving an easy trail to follow."

"You know with the price of beef the highest it's been in half a century, I'm surprised there hasn't been more rustling. Whole herds, I mean, although it's harder to do in Nevada than Montana."

"Too much open country here to move them through, not enough hiding places," she agreed. "Guess you could put them up in a barn but we'd see the hoofprints."

"You have to know what you're doing. You don't have to know much to steal one heifer or steer."

"No, you don't. I think we're going to see more of this, one animal missing here and there. As people get hungrier they'll steal cattle, goats, horses, chickens, whatever they can eat."

"You're right there."

"Well, don't worry about it now. Like I said, I'll pick you up tomorrow and I'll have Tito stay with you for a bit." Tito worked for Jeep.

"I'm fine."

"That's what we all say." She smiled.

What she didn't say was that she was worried that whoever had taken a potshot at Howie would come back.

CHAPTER FOURTEEN

Tired and wrapped in her robe, Jeep, comfortable on her reclining chair in her bedroom, watched the eleven o'clock news. King laid on the floor next to her, Zippy snuggled next to King.

A camera panned an abandoned street, houses boarded up. A steady stream of traffic, much of it black SUVs with tinted windows, slithered down the street. The camera zoomed in as one of the behemoths stopped. A woman wrapped in a short but heavy coat, legs in thin stockings, and wearing high heels tottered from the curb to the window. She climbed in. The broadcast cut to another view: A vehicle stopped in front of a boarded house, its driver remaining in the car, exhaust curling from the tailpipe. A male passenger ran to the boarded-up building's formidable door, knocked, said something, was let in and within minutes returned to the waiting vehicle, which then sped away.

The camera pulled back to reveal Patrick Wentworth, dressed in a three-piece suit with an overcoat and Burberry scarf. He spoke directly to the camera:

"Vice grows unchecked down here. Prostitution is booming. Drug dealing is made all too easy by cellphones and texting. How long before this corruption reaches you?"

The camera then cut to an academic being interviewed by an earnest young man.

"Cities like Hamburg, Germany, have specific areas for prostitution and drugs. By containing it, they prevent its spread throughout the city," the expert said.

The next image was of the standard well-groomed male newscaster. He looked straight into the camera. "Tomorrow we'll show Part Two of 'Reno, the Dark Side.' And now the weather."

Furious and suddenly wide awake, Jeep clicked off the TV. She swung her legs over the side of the chair, stuck her feet into her slippers, and padded down the hall.

Mags's door was open. She was in bed reading Balzac, Baxter next to her.

King and Zippy sauntered in.

"Spoiled brat." King called up to the wire-haired dachshund.

"Jealous." Baxter curled his lips.

"I get to sleep with my daddy all the time." Zippy only inflamed King's jealousy.

"Mags, the damned TV station is doing a series called, if you can believe it, 'Reno, the Dark Side.' "

"Lorraine Matthews?"

"No, the other channel. There's always a political career to be made from stirring up a hornet's nest. They decry vice. The result is a police crackdown, all for show. The vice just moves elsewhere. It's ridiculous. No one has ever stopped these activities since we started walking on two feet."

Mags smiled slightly. "Aunt Jeep, that means there were hookers back in ancient Egypt."

Jeep plopped on the side of the bed. "Someone had to wear all that eyeliner."

"Ha." Mags put down her book.

On his hind legs, King put his paws on the bed.

"King, what are you doing?" Jeep tapped his paws.

"Looking at the wiener."

"Get down before I smack you," Jeep commanded, then bent over to stroke Zippy. "Howie should be discharged tomorrow, so Zippy can go home."

"Goody!" The visitor smiled.

"He said someone has been stealing his cattle."

"You haven't missed any?"

"No. I hope Howie's vigilant once he gets home. He didn't seem to take it all that seriously when I visited him in the hospital. Well, I didn't mean to disturb you. I'm cranky, and seeing Patrick Wentworth on TV just put me over the edge."

"Who's running against him?"

"Anson Sorenson, third-term representative."

"It's early to start campaigning for his seat. I mean, it's a small election." Mags compared this to New York City's congressional campaigning. Wasn't the same.

"Yes, but when you get your name out there, get a head start, that's smart."

"What's Wentworth's voting record been like at Carson City?" Mags named the state capital.

"Nondescript. He's voted for every giveaway program that comes down the pike, but there haven't been a lot. He's definitely one who believes we can handle a lot more people so he's soft on water rights and the environment. Truth is, no one has paid much attention to him until now."

"Well, he seems like a first-class fool. How did he get elected to the state house?"

"The incumbent died. There was a special election. The turnout was very low." Jeep stood up. "Like I said, I'm tired and out of sorts."

"A good night's sleep should cure that."

"Usually does. Did I tell you how happy Howie was, knowing I had Zippy?"

Mags looked down at Zippy, eyes bright, tail wagging. "She's a wonderful dog."

"Thank you." The Australian kelpie couldn't stop smiling. She was going home soon!

"The dog will heal him faster than anything else. Well, good night, sweetie. I'll see you in the morning."

CHAPTER FIFTEEN

Shimmering lights hung from the ceiling like golden necklaces, linked up in the center by a large crystal chandelier. The effect was both illuminating and airy. The High Roller casino had even won a lighting award for the classic ambience. A casino needed to attract conventions, reunions, and weddings to augment gambling, so each of them vied for ways to distinguish themselves. One featured a huge, lush indoor garden, a draw in the desert. Another had an aquatic theme, and then there was always the stereotypical Old West. High Roller pushed elegance. The amazing chandelier demonstrated they had succeeded.

Babs Gallagher had rented this stunning ballroom to gather and entertain the well-intentioned invitees, and then ask them for help in feeding and finding jobs for the Spring Street homeless. She refused to call them squatters.

Every real estate agent had been invited, as well as all the bank leaders, business owners, and of course, the utility heads.

Grateful for any respite from the endlessly dreary wait for spring, the unremitting gloom in unemployment, foreclosures, and the economy in general, those Babs had summoned flowed into High Roller. Just ten percent of those invited sent regrets.

A printed brochure describing homelessness and unemployment in Reno, and a simple plan for getting many of these people back on their feet, rested on a table in the doorway. And Babs did not shy away from the issue of illegal immigration. It had been difficult to determine just how many of Reno's population were hungry, unemployed, and had no way to return to Mexico—and possibly no desire, either. Nor did she downplay their poverty's drain on social services. She included figures on how, when employed, their spending boosted the local economy: foodstuffs and gas, for example.

There were no easy answers to this myriad of problems.

Babs chatted up Lolly Johnson. The utility bigwigs, quite naturally, were wary of any plan wherein they would be asked to restore services with reduced compensation. However, Lolly, if engaged by the project, could petition her husband more effectively than anyone else.

In a small way, the plight of the people on Spring Street and many other streets hinted at what might be headed their way on an even more terrifying scale: no money, no jobs, no services, and worst of all, no hope.

At the High Roller gala, Asa Chartris moved from group to group. He supported Jeep and Babs's idea and had taken to calling them the "Twin Angels."

Mags, running interference for Jeep, felt a strong hand grab her elbow.

"I want you to meet someone." Alfred Norcross took Mags over to Michelle Speransky, who was talking to her counterpart, the senior loan portfolio manager at Heritage Bank—a local bank that had managed to keep its reputation intact.

Michelle smiled. "Jeep Reed's great-niece. I've heard about you."

Mags replied, "Well, I'm glad you're still talking to me."

They both laughed, then Michelle said, "Asa told me you saw the problems with overvalued stocks, derivatives, selling debt, the whole enchilada."

As they continued to talk, Mags suddenly realized that this was the first woman she'd spoken to in Reno who had financial acumen, apart from her great-aunt. All her contacts here had been men, whereas in New York there was a large pool of knowledgeable women on Wall Street. Some survived and others like her, got out.

"So, you're the loan portfolio manager at Reno Sagebrush United," Mags said. "Tough time to have that job."

"Hey, it's better than being the Secretary of the Treasury in the Cabinet." Michelle laughed, then sipped her champagne. "That really is the Gordian knot."

"I think of it as a foreclosure ring of fire," said Mags.

Michelle pondered this. "Yeah, but if only we could put the scorpions who got us all in this mess in the middle of a circle of fire and watch them sting themselves to death." She looked at the tiny columns of bubbles coming to the surface of her champagne. "How do you like Davidson and Fletcher?"

"I'm part-time but I like it a lot. I knew I was going to like it when Alfred Norcross said, 'Our first responsibility is to take care of our clients.' And he meant it."

"You'll find that Reno has a good business community."

"So far I'm impressed. I research banks to see if there's enough value to steer investors that way. You know the figures probably better than I do, but in 2007 Reno had twenty-two banks, not counting branches. Now there are seventeen."

"You know RSU took over Truckee. Blending different styles and people takes time, and obviously some personnel will have to go. Everyone is downsizing."

"You must enjoy your work."

Michelle brightened. "I do. I became fascinated with money when I was in grade school. I can't really tell you why. It wasn't so much what I could buy with it but how money affected people, the decisions they make. Does that make sense?"

"Does to me." Mags added shrewdly, "As an asset manager you'd have to be sensitive to that. I mean, one could use investors' money to prop up the share price of the parent company in the wake of a big drop in the stock price of the bank. Money moves more than goods."

Michelle recognized how sharp Mags was. She not only saw the obvious move of capital, she saw the undercurrents, murky though they might be.

"Yes. It's done every day. I'm happy to say I'm not doing it."

"I didn't mean to imply anything," Mags apologized.

"Actually, I didn't take it that way but if I ever get pressure to do that I hope I have the guts you did to stick it to them and just walk away."

A flurry of people circled them. Two good-looking women drew the men like flies.

Michelle winked at Mags, who winked back.

"See you," Mags said.

The gathering dispersed at six-thirty. Babs had wisely started it at five, kept it short and kept it fun, but saved herself and Jeep the huge bill of feeding everyone dinner. Afterward their little group gathered in a small backroom that held a roulette table. Giant landscape paintings in the classical style decorated the walls.

King, Baxter, and Zippy huddled underneath the stools.

Babs looked at her friends. "I didn't get through to the utilities."

"It's complicated for them," Jeep stated. "I'm not giving them a free pass but perhaps we can figure out other ways to make it easier for them to turn those services back on."

"*How much did you get to eat?*" Zippy asked her two friends.

Baxter grinned. "*A lot of shrimp tails. People kept dropping them.*"

"*They dropped broccoli and asparagus tips, too.*" King grimaced. "*How can people eat that awful stuff?*"

"*They eat even worse stuff than that,*" Zippy whispered solemnly.

"*Like what?*" Baxter's moustache twitched slightly.

"*Poppy eats cooked cabbage,*" Zippy squinted as she relayed this.

"*Eeeww.*" The other two groaned, aghast.

Up above, Jeep absentmindedly put her finger on the roulette wheel's red 22. She glanced at the colorful wheel. "We've made a start. The churches are with us. If we're patient, something will turn up. We will find the right approach, one the utilities can't ignore."

"Give me patience, Lord, but hurry." Babs laughed, and the others laughed with her.

CHAPTER SIXTEEN

"Petaluma," Albert Dalrymple answered.

"You finished high school in California?" was Pete's next question.

Bert—thirty-seven, medium height—nodded. "My brother and I both did. I went to UC at Davis and Bob followed, dropped out after a year, then came over here to go to UNR."

Pete, Lonnie, and Bert sat in an ultramodern office. Bert, a pediatrician, resembled his recently deceased younger brother.

"Great school." Pete smiled, since it was his alma mater.

"After my BA I came over here to med school." He smiled, too. "There were so many opportunities, I stayed."

Pete moved toward the harder questions. "When was the last time you spoke to your brother Bob?"

"Two days before he was found." Bert stopped, then stared at Pete. "You were the officer who found him, weren't you? Now I remember. Your name was in the newspaper."

"We both found him. There were no signs of struggle."

"I remember that, too, from the article. Mom and Dad still live in Petaluma. As soon as they were notified, my wife, Jane, and I drove over."

"Something like this is a terrible shock. I'm sorry to

bring it up but any help you can give us . . . Sometimes a tiny detail that seems unimportant turns out to be significant."

"I'll do anything I can to help you find who did this to Bobby."

"He'd been let go when Truckee Amalgamated was bought out. Do you know where he might have looked for work after that?"

"He first went to other banks. No one was hiring. He tried the credit unions, but it was the same story." Lonnie scribbled notes as Bert replied.

"He wanted to stay in banking, or in some form of finance?" Pete asked.

Bert pulled at his left thumb with his right hand, a nervous habit. "It's what he knew best but as it became clear how bad the market is, how difficult it is to get a job, he would have taken anything. I told him to get a paycheck, any paycheck. When times improve you can always go back to banking."

"Was he bitter? Could he have lost his temper and angered someone?"

"Bitter?" Bert thought about this. "No. He'd have flashes of anger, but mostly—at least at first—he was shocked. As the weeks rolled by, with no job on the horizon, he grew despondent." A wan smile crossed Bert's lips. "But you couldn't keep my brother down for long. He'd get up the next morning, go out and try again."

"Debts?"

"Is there anyone who doesn't have them? He lived beyond his means. Not outrageously. I'm not saying that, but Bobby could blow money here and there. He bought a CTS-V. Great car but he could have saved money and bought a Jetta. But, hey, it made him happy. Me, I drive a Volvo V70. Hauls the kids, the two dogs, Jane, and me. Actually, we both drive a station wagon. Bobby was horrified. He would never get in the car with me. I had to go in his." Bert laughed. "I'd tell him, it's a Volvo, it's the safest car on the road. He'd curl his upper lip and just shake his head."

"He never married?"

"He always had girlfriends. Even in high school he was more popular with the girls than I ever was. Losing his job sobered him, though. He told me once he was back in the saddle and cleaned up his debts, he was going to settle down and have a family. As he grew older I knew he was starting to feel lonely, and starting to worry that he was getting too old to handle kids. They get up at two in the morning with a stomachache, you get up..."

"Did he have a girlfriend when he was killed?"

"He'd been seeing a nice girl. Some other ones helped him spend his money. I'm not saying she didn't enjoy his money but this one had sense. Jane and I liked her but then it seemed to fade off."

"Her name?"

"Emma Logan. Works for Dr. Marahbal."

"Can you think of any enemies your brother might have had?"

"That would want to kill him? No. If Bobby had a fault it was that he needed to be successful. If he couldn't be successful, he had to look successful. Sometimes when people observe that they don't like it. He seemed superficial to them. But he wasn't the kind of man to walk away from debt. He never left anyone holding the bag that I knew about, anyway. He could talk to anyone and pretty much did." Bert laughed again, remembering his voluble brother.

"Drink? Drugs? Gambling?"

"Normal. I mean yes, he could take a drink or two. He partied at UNR, but still made his grades. He got over that once he had to show up at work every morning. Guess we all do. Drugs? In high school, a joint here and there. He had sense about that."

"Gambling?"

A moment followed this query.

Bert pulled his left thumb again. "He went through a bad patch. Went to Gamblers Anonymous. That was five years ago. He really did clean up his act. As a doctor I can tell you that gambling releases the same endorphins, the same chemicals, that produce the euphoria that alcohol, drugs, and sex do. There's so much about the brain we don't understand but we do understand that there are specific locations that have to do with happiness. As a pediatrician I see the developing brain, which works differently than the adult brain. For one thing, chemicals like alcohol affect the developing brain more seriously than the adult brain. There's no doubt in my mind that the long-range impacts are far more damaging than we think, but they take years to show up. This is a fascinating new field."

Pete, letting him rattle on, responded, "How do you keep up with the newest research?"

"Can't. I try. If I were a young man in med school I would specialize in this area. I don't know if you know, Deputy Meadows, but each year, every physician in Nevada must take and pass thirty course hours. You can select them—such as a weekend course in San Francisco on air passageways. Just about anyone in ER would try to attend that. As a doctor, one is always learning—that is, in addition to what you learn from your patients and from other doctors."

"Did Bob have your curious nature?"

"Actually, he did," Bert replied in a strong voice, happy to remember their shared traits. "Not about science or math. Just hated them. He liked business, obviously, but he also really liked conservation. If he had it to do over I think he would major in environmental studies but that wasn't offered when we were in college. I don't think it existed."

"Dr. Dalrymple, you've been a great help. Getting a sense of someone's character is as important as getting the facts. Any other interests, say, something that developed as he got older?"

"Now that you mention it, yes. Just recently, he really got interested in politics, which only escalated with the banking crisis. He swore the crisis had started in Washington, though he admitted the banks didn't do themselves any favors. That crisis is still everywhere: Ireland, Greece, Portugal, all of the EU nations will be dragged down. And Bobby swore things weren't all that great with China's banks, either. He said we'd never ever get the truth about China. You know, he became so passionate about this that he offered his services to a fellow running for Congress—Wentworth."

"As a consultant?"

"Yes. He offered to explain the crash, the buyouts, the bailouts, and what Bobby thought would happen next. In the past, my brother kind of went with the flow. I don't say that in a critical way but this crisis finally provoked him to think for himself. Painful as losing his job was, it might have been a good thing."

"Was Wentworth interested in what Bob had to say?"

"Didn't care. Didn't understand any of it. Bobby said his whole focus was drugs, illegal prostitution, stuff like that. Emotional issues. He said that man was too stupid to apply himself to economic issues."

"I see."

Back in the squad car, Pete turned to Lonnie. "What do you think?"

"I think Bert loved his brother."

CHAPTER SEVENTEEN

"We have no suspects at this time." Pete, never relishing TV interviews, particularly disliked this one since the reporter was his ex-wife, who looked fabulous.

"Thank you for your time, Deputy Meadows." She smiled, turned back to the camera, and said a few closing words.

When the camera was off, Lorraine waved Pete over. "Thanks. Someone is banging on the station about the Dalrymple murder. It's been a week . . . you'd think the police were doing nothing."

"Lorraine, no one builds a political career praising the Sheriff's Department." Pete half smiled.

"Or anything else. Find a fault or make one up, then promise to fix it." She flashed her megawatt smile. "Hey, I wouldn't have a job without this media manipulation. I shouldn't complain."

"We both have, um, distinctive jobs."

She changed the subject. "You doing okay?"

"Sure. How about you?"

"Okay. It's good to see you looking so well." She climbed back into the mobile van. He watched her drive off.

Once in the squad car, Pete exhaled, "That wasn't as painful as I thought it would be."

"I never saw her in person before." Lonnie whistled. "She's more beautiful than she is on TV."

Lonnie had become Pete's partner after his divorce.

"Pretty is as pretty does."

"You get the lookers, Pete."

"What I'd like to get is any kind of lead on who killed Dalrymple. I'm willing to bet you five bucks that thanks to Patrick Wentworth there's going to be more violence on Yolanda Street. He's poking around in a snakehole."

"He doesn't have to deal with what crawls out."

"That'll be our job. Meanwhile, municipalities and counties are cutting budgets because the economy's in the toilet. We can't be everywhere."

Lonnie slumped down, looked out the window as the wind kicked up a swirl. "I've been thinking about the department's tight budget. If they lay people off, I'll get a pink slip. I haven't been on the force that long."

"No use worrying about what might not even happen," Pete advised. "The sheriff will freeze hiring but it's another thing to lay off trained officers."

"Hope you're right." Lonnie sat up straighter.

That afternoon, Babs Gallagher visited Howie Norris at the hospital. Years ago at the bank, he'd given her a leg up when she bought her business. Afterward she steered her clients to Reno National, as it was then called. Babs would forever be grateful that Howie had lent her the money to buy Benjamin Realty.

Thirty years ago, few commercial loans were made to women in Reno—or anywhere else, for that matter. Miles Benjamin, the founder of Benjamin Realty, recognized Babs's gift and drive. As Miles aged, she became his primary broker. When he passed, he left his heirs the terms by which he wanted to sell the business to Babs.

They were good terms and his progeny had no desire to work as hard as their father.

Babs had gone to two banks. The only way they would give her a loan was if her husband co-signed. John Gallagher would have done so but Babs, enraged, refused his offer.

When she called on Howie, he'd already heard about her visits to the two larger banks. He listened to her proposal before carefully poring over her paperwork. Within two days, he made her the loan.

The president of the bank raised his eyebrows at providing that sum to a woman, but he didn't question Howie. The man had a sterling record, and the best business minds know that if you're going to hire someone, you'd best trust his judgment. If not, get someone else.

Howie pushed forward a number of entrepreneurs in Reno. He recognized talent both within the bank and without. The heyday of personal banking was also his heyday.

Asa Chartris, another of Howie's past protégés, was sitting at his bedside when Babs entered the hospital room.

"Babs." Asa rose and kissed her on the cheek.

"If anyone should be kissing good-looking women, it's me." Even flat on his back in a hospital bed, Howie beamed at the sight of someone he liked immensely.

Babs leaned over and Howie kissed her cheek.

"You don't look so bad," she said.

He grinned. "Figured if I was on my butt I might as well beautify myself. Got my hair cut, got a shave. I'm ready for action."

"Dizzy?" Babs asked.

"No, I never was. The wound stings but it doesn't hurt. I had a headache because I hit my head hard when I fell. I was just telling Asa about it."

"What a bizarre thing." Babs pulled up another chair

so she and Asa both sat beside Howie, who was propped on his pillows.

"I'll be released later today. Jeep's picking me up. She won't let me stay by myself, though. Says she's putting someone in the house with me. I'll be fine." He pursed his lips, then said with surprising force, "I didn't have a stroke. I know that's what's running through some people's minds. I'm old. All I remember is the sound of a gunshot, a terrible sting to my head. I don't remember falling."

"Jeep's right." Asa nodded. "It's best to be cautious after hitting your head, to say nothing about being shot."

"Maybe it knocked some sense into me." He smiled.

"Did Jeep tell you of our project?" Babs wanted to get Howie thinking about other things.

"No."

Babs explained the Spring Street project.

Howie smiled, reaching for her hand. "Smart. You just might restore some value to those homes. Better an asset than a liability."

"Babs, it's a good idea and like all good ideas it will be met with resistance." Asa smiled grimly, his handsome face framed by steel-gray curly hair. "When you're ready with more concrete proposals, come talk to me. If we put our heads together, we can make a more effective presentation to the board. They'll need to see improvements and stability. I'm all for what you're doing. After all, my department is foreclosures and it's been hell."

"That's just it, Asa, these people have no services. They're living in cold rooms using only the fireplace. They have camp stoves. No water. They're doing the best they can. They can't possibly improve the properties."

"Not without jobs." Asa's brow furrowed.

"That's the bitch," Howie blurted out. "Maybe I can get some hired for the school bus expo."

"Jeep and I want to approach SSRM regarding the

power and gas services. We think that will be our biggest fight, getting those turned back on before the inhabitants have work. They won't be able to pay for a while."

Eyes now bright, Howie pointed his finger in a friendly way at Asa. "Reno National had what I always called a slush fund. Can't imagine Reno Sagebrush United doesn't."

"There are some emergency funds, so to speak."

"Well, if the bank pledges a small portion of that to pay the difference in service rates, then the utilities can reduce their rates until people are employed."

Asa considered this. "Let me see what I can do."

By the time his visitors left, Howie's mind was fully engaged and whirring. His cheeks glowed with color.

Help someone else, you always feel better about life. Howie suddenly felt as though he had a purpose, and being an old man with a bullet's crease on his head was irrelevant to it.

CHAPTER EIGHTEEN

March in the Northern Hemisphere can be an explosion of color if one lives in Charleston, South Carolina, or silent with snow if one lives in Medicine Hat, Alberta, Canada. Reno tended to follow a pattern similar to Medicine Hat's, although in latitude it was closer to Charleston.

This night, a lack of cloud cover allowed the earth's heat to escape. Black as the Devil's eyebrows, the sky, crystal clear, curved over the Peterson range and all the small spur ranges to the east. In the main, the earth in Washoe County looked like an accordion pulled wide apart. Low ridges had small or large valleys between them only to fold back to more ridges.

The early settlers, depending on their money and their line of work, set their homes with the backs to the wind or just under the lip of a rise in the land. While they hoped it would offer protection from the wind, very often it didn't. The winds of the northern desert have a way of finding you no matter where you tuck up.

Horses and cattle would walk single file at sundown to their sheds or barns, content to be inside shelter. Birds, feathers and down warming them up, would build sturdy nests, many with high sides. At sundown they'd nestle in, the wind skimming over the top of their nest.

Snug in their dens, coyotes and ground squirrels successfully manage to escape the chill winds. Den dwellers drag in hay, bits of blanket—whatever they can find to fluff things up. Hay and straw prove good insulators. Coyotes will hunt at any time but they prefer the night, less commotion, less people. Returning to the den after a night hunting was indeed a pleasure. The wearied animal would curl up, tail around its nose, and fall asleep, often to awaken to a den entrance snowed in. Digging out usually took little time unless a storm was fierce. But being prudent, most coyotes had alternate entrances in different directions. Naturally, one wouldn't get as much snow blown in as the others.

This March night a single male, called Ruff, weighing about thirty-five pounds, walked near Jeep's house. Sometimes the lid on the garbage cans could be removed if not tightly secured. The treats were worth the risk of venturing this close to the house.

Carlotta had bought new heavy rubber cans, which were stashed behind a low palisade to hide them. She was careful about what she threw out, what she put in the compost pile, and what she recycled. Even so, there were always goodies left over for these garbage cans. While the coyote couldn't read which cans were marked for metal, glass, etc., Ruff could certainly smell which ones contained dog food cans, chicken bones, and bits of gravy. Ah, the heady scents!

Since King and Baxter would devour fowl bones left in the compost pile, Carlotta put them in the cans. As to T-bones, Jeep and Mags, when finished, gave them to the dogs out on the back porch. King and Baxter would gnaw to their complete delight. What could be better? Sooner or later they'd forget the bone and drop them somewhere. Ruff especially enjoyed those bones.

Two big bones rested on a mat on the back porch. Boldly, he hopped onto the porch and picked them up.

Jeep slept with a window cracked about an inch, so King heard him as he slept on the rug by the bed, the bedroom facing the back. She believed fresh air, no matter how cold, was healthy.

King tore down the stairs. Baxter heard the claws click on the stairs, so he left Mags's bedroom to rush after the big dog.

King bolted through the door in the mudroom off the kitchen. Ruff heard him coming across the wooden kitchen floor and was already loping toward the cattle shed.

King flew after him with Baxter on his heels.

The coyote had a head start. They chased him to the top of the ridge, where all three creatures stopped. Ruff dropped the two steak bones that he'd been able to carry, thanks to a long jaw.

"If I catch you on my porch again I'll kill you," King threatened.

"Yeah." Baxter growled.

Ruff blinked his golden eyes, viewed Baxter and laughed, little puffs of air escaping him, laughing just as other canines do. *"One bite, worm dog. Lunch."*

Baxter bared his fangs, crouched, and crept forward.

King blocked his path. *"Get over it."* The powerful shepherd mix, bigger and heavier than the coyote, looked at the intruder. *"It would take you more than one bite. He's scrappy."*

Thrilled at the praise, Baxter came around to stand next to King.

The coyote was amused by this odd couple. *"You eat good at the ranch."*

"We do. How many of you in your pack?"

"Only me. I don't have a mate yet. There are females north that I know but they're all taken."

"Young?" King inquired.

"I am. Up where the old man lives, dens everywhere. Clever girls, too." The golden-eyed fellow meant Howie Norris. *"I'll find a mate. Takes time."*

"*That's what my human says,*" Baxter piped up, intrigued to be talking to a wild animal—not something he'd ever done in Manhattan except for chattering squirrels.

"*About coyotes?*" The young wild animal was curious.

"*No, about herself.*"

Ruff laughed. "*I don't understand human mating.*"

"*I don't, either.*" Baxter laughed as well.

Chiming in, King believed he had the answer. Maybe this time he did. "*They think too much.*"

"*Or not at all,*" Ruff replied. "*Look what they're doing to our home. Moving us out with all their houses, sucking up water. They'll kill us all and then themselves. That's what I think, anyway. When I have a mate, I wonder what she'll think.*"

Baxter said, "*Where I lived with my human, there are nine million people from about five in the afternoon to nine in the morning. Then people come in from surrounding states to work and it's about twenty-two million people.*"

"*That's impossible.*" Ruff sniffed the air for a moment. "*There's no way to feed that many people.*"

"*The humans truck in food and they even fly it in. Really.*" Baxter sat on his haunches.

At first resistant to the little dog, King now knew that Baxter was truthful and he actually liked him.

"*All that food?*"

"*Even your kind is moving in.*" Baxter meant coyotes were coming to Manhattan.

"*City life is bad. I'm happy with two big bones and all this land.*" The young canine smiled. "*I can kind of imagine nine million ground squirrels or bugs, maybe. But people. It's insane.*"

"*Is kinda,*" King agreed.

"*They really will kill us all.*" Ruff sighed.

"*You especially. If they see you, they'll shoot you. Not*

Jeep, though. If you don't kill any calves or snatch the barn cats, she'll let you be. She believes we all have a right to live and your kind was here before her kind," King stated with pride.

"Is she the old lady with the baseball caps who walks funny?"

"That's my human. She's really really old but she's tough and she loves all animals." King sat down, too.

"Mine is young and beautiful. Truly beautiful," Baxter boasted.

"And she doesn't have a mate?" Ruff was incredulous.

Baxter's ears dropped a little because this worried him, too. *"No."*

"Young, beautiful. Alone. I never will understand humans. I don't even understand how they walk." He picked up his prizes. *"I'll see you again."*

The two domesticated canines watched him start off.

The coyote stopped for a moment and dropped his bones again. *"I'm Ruff. Who are you?"*

The domesticated animals gave their names. He smiled, picked up his bones again, and loped away.

"Cold. Let's go home," King announced. *"Do you ever miss where you used to live?"*

The little fellow, alongside his friend, trotted down the hard frozen slopes toward the house. *"At first I did. More smells. But now I don't at all. Mags hardly ever puts a leash on me. I can go where I want. The only cars, unless we're in the truck, are the ones on the ranch. And the animals I see and meet are exciting. I wouldn't go back for anything."* He paused. *"And I like you. I never had a dog friend before."*

King, surprised, replied, *"I like you, too, you little sawed-off shotgun. We can talk. When Momma died, I was so lonesome. I love Jeep but it's good to have a friend who understands."*

CHAPTER NINETEEN

Sitting in George W.'s large office—the maps on the walls identifying aquifers as well as surface water—Twinkie and Bunny listened.

"All right, can you keep out of John Morris's way?"

"Hell, yes. I don't want to see him," Bunny replied immediately.

Less emotional than Bunny, Twinkie commented shrewdly, "John Morris is our nominal boss."

"True, but I had a long talk with him yesterday. Enough time has passed for him to realize our number-two team is good but not as good as you. You probably know that Pump 14 blew out. Yes, it was fixed but in your absence it took much longer than it should have. He is your nominal boss, Twinkie, you're right, and in my experience, people who are bosses expect a certain amount of deference. My advice is tip your hat, keep your mouth shut, and complete your assignment, even if you don't like it. You're in the truck, not here in the office, so you ought to be able to do that."

Bunny folded his hands in his lap. "Thanks. You cleaned up my mess."

George W. smiled. "Morris is not the easiest guy to get along with. He's new on the job. Either he'll settle in or he'll ship out. SSRM has enough to deal with without difficult personalities in the home office."

"Thank you." Twinkie echoed Bunny's gratitude.

Once back in the truck, out on the road, they drove out to Red Rock. A pipe had broken two miles south of Pump 19, a pump about halfway up the Petersons, placed there to capture an underground creek running down the east side of the range.

When the pipes had originally been put in, in 1967, they were good. The fact that they'd lasted this long bore testimony to that. SSRM was replacing older equipment in an organized way. The bad economy delayed this program. The burst pipe was in a section due for complete replacement.

Fortunately, it took the two of them only three hours to section out the damage, fit a new insert, and seal it. Just to be sure, they drove up to Pump 19, removed the housing and checked it, too. It was fine.

Coming down the service road to Red Rock Road, Twinkie said, "Howie Norris is supposed to come home tonight. Jake Tanner told me."

Jake Tanner ran a small ranch, also making a little money doing odd jobs as he had a Ditch Witch, a backhoe, and a sizable bulldozer, plus a couple of good tractors. He could also repair his own equipment. Jake's distinguishing feature, apart from an Old Testament beard, was his intense interest in everybody else's life. Gossip was manna from heaven for Jake.

"Speak of the devil." Bunny laughed.

Jake, slowly driving his backhoe, had turned onto a ranch just below Pump 19.

The SSRM truck pulled in after him.

Seeing Twinkie and Bunny, Jake hopped off the backhoe after cutting the loud motor.

"How de do."

"What are you up to?" Twinkie turned off the truck motor.

"Drainpipe." Jake pointed to a brand-new drainpipe, its swirls making it look like a silver Dairy Queen.

"Ronnie Hartnett ran over the end when he went off his one. I'm putting in a new one."

"Ronnie doesn't drink," Twinkie noted.

"It's the diabetes," Jake said solemnly. "If his blood sugar goes he sometimes blacks out. Looks like that's what happened. He's all right."

"I saw an ad in a magazine that said they now make contact lenses that tell a diabetic when their blood sugar is dropping. Isn't that something?" Bunny marveled.

" 'Tis. If you guys got a minute, let's go to Howie's."

"Why?"

"Jeep told me where they found him. I thought maybe we could jimmy rig his fence line. With two to pull the wire tight, the third can tie it to the post. Pulling is a tough job."

Squeezing into the cab of the work truck, the three drove the mile and a half to Howie's, which backed up on the Harnetts' ranch. Howie kept a pretty big spread. No one had the ten thousand acres that Jeep did but Howie, over a long life, had amassed two thousand acres. He was land poor and had little cash but that was okay with him. Jeep owned the water rights. She'd bought them when he first started ranching with only three hundred acres. Since he and Ronnie were childless and knowing that Jeep had children and grandchildren, Howie sold her the rights every time he acquired more land. Anything to keep the water out of SSRM's hands once he passed away, for the new owner of his land could sell the water to whomever they wished and SSRM paid top dollar. Howie trusted that Jeep's descendants would protect the valley's water as he wished it to be protected.

Twinkie pulled into Howie's drive. The three men hopped out on a cold, perfectly clear day.

"She said they found him over that little rise there."

They walked over and it was easy to find the spot because dried blood still stained the small rocks and the light-colored soil.

The three kept walking toward the ripped fence line. Being workmen, they wore heavy gloves and their equipment belts. Even with three of them hard at it, the repair took a half hour. Splicing and reinforcing the damaged wire demanded patience.

Heading back, they paused when they reached the slight rise.

Twinkie, seeing the boulders, headed over. He noted a coyote den. The coyote wasn't there. Bones, mostly chicken, were scattered in front of the opening. A few features bore testimony to the fact that it was a white chicken, probably a Leghorn.

Twinkie walked around the boulders. As usual, the coyote had been industrious, making more than one entrance and exit.

Bunny and Jake started back.

Twinkie caught up. "Coyote den. I can usually smell them." He tapped his nose. "I should work for a company that makes perfumes. I could have made big bucks."

Bunny laughed. "Yeah. Eau de Varmint."

They walked back to the SSRM truck, chuckling over the vision of Twinkie sniffing test tubes of orange, lavender, and musk. Howie had parked his truck alongside the old corral so any visitors could park on one side of the circle or in front of the house.

When Twinkie opened the door to the truck, his boot tip hit a rock. He kicked at it, then looked down and picked up a section of ingot. It was black. He turned it over. He rubbed it in his hands. "I'll be."

Already in the truck, Bunny and Jake wondered what he'd found.

As he approached, Bunny opened the door and yelled out, "Twink, get in here and shut the door. It's cold."

Lifting himself up, for the company truck lacked running boards, Twinkie dropped the ingot piece into Jake's hands. "Look at this."

Bunny peered into Jake's palm. "Gimme that. Your beard's in the way."

Bunny rubbed the small but heavy piece of metal on his overalls. A dull gleam began to appear. "Will you look at this?"

All three men intently studied the piece of ingot, which showed a small Sunrise stamp.

"Sunrise Mine. The big silver vein that played out. Weren't there murders at Sunrise?" Jake asked.

"Back then everybody shot up everybody else. A form of population control." Bunny rubbed the ingot piece some more. The mark got brighter.

"Remember in high school, maybe it was eleventh grade, we studied Nevada history?" Twinkie looked at the other two. "I studied Nevada history, don't know what you two did. I kind of remember the story of that mine, a couple of murders followed the murders at a bank. The robbers were brothers. One was caught, the other got away. The one that got caught hung himself in his jail cell."

"It's another one of those stories with the lost treasure, just like the lost army post, Fort Sage." Jake stroked his long beard.

Bunny leaned back in the bench seat. "You'd think someone would have found it by now."

"Maybe someone did." Twinkie took the silver ingot piece back.

CHAPTER TWENTY

Sitting in her high-tech office at Reno Sagebrush United Bank, Michelle Speransky crossed her legs and leaned forward in the desk chair. "He considered himself irresistible to women. It's wonderful he could maintain that delusion." She offered up an appealing, sparkling laugh.

Pete smiled, for her charm was infectious. "Was Robert Dalrymple competent at his job?"

"As competent as anyone could be at Truckee Amalgamated. Loans were being handed out so fast we couldn't keep up with the paperwork."

"You left?"

She nodded. "I saw the handwriting on the wall and found another job at a better-managed bank. Asa Chartris hired me here at Reno Sagebrush United to be the senior loan portfolio manager. The irony is that this bank then bought Truckee Amalgamated. I have the delicious pleasure of having one of my former bosses work under me." She smiled broadly, revealing even, white teeth. "I know, it's not ladylike to gloat."

"But it's human." Pete could imagine the satisfaction. "Did you ever suspect that Dalrymple dabbled in drugs?"

"Robert was an overgrown frat boy. I expect he did everything. But he never showed any signs of dependence on drink or drugs."

"You say he was immature. Did other employees feel that way?"

She leaned forward even more. "Because he was conceited as well as immature, he was incredibly easy to work with, if one was a woman. All you had to do was tell him he was brilliant. The egoist is the easiest man for a woman to manipulate. I'm not telling you anything you don't know."

Michelle was attractive and in her early forties. Dressed in a long suede skirt, boots, and dark green cashmere turtleneck, she exuded good humor and confidence.

She had every reason to be confident. She'd called the mortgage collapse before it happened. Impressed with her acumen and forthrightness, Asa hired her. He, too, felt that the house of cards called the banking system could collapse and he wanted someone on board who possessed a cool head, the ability to steer away from the herd. Because of officers like Asa, and people on the way up like Michelle, Reno Sagebrush United had not faltered in the recent crisis. They still had plenty of cash to lend but no one, not Asa nor Michelle, could have predicted the appalling foreclosure rate in Nevada. Yes, there was money to lend but to whom does one lend it?

Pete and Lonnie, too, recognized that Michelle was an astute observer of human behavior as well as a sharp businesswoman.

Pete asked, "Did you keep up with Robert Dalrymple after Truckee folded?"

"No. We weren't friends. We weren't enemies, but he's not someone I would make an effort to stay in touch with."

"We have a list of people from Truckee who were hired here at Reno Sagebrush. It's not too long. We've spoken to each of them. Some of them thought that Robert was a regular, likable guy."

She clasped her hands around her knee. "He was likable, really. But apart from his perhaps-too-obvious interest in women, he ran with the pack. When people spouted golden statistics and government officials painted rosy pictures, everyone in the pack was certain a crash could never happen. It was impossible. And when you have a company that's publicly traded that needs to show increased earnings every quarter, it takes a brave man to say, 'Hold on. Not so fast. Let's look at what they're not telling us.' Robert was basically just another sheep. He looked good. He sounded good. He could quote all those positive numbers but he didn't think for himself. No real head on his shoulders. Down he went."

"Did he have enemies?"

She shrugged. "No more than anyone else in this business."

Pete slipped in the vital question. "Do you think he was honest? Could he have diverted bank funds?"

She dropped back in the chair, uncrossed her legs. "I wouldn't know. I never saw or heard of anything—you know, like under-the-table payments. He made a lot of loans to a lot of people and I doubt all those people were upright citizens. Was he a crook? I don't know, but I do know he couldn't get a job after Reno Sagebrush bought what was left of Truckee. That points to something, whether it's a whiff of something unpleasant or incompetence."

"Was he a big spender?"

"Yes. Expensive clothes, watch, car. Ski vacations to Banff. Well, let me backtrack. Maybe he wasn't outrageously extravagant but he spent money to impress others, more than I would. So that's a matter of personal judgment."

"Were you surprised at how he died?"

Her brown eyes widened. "Yes. We all were. How did he wind up down there with his throat slit?"

"That's what we're trying to find out."

"I can't pretend I miss him and I can't even really pretend that I care too much, but it was a terrible end."

"One last request. And we both appreciate all the time you've given us. Do you know or can you direct us to who might have a list of those employees from Truckee Amalgamated who did not get hired by another bank?"

"That's a lot of people." She took a breath. "I don't have that information but the former director of personnel works here. He might know."

After thanking Michelle, the two called on William Elgar. He had suffered a demotion since he was no longer the director of personnel for Reno Sagebrush, but at least he was working, which was a blessing.

William didn't seem to mind the unplanned visit to his office by the police. "I can get you that information. Unless it's a rush, I can have it by tomorrow. It's in my computer at home. I used to take a lot of work home. Still do."

All three men knew that William Elgar should not have bank information at home. No one said a word. If one is fired from a bank or brokerage house, one is escorted out of the office after clearing out personal items. The escorts are from the Sheriff's Department or they are private security officers. Customer lists were particularly valued, even if the employee brought in the customer. The bank "owned" that customer and customer information was supposed to be secure. Anyone with brains took home information in increments so no one would notice. Often, the desire wasn't to steal customers but to preserve one's work, keep track of associations and discussions. Clearly, William had brains. He promised to email the information to Pete.

After leaving the bank, the two pulled into a nearby diner for a cup of coffee.

Sitting at the counter, Pete stared at the menu. He wasn't hungry.

Of course Lonnie was always hungry. He ordered a bacon cheeseburger with fries.

"If you're ever shot, blood won't flow," Pete said. "Instead, pure grease will ooze out of your body."

Lonnie looked at his partner. "Jealous?"

"I can't eat that stuff anymore. I don't know how you can stomach it. I can't eat a lot of salt anymore, either."

"That's what happens when you're in your thirties."

"Maybe." Pete sipped the good coffee, the reason they had stopped at this place. "We've questioned Dalrymple's family, any associates we could track down. Not one person thought he was on drugs. And his mother and father swore they saw no physical signs of addiction."

"Parents sometimes don't."

"True, but everyone sings the same tune and his lab reports came back clean, which means you owe me five dollars."

"That doesn't mean he wasn't making money from the trade." Lonnie fished in his pants pocket, retrieved some bills, peeled off a fiver, and smacked it on the counter.

"Or borrowing money from those in the trade. There's ready cash, no taxes, no records. His bank account looked like a river at low tide." Pete, with a broad smile, picked up the money.

"Well, so does mine and you've got some of it." Lonnie laughed as the huge burger and fries were put in front of him. "Thanks, Vern." He smiled at the waitress.

Pete called Vern back. "Changed my mind. A bowl of today's soup."

"Chicken noodle with lots of chicken." She smiled.

"Good choice. Will warm you up on a cold day. I don't think spring will ever come."

"I know the feeling." She left and Pete returned to the subject. "What I think we should look at is, did Dalrymple make any loans on houses in Cracktown, houses now in foreclosure?"

"I bet he made loans on houses in foreclosure all over Washoe County."

"I want to know," Pete replied.

"Why would someone kill him over foreclosures? If that's the case there will be a whole mess of dead bankers."

Pete put the cup in the saucer with a little click. "I have a feeling about this."

"I think the guy was just trying to keep ahead of his bills."

"You're right, but based on what we've learned this was a guy with a big ego. Dalrymple might not be the kind of guy who could face being seen as a failure, or even doing with less. He strikes me as the kind of guy at the faro table whose chips are down and he still dreams of a big haul so he bets them all."

Pete paid for lunch with the five dollars he won from Lonnie, gave Vern a wink, and added a good tip. He walked out with his arm around Lonnie's shoulder.

"Thanks." Lonnie smiled, then touched Pete's hand draped over his shoulder.

"Does this mean we're having a bromance?"

"Asshole." Pete dropped his arm, laughing as he did so.

That evening Jeep picked Howie up at the hospital. He teared up when he got into the truck and spotted an ecstatic Zippy, so very happy to see him.

Mags sat in the back with King and Baxter. Jeep's new truck had the extended cab, not the double doors, but there was enough room in the back for the dogs and Mags, plus gear.

Later, upon first entering his house, the old man stopped. "Oh, Jeepy." He hugged and kissed her.

Jeep, Carlotta, and Mags had cleaned up the whole place. It hadn't been so bad, but now it sparkled. They'd put flowers in a vase on the kitchen table and filled the refrigerator with Carlotta's stuffed pork chops, salad made with everything but the dressing, and baked potatoes that just needed to be warmed up. Cereal, bread, butter, everything he needed, plus a six pack of Land Shark Beer.

Also at the house was Tito, a young workman from Wings Ranch.

Howie had finally accepted that this was the way it would be for a while, and Tito was an easygoing young fellow.

"You have a lot of chores. You're going to need his help," Jeep said, and glanced in Tito's direction before turning back. "Enrique and I will bring the cattle back tomorrow. Your fence is already repaired. Twinkie, Bunny, and Jake did it."

"I'm fine."

A knock on the door sent a barking Zippy in that direction.

King and Baxter showed interest but it wasn't their house.

Jeep stood up, then sat down as Mags headed for the door. "Howie, I forgot. Twinkie's coming over. He called me and I told him when we'd get you home. He has something he wants to show you. He wouldn't even tell me."

Twinkie walked in, almost as glad to see the old fellow as Zippy had been. "Howie. You shaved." He laughed.

"Didn't know I was this handsome, did you?" Howie

stood up and the two men clasped hands. "Sit down, Twink. Take off your coat."

Mags took Twinkie's coat. He reached into his jeans pocket and placed the piece of silver ingot on the table.

Jeep immediately knew what it was. She'd made her first fortune in mining because she could read the earth from the air and on the ground. "Where did you get this?"

Twinkie told them.

Tito examined it when it came to him as it passed from hand to hand. "Big enough."

"Yes, it is." Jeep stated the obvious with puzzlement: "Silver doesn't just lay around on driveways."

"Was here. Right out front." Twinkie repeated where he'd found the ingot section.

"Wonder why the boys didn't find it?" Mags said, meaning Pete and Lonnie.

"Probably parked on it." Howie chirped up as he rolled the small heavy silver in his hand.

Tito had heard the discounted stories. "Maybe someone did find the old treasure."

"Anything is possible." Jeep smiled. "That's one thing old age teaches you. You know, the conditions in those mines took such endurance. Often men worked with water up to their ankles, the temperatures might reach one hundred twenty degrees, and there was always the danger that an airshaft would be clogged and you wouldn't know it until it was too late, when you got sleepy. Those old Nevada people were tough."

"Still are." Howie was fascinated with the silver piece.

Mags held out her hand. Howie dropped it into it. She studied the Sunrise mark.

Jeep was as intrigued as everyone else. "Well, neighbor, maybe you do have the Garthwaite treasure on your land."

"Ronnie and I crawled over this land for fifty years. How could we miss it?"

"Maybe you were looking for the wrong things. You know the Garthwaite boys didn't bury it down by the creek bed. They were smart enough to know what happens when the mountain snows melt. Whatever they did, they made it look natural. No one ever said there was a mine here but in the early part of this state's history everybody and his brother were digging. Could be a small little worthless hole. The Gathwaites might have known about it. Hid their stash. Camouflaged the opening. Time did the rest."

"Let me pay you for the value of this silver," Howie offered. "Finders keepers."

"Thank you, Howie, but it really belongs to you."

"Do you think whoever took a shot at me dropped it?" Howie's voice rose in excitement. He looked at Tito, Jeep, Mags, and Twinkie. "You think?"

"It's possible," Jeep replied, now completely fascinated. She turned to Tito. "I'd keep a gun close at hand if I were you. You, too." She now looked at Howie.

As the humans left, Zippy said to King and Baxter, *"Whoever did this will be back."*

CHAPTER TWENTY-ONE

Patrick Wentworth's Reno office was in a storefront on Plum Lane, the main road from town to the airport. "Wentworth for Congress" had been neatly painted on the front window. He also had a small office in Carson City.

In keeping with Wentworth's "I am a man of the people" stance, visitors to his Plum Lane office encountered no hallway, waiting room, or receptionist. Computers on three simple desks for the volunteers hummed as the phones rang. The candidate's desk, exactly like the volunteers', was in the rear, behind it a small conference room with some chairs and a coffee table. No phones jangled or computers hummed there.

In general, Patrick didn't put on airs. Raised in Reno, his father had welded for a living, often suffering from welder's blindness caused by the flash. Even after the temporary blindness went away, his eyes would still hurt. Patrick's mother, a first-generation American, had worked in a local elementary school cafeteria. Sophia's parents had left Chile for America. Like so many people south of the U.S. border, her coloring was stunning, her eyes dark liquid brown, her lips chiseled. To some extent her beauty had been passed on to her middle son, Patrick.

Like so many people in public service he had started out with the goal of doing good for the people, then settled for doing well for himself. There were times when Patrick grumbled to his campaign manager—his older brother, Norton—that if only their mother were Mexican or Hispanic they'd clean up that vote. Such talk presumed that anyone Hispanic cared nothing for the issues.

He was wrong about that, but Patrick was right about other things. Raised a Catholic, he saw that his religion would be of no great benefit to a political career in Nevada. Not one for much religion anyway, he left the Church and allied himself with the evangelicals, riding their coattails into office the first time. He was careful, though, not to sound too strident on what he termed "personal choice" issues.

More than anything, he wanted to sidestep the backlash against people in office who had voted for any kind of state or federal spending. Naturally, as part of his job, he had voted for some state spending. He was attacking vice in Reno in hopes of deflecting any criticism of him on throwing money around. Given the level of Nevada's state government programs, he hardly spent much of the taxpayers' money. However, the public remained virulently anti-incumbent. He needed his incendiary anti-vice approach or his political career was dead in the water.

Patrick looked up from his desk when Michelle Speransky walked into the campaign headquarters. So did Norton. Without saying a word, they headed to the small meeting room in the back. Patrick followed them in and shut the door.

After sitting down, she wasted not one moment. "Lay off Cracktown."

"It's a good hook." Patrick defended himself.

"No doubt, but you're drawing attention to an area in which our bank has a great deal of holdings."

"They're worthless without me. If I clean up that area,

people will buy there again. I'll clean the vermin out for you," Patrick bragged.

"Wentworth, Robert Dalrymple was killed there. All you're doing is stirring up scrutiny at a bad time. Drugs, prostitution, crime—the far right eats this crap up. They live for it. My bank does not. We'll eventually remove the squatters, but you're stirring up the criminal element. It's not like they can't watch the nightly news or your campaign ads. You're bad for their business and right now, ours. Just let this alone."

Patrick held the quaint opinion that speaking his mind was always a good thing. "Michelle, I have an election to win."

Her face flushed. "And I have assets to protect. In the long run, Reno Sagebrush can do more for Reno than you can in Washington."

Norton, seeing his temperamental brother about to go off, said smoothly, "There's a lot of truth to what you say, Michelle. As a banker, I would guess you have little affection for Congress."

She smiled. "They're cowards. They can create all the regulatory commissions they want. They are in this as much as the banks and they loosened the lending regulations, not us. The bottom line is, they aren't as intelligent as people in private enterprise. They never are. It really doesn't matter what they do, it's smoke and mirrors for the public." She checked her watch. "I've got to go. Sorry I didn't call you first. I didn't know if I could get away. Just lay off, Patrick."

"I'll have to think about it," he replied stubbornly.

"You'll have to think about your campaign contributions, too." She stood up, smoothed her skirt, and walked out.

As to who had the biggest balls in this meeting, there was no doubt.

Furious, once she was out of earshot, Patrick sputtered, "Bitch."

Norton cracked his knuckles. "Calm down."

"I'm running this campaign. I'm getting a lot of traction from this cleanup campaign."

"Traction is one thing, votes are another. And how do you propose to pay for the campaign ads if businesses like the bank withdraw support? Look, they gave to Anson Sorenson, too. That's smart business. But their contributions to our campaign paid for some of the TV ads. We'd be nowhere without that money."

"I'll look like a coward."

"Pat, public memory lasts about two days. Forget it."

"All of a sudden I shut up about Cracktown! What do you mean no one will know? And there *has* been a murder there. A man getting his throat slit is news. Too bad for him, but good for me."

"Don't be an idiot. Who's to say you won't get yours slit?"

"Oh, bullshit."

Later, Norton called their mother, recounting the meeting and ending with, "He's going to shoot himself in the foot."

With deep knowledge of her impetuous middle son, whom she loved, of course, Sophia sighed. "It won't be the first time."

CHAPTER TWENTY-TWO

"I wasn't sure. I mean, that it ended." The clear blue eyes of Emma Logan, Robert Dalrymple's girlfriend, looked into Pete's deep brown ones as he sat across from her in her high-rise apartment. "I mean, uh, no fights or, well, I don't know. Robert returned my calls and texts and all but the last few weeks, I didn't see him."

"Any idea why?" Pete crossed one leg over the other as Lonnie silently scribbled in his notebook.

She pushed back a stray lock of blonde hair. "Uh, well, he said he was working on a deal."

"Did he tell you about it?"

"Kinda. He said he wouldn't go back into banking but he was really glad he had put in those years. He said he was going to start a business linking up real estate investors, as well as people buying homes, with the proper lenders—kind of like a mortgage broker. Robert knew all the banks and bankers. He said after he closed this one deal he'd have his start-up money."

"But he didn't say what the deal was?"

"No."

"Did he say who he was working with or trying to work with?"

"No."

"Did you see him take drugs?"

"Never," she answered quickly.

"What about friends? Did you ever see his friends, acquaintances, take them?"

"No. Robert could knock back a drink or two but I never saw anything to worry about."

"Did he have a temper?"

This surprised her. "Uh, well, he could get irritable sometimes but he didn't lose control."

"Irritable how?"

She looked at Pete curiously, trying to figure out this line of questioning. "Curse at someone who cut him off in traffic. Stuff like that. He threw a cellphone across the room once."

Pete smiled. "Understandable."

"Officer Meadows, I don't know why it didn't work out better between us. I don't know why he was murdered. Don't you think I've gone over this in my mind? Thinking of every conversation we had, thinking of the people I met with him. Remembering how much he liked to drive up to Virginia City; he liked the curves in the road. He read every car magazine in the universe." Her face crumpled. "And then I think of him tied up, blood everywhere." She held up her hands in mute appeal.

"Miss Logan, if it's any comfort, his death was quick."

She blinked. "But why?"

"That's what we're trying to find out. Given where Robert was found, drugs would seem the obvious motive, but you and everyone we've questioned said he was clean." He paused. "Did you think he was arrogant?"

She tilted her head. "Oh, he liked to brag, cock of the walk or what-have-you, but not around me, around other men. I don't know if I'd call that arrogant. I just figured it was a stupid guy thing."

Lonnie smiled as he wrote in the notebook.

Pete nodded. "Lonnie and I understand that. Did you ever meet his parents or his brother?"

"We'd have dinner with his brother and his wife sometimes. Very nice people and they were kind to me. I got the feeling they, oh, I don't know, they were waiting for Robert to grow up, settle down. Maybe I was, too."

"When did you last hear from Robert?"

"He texted me. I saved it." She handed Pete her iPhone after retrieving the message.

Pete read the text aloud. "Another week. I'm sorry I haven't seen you. I miss you. Your big guy." Without thinking Pete said, "But he was only five nine."

She shrugged. "His penis. He always referred to it and himself as 'big guy.' I called him that, too. It made him happy." She again turned her palms upward.

Lonnie smiled.

Pete nodded, then added, "I think we can chalk that up to another guy thing."

She smiled a sad little smile. "Robert had his faults but he was basically a good guy."

"Did he ever speak to you about a gambling problem?"

"He was over that, and I never once saw him go into a casino. When we first met, he had money. He bought me jewelry, took me to the best restaurants. I thought he really liked me. If I mentioned something I saw in a magazine or in a store, he'd surprise me with it. Even when he was laid off, he was never cheap. I mean, he would always bring me a little something: flowers, a magazine, a silly pair of socks with chickens embroidered on them. Even so, later on, I knew he was worried to death about money." She blinked again. "I shouldn't have said that. I hate the word 'death' now that Robert's dead."

"I'm sorry, Miss Logan. He seemed like a good guy."

"He was." She thought for a moment. "I take that back about his gambling. He would always bet for the Phillies to win. You know, five dollars. I could never understand why he was so nuts about baseball in the first place. It's s-o-o slow. But the Phillies? Robert had never been to the East Coast."

"Miss Logan, the best way I can explain that is to tell you that baseball is the most serious thing that isn't important."

She smiled. "Another case."

"I have my moments, but not for the Phillies."

Emma rolled those big blue eyes.

Lonnie cleared his throat. "Miss Logan, did Robert ever mention anyone at Truckee Amalgamated that he didn't like?"

"His boss, Carl Giannini, bored him to death, always going on about the good old days. The former bank president bored him, too, stuff like that. Michelle Speransky, her ambition got under his skin. He thought she was the smartest person at the bank but that she would roll over anyone if it advanced her career. He said she wanted to be president of the bank."

"I'm sure a lot of people are like that in business," Pete said.

"That's what Robert said. That the whole bank seethed with ambition, and then fear when people started getting laid off. But he swore those on top would cream off the government bailouts. The public would never see that taxpayer money being given out in loans. He said the American public was being cheated blind and was too dumb to see it. He even went to the guy running for the House of Representatives. Said he could help him, but the guy didn't want it. I should remember his name, his face is plastered all over Reno."

"Patrick Wentworth."

"Robert said he was really stupid. But Robert said that about a lot of people. He could never understand why people couldn't see what he could see."

"Was he political?"

"Sort of. Getting laid off changed him and that was

one of the ways. He read lots of newspapers and magazines. He'd go to Sundance Bookstore for the latest books and one of the owners, Christine Kelly, would call him when a new book about Wall Street or the economy would come in. I thought maybe he was going out with her."

"Was he?"

She shook her head. "No. She's very attractive but he really was reading all this stuff."

"What other ways did getting laid off change Robert?"

"He was quieter, I mean for him. He was a 'can do' guy even when he was worried, and he was really worried, I could see it. He just didn't want to talk about it. Said for me not to worry. He could handle it."

Pete exhaled softly. "You've been very helpful and I appreciate you taking all this time and allowing us into your apartment. You have a nice view of the river."

"I like to watch the water roll over the big rocks," she replied.

"Ever open your windows to listen?" Pete smiled at her.

"All the time."

As the two men rose to leave, a little Yorkie woke up, yawned, and bounced over to Emma. She scooped him up, kissing him.

Pete asked, "What's the dog's name?"

"Velcro, 'cause she sticks to me."

"Well, we thank you and Velcro," Pete said as he and Lonnie left the apartment.

Waiting for the elevator, Lonnie said, "We're getting a range of opinion about Dalrymple."

"They aren't miles apart but he seems to have been a guy who rubbed some people the wrong way without trying and others liked him just fine."

"Ordinary?"

"Lonnie, I'm not so sure. His death was anything but. We're missing something." On the ground floor Pete added, "We're missing something over at Howie's, too."

The glass door made a whoosh sound as the two young officers stepped into the cold, sparkling Nevada air.

"We've crawled all over that ranch. Too bad so many people had driven in. We might have gotten a print of tire tracks."

"Yep."

"Think someone's going to rustle all his cattle?"

"I don't know, but if they do they'd be smart to wait for a snowstorm. Like I said, we're missing something in both cases."

"Stuff will show up." Lonnie opened the squad car door. "Always does."

CHAPTER TWENTY-THREE

"*They could share, you know,*" said King, thrilled by the enticing aroma of fried chicken wafting into the backseat.

"*Maybe she saved some for us at home.*" Baxter, too, was hopeful the largesse would be shared.

The deep rumble of the big V-8 provided a counterpoint to their conversation and that of Jeep and Mags in the front seat of the truck.

"*Mother says that I can't eat chicken bones. They'll splinter and I'll die. I don't believe it. Not for one minute. She's just being selfish about chicken. Look, we ate chickens in the wild. If dogs had died you and I wouldn't be here. Human selfishness, I tell you.*" King's ears pricked upright.

"*It is a suspicious theory. Mags tells me that when she's eating chicken at the table and she won't give me any. Did you ever notice how much they dress up selfishness? It's always something else.*" Baxter twitched his well-groomed moustache.

"*The entire back of this truck is full of food. What's a little chicken thrown to us?*" King stood up to look through the center console out the front window. "*What a clear day.*"

"*Back home it's spring by now. Daffodils in Central Park, light green buds on the trees. And, oh, the smells.*

All those hot dog vendors." Baxter closed his eyes for a second.

"A hot dog vendor?"

"They don't have hot dog vendors on the streets of Reno?" Baxter couldn't believe this.

"I don't know. Tell me what one is."

"Sometimes you'll see them in winter, but they are always out in spring, summer, and fall. It's a person, usually a man, with a stainless-steel cart with an umbrella." Baxter smiled in remembrance.

"I've seen one or two now that you describe them."

"It can get hot in Manhattan in the summer. The fellow needs shade plus you can see the umbrella from far away. In this cart there's a well with hot water. You stand in line, hand him money, he spears a long skinny hot dog, puts it on a roll that is kind of protected with waxed paper. You get your change, maybe you give him a tip, and then you put on ketchup, mustard, relish. The smell, King, the whole city smells of these wonderful, wonderful hot dogs. And my mother always bought me one when she ate one. We'd sit on a park bench together and eat our prize. They're all over the city."

"I'd like to do that," King said wistfully.

"I think these vendors make a pretty good living. At least, I'd think so just because of the smell."

"Carlotta makes hog dogs," King noted.

"Yes, but it's not the same." Baxter did not say this in a superior fashion.

"Finally." The truck stopped at Donald Veigh's Spring Street squat.

Donald, old jacket on, hurried out of his house. Mags called out to him.

He climbed up on the back of the truck crammed full of groceries. "Wow. This is a real haul."

"We had some extra help today. Treasure City gave us

a lot of food because the casino food manager over-bought." Mags smiled.

She didn't say that in years past Jeep had assisted him in some business dealings. He owed her one.

Jeep got out from behind the wheel. She looked on as the two of them began removing the large plastic containers. The aroma affected her as it affected King.

The two dogs clambered down from the backseat. Baxter, with his little short legs, had learned to go down into the footwell, then out onto the flat running board, which retracted when Jeep started the motor. From there, he could make it down to the pavement. Baxter, ever resourceful, rarely asked for help. Wishing for one chicken wing, just one, he watched the containers carried into Donald Veigh's place.

Jeep pitched in and carried small containers.

Once the truck was unloaded the three humans stood in the empty living room.

"Donald, do people around here make coffee?" Jeep inquired. "I know they can't use electric pots."

"Mostly people use the plain kind, you know like chuck wagon cooks. Heat it over an open flame. That's what I use anyway."

Outside playing, the dogs chased each other into the next yard, 230 Spring.

A skinny Manchester terrier scooted out from behind a dead bush at Donald's to follow the two dogs.

"Who are you?" Baxter turned his head.

"I live next door. Help me." The little dog trembled in the cold. He was skin and bones, no fat to fight the frigid temperatures.

"Stick with us. We'll get you food," King said.

"There are lots of us down here. We have to avoid Animal Control. They take us to pens. If no one claims us, I hear they kill us. So we hide. There are fewer and fewer of us. It's been a long hard winter." The small

black and tan tried to nudge them to the front door of 230 Spring Street.

"I can smell him now," King barked.

Their sharp ears detected a rattle and wheeze.

"Let's get Mom. This isn't good!" Baxter tore off to Donald's.

As Donald's door closed, the two set up ferocious barking, scratching on the door.

The skinny dog, upset, watched.

Jeep opened the door. "Settle down. We didn't leave for Tunis. We're right here."

"Come quick!" King danced on his hind legs.

"Trouble." Baxter howled.

Donald thought the two dogs must be sick or something. Jeep and Mags, being dog people, knew otherwise. They hurriedly followed their two companions out the door. Donald, puzzled, brought up the rear with the starving dog.

Donald wondered if they weren't having a moment, as his late mother would say. But they were good to him and the neighborhood. They'd brought all this food and other people could pick up their portions at will. This saved time for Jeep and Mags, plus it gave Donald an opportunity to know his struggling neighbors better. So what if the girls were a little tilted? He'd tag along.

King reached the door first, scratching frantically.

Baxter repeated himself, *"Trouble, Mom, trouble."*

"It is trouble," the little dog barked.

Jeep boldly opened the door. A young man, a boy in his teens, crumpled to the floor, wheezing. The terrier ran to him, licking his face.

Mags reached him before Jeep did. Donald, too, knelt down at his side.

"Faint pulse!" Jeep said, holding the wrist of the painfully thin young man.

"230 Spring Street. Ambulance." Mags, on her cell, described as best she could what lay before her: a young man, no wounds that she could see, who was having great difficulty breathing.

The cold room didn't help his condition. He opened his eyes. A dreamy look crossed his face. He reached up to touch Mags's beautiful face, then his hand fell to his side. A rattle, a twitch.

"He's gone," King said, knowing the humans did not yet know.

Sensing his human's distress, Baxter walked to Mags, sitting tight next to her leg.

In the distance, a siren wailed. The little dog wailed, too.

CHAPTER TWENTY-FOUR

"Loneliness," King stated emphatically.

"*Right*," Baxter agreed, which was always the best strategy in getting along with the larger King.

Though in this instance, the wire-haired dachshund actually did agree. "*People need one another.*"

"*They do but then again they miss a lot, they even miss their own mating odors. They can't always connect because they listen to talk. Can you imagine living with such dull senses? If they had better senses I don't think as many would be lonely.*"

Baxter replied, "*Remember, their sight is good. And they think about things we don't so I like living with Mags. I learn things.*"

King swayed a bit in the backseat of Jeep's truck. "*Really? Like what?*"

The scrawny little dog was there, too. Jeep murmured, "We couldn't save the kid. We'll try to save the dog. Starved, too." Jeep was terribly upset. She couldn't bear to see an animal or person mistreated or abandoned.

"*She reads me things,*" said Baxter. "*I like that. She tells me what happened before I was born and what she thinks will happen.*"

King harrumphed. "*Who cares about what happened before we were born? And whatever is in front of us, we'll find out when we get there. Why worry?*" King spoke with his usual sense of authority.

"My human says the past is prologue. She thinks about this stuff all the time. She read a book about the crash of 1907. She's reading everything about bad times except for the Great Depression. She says everybody is studying that and it seems that they're learning nothing from it. She'll go elsewhere. She read me stories about the South Sea Bubble and the Tulip Craze. I like that she wants me to know."

"Maybe she doesn't have anyone else to talk to," King teased.

"She has Jeep and Pete." Baxter flopped onto King as Jeep took a sharp turn. *"Sorry."*

"Not your fault. Momma's at the wheel."

And so she was.

Mags, strapped in, figured she was up high enough that if Jeep did get them into an accident it might not be so bad. She knew not to criticize her great-aunt's driving. After all, if she could fly big, complex planes, she could handle a new Ford pickup. Mags repeated this to herself whenever her great-aunt was scaring the bejesus out of her.

The pint-sized stray, warm for the first time in months, fell fast asleep, whimpering in his sleep.

A furious Jeep hurried to the local CBS affiliate. It would have been easier to simply call advertising but Jeep preferred face-to-face meetings, and she was going to have one.

The station's utilitarian building was located in an industrial park east of the airport. She pulled in, opened the windows a crack for the dogs, hopped out, and locked the truck.

Mags followed, hoping her beloved great-aunt was not about to suffer an intemperate moment.

The dogs watched the two humans walk across the tarmac.

"We weren't going to suffocate," King complained.

"It is kind of cold but not as bad as it was." The little guy inhaled the bracing air sifting in through the cracked windows.

"What did you mean when you said Mags told you about the Tulip Craze?" King asked.

"In Holland way back in 1634 those people paid what would be hundreds of thousands of our dollars for tulips. Tulips."

"That can't be true. You can't eat tulips. They blossom and die."

"It is true. But a person can store the bulb and it will bloom again next spring. Mags reads me everything. It really happened."

King's ears pricked up. *"Do you ever wonder why you love someone from such a demented species?"*

"No. I just love Mags. I don't much care about the rest of them," Baxter hastened to add. *"I love Aunt Jeep and I like Pete and Enrique and Carlotta, but my job is to protect Mags."*

"Baxter, if dogs left humans they would perish. They just can't fend for themselves," King said solemnly.

"Perish." Baxter repeated in enthusiastic agreement.

They both looked at the canine ragamuffin sound asleep, and Baxter then curled around him.

As if echoing the dogs, Jeep, standing not sitting, said, "Perish. It is unconscionable that someone should starve in Reno."

The advertising director, standing because Jeep was standing, swept his hand toward the leather and steel sofa. "Miss Reed, Miss Rogers, please sit down. And I quite agree. Tell me what I can do."

Realizing he was a decent man, Jeep turned around, looked at the sofa, and plopped down.

Mags also sat, smiling at the director, Jonas Forloines.

He was in his midforties, slightly balding, clean shaven, and dressed a bit more colorfully than a lawyer or an insurance executive, which is to say he had his coat off, wore a French blue shirt with an expensive silver tie and expensive cuff links bearing the CBS logo.

"I will be happy to discuss a contribution from our station manager," Forloines said as he returned to his desk chair.

"Oh, Mr. Forloines, I didn't expect that and I'm sorry I blew in here and just, well, perhaps stated my feelings too forcibly." Jeep realized she had done just that.

"If I'd seen what you've just seen, I'd be upset, too."

"What I want to do is to create a series of ads highlighting the problem. I don't know a thing about how to do this. You do. I'd like to run these ads, say, once with the morning news and once with the evening news."

Mags interjected quietly, "Aunt Jeep, there are so many different news programs now. Perhaps Mr. Forloines can help us identify the time with the most viewers. You'd like your dollars to reach the widest audience."

"I can certainly do that." He swiveled around in his chair to pluck glossy folders from a beautiful enameled shelf running the length of one wall. "These give you a breakdown of advertising rates, news times, prime time, everything. Allow me to make a suggestion."

"Anything." Jeep meant it.

"Don't preach. Create a powerful visual image. This is a visual medium and words are always secondary to the image. State what you wish the viewer to do and know, giving an address, email, or whatever. But take time to find that image or images. I know the station manager would love for me to talk you into a three-minute ad but, Miss Reed, two is more effective if you've got it right."

"Thank you, Mr. Forloines."

"Of course, I know of you, but I've never had the

pleasure of meeting you. I know you can buy this station if you so wish but that doesn't mean I want to waste your money. What you've told me upsets me. No one should go hungry or suffer from cold in Reno. I will do my best for you and I will talk to the station manager about some contribution, be it financial or a discount on running the ads. He'll suggest public service, but you simply won't reach your target audience, which I understand to be all of Reno." He smiled. "Most stations, and ours is no exception, wedge the public service ads in the least expensive time slots. And I can't fault anyone for doing so. It's advertising that keeps us in business."

"I understand that and I am grateful for your candor."

He smiled a little and shook his head. "Not everyone agrees with you on that, so that's music to my ears." He paused. "Right now people's idea of foreclosed homes is the deterioration down on Yolanda Street, that area."

"The part of town Patrick Wentworth is trying to build his career on." Jeep leaned forward putting her hands on her knees.

"Yes. His campaign ads aren't brilliant, aren't particularly well shot, but that's part of his shtick, to make it look like the footage is from an amateur with a handheld. I can assure you it isn't. But it's subtly meant to convey honesty and integrity—that he's not paying a big ad agency for slicked-up ads. Again, those ads aren't brilliant, no special compelling images, but the cumulative effect is clear: bad doings in your town and I'll fix it. You'll be safe."

"Yes, I've watched them, too," Jeep said without enthusiasm.

"I'm waiting for the incumbent, Anson Sorenson, to mount his campaign. He's awfully slow. He's underestimating Wentworth."

Jeep said sincerely, "Mr. Forloines, thank you for taking the time, and for withstanding my outburst. I'll be in touch, as they say." She looked at her great-niece, "What do they say?"

Mags touched her aunt's hand. "It's a wrap. At least I think that's what they say."

"And the check will be with it, even better." Jeep smiled.

On that note the two women left the station. Walking out the front entrance, Mags asked, "Do you have an agency in mind?"

"Holland and Fille. First, I want to call Babs, and set up a meeting with her there tomorrow. Oh, will you call the hospital on your cell and see what you can find out?"

Mags called West Hills Hospital, described the patient, and gave the time of the ambulance call. "We don't know his name." Before getting into the truck, Mags had her answer. "I see. If you can establish his identity and find the next of kin, let me know." A pause. "Yes, yes, it is. Thank you."

Once in the truck, she looked at her aunt. "Starvation."

Jeep inhaled sharply. "Call the *Reno Gazette-Journal* and get them on the story."

"Aunt Jeep, if I might suggest. Let me call CBS. Give them the story first."

"Yes, yes, of course." She didn't start the motor. "This is the richest nation on earth. Our agricultural wealth is so great we can feed millions above and beyond our own population and a young man starves to death in Reno, Nevada."

"Aunt Jeep, I feel terrible. What a dreadful thing to die so young, so alone."

"What about the homeless dogs, cats, and horses?" King allowed himself an indignant moment.

"They think of themselves first," Baxter said. *"But they're letting this little guy come home with us. That's a start."*

"If King and Baxter hadn't started barking and pawing at the door, we'd have never found that poor soul. As it was, too late." Jeep finally started the motor.

"Right next to Donald Veigh. He said he thought he saw a light in there but he didn't want to snoop around. If we hadn't checked up on Donald, if we hadn't brought King and Baxter, who knows how long before he would have been found, months? A year?" Mags slipped her cellphone into her purse. "Aunt Jeep, let's get to your advertising company first thing tomorrow. I doubt this would be too useful for Wentworth's campaign, after all, since there's no drugs or prostitution, but still, if he can find a way to use it, he will."

By the time they reached Wings Ranch, all parties had been contacted, nine A.M. tomorrow, Holland and Fille.

In the house Jeep fed the hungry dog. He ate with such pleasure. Mags brought down some old towels to make a bed for him in the warm kitchen.

"He'll need a trip to the vet. Poor little thing," Mags said. "Skinny. Can see every rib. Like little bent toothpicks."

"That's his name then. Toothpick." Jeep put her hands on her knees. "You know he loved that dead boy. The kid couldn't feed the dog or himself." Tears ran down her face.

Seeing this, Mags got misty herself. She put her arms around her great-aunt. "We did what we could."

"Too late. Too late."

King licked Jeep's hand. Baxter went to Mags.

Toothpick also licked Jeep's hand. *"Thank you."*

Jeep cried all the more.

CHAPTER TWENTY-FIVE

George W. walked along the Truckee River with his boss. Twice a month, the two had lunch outside the office. They'd become friends. Then, too, there were matters best discussed in the office and others best explored elsewhere.

Brilliant sunshine bounced off the fast-flowing Truckee onto the buildings on its banks. Both men wore sunglasses, a staple in Nevada.

"This will come back on us," said George W., hands deep in his pockets.

"George, there are about one hundred sixty-four thousand houses in foreclosure in Reno. We can't turn service back on for all of them," Darryl Johnson replied without anger. "This is a problem for government, not Silver State Resource Management."

"Darryl, it's government that got us into this mess. Them and the banks. And the banks are sitting on a hell of a lot more money than we are. Must be wonderful to get billions of dollars for failing." George W. felt only disgust for the current situation. "In truth, it's the banks that should pay for some restored services on those foreclosed homes. The electric company and the gas company should pitch in, too. We need to approach the banks."

Such a revolutionary idea would never have occurred to Darryl, which is not to say he wasn't listening. Most leaders reject the unusual, the innovative, especially if it will cost them more in the beginning. They might accept the new in technology but not when trying to solve people problems. The homeless were a people problem, an ever-growing people problem.

Darryl's willingness to hear off-the-wall ideas, as well as potentially applicable ones, made him a dynamic leader.

"Well"—he pondered this—"It's going to be a tough sell. First thing we have to do is determine how many people are in this situation. Then we have to winnow the wheat from the chaff."

George W. wasn't sure he was hearing right. "What do you mean?" The big man smiled because Darryl's brain was already clicking along.

"Patrick Wentworth defines squatters as the crackheads in the Yolanda Street area. Obviously, if we turn on water there the whole county will be in an uproar. Decent people pay their bills, drug addicts and dealers don't."

"Right."

"So the first order of business is trying to come up with reliable statistics on how many nonaddicts are holed up in these foreclosed houses."

"Right." George W. saw his point.

"Last night's coverage of that poor kid who starved to death, sad though it was, might turn out to be a help. A young man dies alone, cold, starved. His story arouses sympathy. It aroused mine." A long silence followed. "Let's talk to our department heads on this, especially marketing. They know how to reach their counterparts in other companies. We need to work on this in-house first."

"What about the banks?"

"I don't know. We're all going to have to find the road in. It's so highly political." Darryl shook his head.

George inhaled the sparkling air. "Seems to me, one or both of our senators could help on that. It was the federal government that bailed banks out. So those funds should be flowing back into the community. Like I said, this is a big order. Leave it to Babs Gallagher to throw out the first pitch."

This perked Darryl up. He liked a challenge. "Babs Gallagher knows the bankers and she knows real estate. What made you think of her now, just out of curiosity?"

"Twinkie and Bunny. She felt responsible for them after they'd riled up John Morris."

"Yes?" Darryl stopped walking for a second.

"Not only are they the best repair team, they keep their eyes open. Bunny has been spending time on Spring Street. There's a little girl there, he says she'll be in kindergarten next year. He feeds the child and her mother. He's frantic to find a way to keep the kid warm. Now he drags Twinkie down there. There are other kids. So Twinkie's on the team. You know, my boys, rough and ready on the outside, big teddy bears on the inside."

Darryl smiled. "Ever think about that, George W.? How men who work with their hands, maybe they don't have college degrees and can be quick with their fists, but step up to help and so often those of us in three-piece suits just walk on by."

"I do think about it, Darryl. I don't want to be one of those men."

"I don't, either. Damn you, you've thrown me the biggest curve ball here since I've been president of SSRM." He paused. "And you know what? I'm going to hit that damned ball right out of the park—with or without the bankers on the team." He clapped George W. on the back and they both laughed.

* * *

As Darryl and George W. walked back to SSRM's sleek offices, Pete and Lonnie sat in different offices, fancy bankers' offices, in which also sat Reno Sagebrush VP Asa Chartris.

"No reason to fault Dalrymple's performance. We had to downsize and his performance wasn't outstanding at Truckee Amalgamated. This happens in buyouts, a portion of workers from the purchased firm are let go."

"Were you the one who fired him?" Pete asked.

"No. Each department head broke the news to those affected in his department."

"Did you ever meet Robert Dalrymple?"

"No, I only reviewed his records, which as I said were good but not outstanding. Thirty percent of Truckee Amalgamated people lost their jobs in the buyout. Payroll is one of the first places any business looks to save money. The payroll taxes alone can bring you down, it's not just salary. Then there's health-care costs. The expense of keeping an employee who's not top-notch just isn't worth it."

"But Reno Sagebrush retained some of Truckee Amalgamated's people?"

"The smart ones who foresaw this whole mess, and there were a few. Maybe fifty people. They were a smallish bank. We have also inherited their foreclosures, their debt."

"And bailout money?" Pete, no fool, asked.

"Yes." A pause followed this admission. "The problem is how to lend it. It sounds simple but it isn't. Our industry is taking a beating on this. My department and the loans and mortgage department are reviled."

"People are angry. Is it possible someone whose house was foreclosed on by your bank might target one of your current or past employees, say, Robert?"

Asa threw up his hands. "Anything's possible. I'm surprised some of us haven't been hung from lampposts along with members of Congress. The anger is hot and it's comforting, I suppose, to blame an easy target, anyone."

"Human nature." Lonnie let that slip out, then quickly returned to his notebook.

"Mr. Chartris, Robert's girlfriend told us that he planned to start a business, to be a liaison between people seeking loans and the banks, and that he almost had the capital. I wondered about the viability of that as a business—can't anyone just walk into a bank and ask for a loan? I talked to Michelle Speransky about this. She's been very helpful. She thought Robert might be on to something because, according to her, even though there are federal guidelines about lending money, there are institutional variations. In her estimation, being able to offer a client access to different banks was a good idea."

"Redlining is one of those peculiarities." Asa noted the old practice of drawing a red line on a map around districts thought to be bad investments. Loans were not made in that district. "These days dividing up the map goes on in a more sophisticated way. By that I mean it's all computer generated. There are numbers given for an area's citizens' credit ratings, numbers for prime business locations. It's foolish—one of the reasons we're in this mess. Redlining, at least, was based on direct observation, not that I agree with it because some of it was discriminatory against Hispanics. It wasn't just their salaries, you know. Decisions now are based on computer numbers."

"Miss Speransky said some parts of town might look better to the head of the loan department in bank A and another part of town or the county looked better to the head of the loan department in bank B. Knowing the individuals at the right bank might facilitate a loan. This was Dalrymple's plan. Would it work?"

Asa leaned back in his chair. "Let me put it this way, I wouldn't base my future on such a business."

While not a business major, Pete had a lot of common sense. "Why not? Too many commissions? The real estate costs, plus Robert's fee? Then the points to the bank for making the loan?"

"Exactly." Asa looked more intently at Deputy Meadows.

"Well, Mr. Chartris, what if in order to bring the two parties together, it was the bank that paid Dalrymple's commission? Given the number of bad loans, the bank really can't afford more bad debt, so if Dalrymple had vetted the client, that would be a plus."

This startled Asa Chartris. "Uh—I suppose."

"Have any of the former employees of Truckee Amalgamated threatened this bank or its workers?" Pete asked.

Asa was startled at the shift in topic. "Not that I know of. Look, when it all hit the fan, Truckee Amalgamated couldn't do anything other than what it did. Any smart business person could see that. Sometimes you get the bear and sometimes the bear gets you. Look, all the banks had problems. Our timing was better than Truckee Amalgamated. We ran faster from the bear than they did."

Back in the squad car, Pete drove past a casino. Its moving marquee showed dancing girls. "Mags can find the money trail if anyone can."

"Of course, that's why you want to see her every waking moment." Lonnie chuckled. "Because of her beautiful mind."

"How'd you guess? And I don't see her every waking moment. I work out at five-thirty in the morning. Baseball practice starts next week. I do take her to the shooting range though, kill two birds with one stone." He grinned, then switched back to the murder. "Lonnie, Dalrymple was killed over something he knew. Information can be a form of stolen goods. He was on to something and, like a lot of guys with their line in the water, he was sure he'd snag the biggest fish."

"Instead, he got snagged."

"I keep asking myself, what would provoke someone who wasn't insane to kill? Or—who knows?—maybe the killer is insane."

"Pete, I think there are as many reasons to kill as there are people."

Pete stopped the car, waiting for the green light. "The more I think about the body being dumped, warm, in Cracktown, the clearer one thing becomes: Robert Dalrymple was naïve."

"They got him first."

"Yes, they did."

CHAPTER TWENTY-SIX

While Mags waited at the foot of the Washoe County courthouse steps, she pulled her scarf a little tighter against the cold. A block of properties in foreclosure—held by Western United, a huge regional bank—was up for sale.

All counties in the United States sell foreclosures on the courthouse steps, houses to which heirs cannot be found after owners die, or those encumbered by years of back taxes. Each county devises its own special wrinkles but basically the properties for sale are advertised in the paper for a month to six weeks before the date. The sale time is often in the morning or at noon. A cash deposit or cashier's check needs to be presented as earnest money. If the property goes for more than potential buyers considered, that creates a scramble. Unfortunately, no such scrambling was happening.

For years, few properties came on the market this way. Now there was a flood.

Western United owned many properties in foreclosure south of Reno, a fairly upscale area closer to Tahoe.

A few real estate agents attended the auction on the courthouse steps, wishing to gauge the market.

The resell head of the Reno branch of Western United stood in the crisp air, as did Michelle Speransky, Asa Chartris, and an attractive middle-aged man.

After chatting with Mags, Babs joined the business crowd.

Wishing to give Davidson and Fletcher timely information about the banks unloading toxic assets, Mags thought she should observe closely.

At noon, a short lady wearing a wool skirt, lavender sweater, and a full-length coat appeared upon the top step. She pulled out papers and, without a megaphone, reminded the assembled that a ten percent deposit must be made on the winning bid, then began reading off addresses.

Walking up behind the public official was a young man who would take the down payment and record the transaction.

"63 Mountainside," the woman called.

No response from the crowd.

She repeated this address two more times, then moved on. The whole list took less than a half hour. Fourteen properties—each of them once in a hot neighborhood, the kind where kitchens boasted granite counters, and foyers were marble—did not sell.

The grim mood washed over all of those at the courthouse, including the two officials. Shoulders slumped, they walked back into the courthouse, the doors closing behind them reflecting the light.

Babs returned to Mags. "Not even a glimmer of interest."

"It is depressing," Mags agreed.

Michelle came over. "Ladies, good to see you, despite the circumstances. I wanted to see for myself how our competitors were faring. Our head of resell urged me to do it and Asa, too. Not a pretty picture."

Wearing supple maroon deerskin gloves, Babs rubbed her hands together. "This is going to take much longer than we'd hoped."

"It's not really like the thirties where federal money

kick-started the economy." Michelle studied economic history, as did Mags.

"Exactly." Babs's face flushed. "Then they put the money into work programs. Yes, some went to industry, but a lot of it went into getting people back on their feet, earning a salary."

"Too simple. Everyone wants to complicate things to make themselves look smarter. All they're doing is dragging us down." Bitterness crept into Michelle's voice. "Of course, I enjoy getting ahead of my competitor, but I don't wish this on any bank and, you know, we'll soon be selling off our foreclosed properties and will have to meet all the federal and state guidelines for resell. It's a disaster."

Mags, with a sneaky smile, said, "FDR was saved by the advent of World War II."

Babs gave Mags a sharp glance. "Certainly let's not wish for that."

"I'm not, but I'm not fooled by thinking all the programs of his administration were necessarily what revived the U.S. economy."

Once again Michelle took Mags's measure. "Well, you don't toe the party line, do you?"

"No, and I learned that the hard way. To switch back to what we just saw: What happens now?"

"If we're left alone by regulators," Michelle said, "Western United can seek its own private buyers, perhaps selling large numbers, packaged so to speak, to an individual or corporation. If banks are further impeded by regulation, then Western United will sit on those foreclosed homes for months, maybe years. The assets will deteriorate; homes need to be kept up. It's like a snowball on a hill."

"Sort of like banker and real estate insider trading." Babs got it instantly, but then, she would.

"Well, the public is suspicious after all that's happened. Hard to blame them. I wish I had an answer." Mags turned to Babs. "Why can't a realty company or a syndicate of companies from out of town buy blocks, sections of subdivisions?"

"We could if we had the money," said Babs. "Then we'd need more capital to do the repairs. You saw Spring Street—and all in all, it's in a condition that is fairly easy to rehabilitate, for now. So there are two large outlays of cash and then you have to advertise. Plus we'd have to pay the water, power, and gas services until the properties are sold. You can't show a house without electricity. You can see why no one is stepping up to the plate."

"I'm still holding on to the belief that these properties are assets," Michelle said.

"I'm glad I came down here," Mags said simply.

Michelle sighed. "I doubt you can return to Davidson and Fletcher with a recommendation to purchase Western United stock."

"You know I can't." Mags smiled tightly.

"I understand that. However, if people don't reinvest in banks it keeps the downward spiral spinning." Michelle shook her head. "I wish I had an answer. I mean, I wish I could convince you and other people in your industry to put money back in."

"Hard sell." Babs shrugged. "Well, ladies, we haven't solved the problems of the world today but it was still good to see you two. When I was your age, the only women here would have been those who worked for the county—like the recorder who stepped outside—or women with their husbands, the two of them intent on picking up a property. Whenever I get blue about all this I remind myself that some things have changed for the better."

"You flatter us." Michelle reached out and touched

Babs's forearm. "How do you know we won't make it worse?"

Babs laughed. "Honey, could it get any worse?"

Driving back to the office in the old big-ass Chevy truck that Jeep had given her, the 454 engine rumbling like a distant thunderstorm, Mags wondered about Babs's question. She banished dark thoughts. Concentrate on moving forward.

CHAPTER TWENTY-SEVEN

"We think of prostitutes as women. We're wrong." Patrick Wentworth—dressed in Wranglers, cowboy boots, a Western shirt, and a lined leather vest for the cold—spoke to the camera.

230 Spring Street was behind him.

Knocking back their morning caffeine blast, Jeep and Mags, along with Carlotta, watched the tiny TV in the large kitchen. The huge old round clock read seven-fifteen A.M.

"Brad Heydt, twenty years old, was found dead yesterday by his neighbor, another squatter here in the Spring district. He was a rent boy, a male prostitute, and he died of AIDS. Spring Street is four blocks away from Yolanda Street, Cracktown. Vice is spreading over our city like a stain. Vote for me and I'll clean up this filth."

"I will kill that bastard. With my bare hands!" Jeep slammed the table so hard that coffee jumped out of the cup. "He died of starvation. This is an outrage. I will kill Wentworth!"

Carlotta, bracelets jingling, wordless, wiped up the mess and refilled her mother-in-law's cup. She loved Jeep, had seen all her moods, and knew to keep quiet for a bit.

"Oh, Aunt Jeep, that poor kid."

"Who did Wentworth pay off to find out that boy's identity? And where are his next of kin? I will kill. I mean it." The old lady's face, now crimson, bore a frightening determination.

"Oh, Momma"—Carlotta twirled her hand upward—"make it slow. Swift death is too good for him."

After this brought a bark of approval from Jeep, Carlotta winked at Mags while she patted her own heart. Carlotta feared intense emotion might set off a heart attack in Jeep. The fact that the Reed line was notoriously long-lived did not dissuade her from her worry. Carlotta lived to love, to nurture, to fret over everyone whom she cared about, which seemed to include just about the whole world. The moment she'd met someone, anyone, she knew, just knew, they would be good friends. She was right.

Jeep put her head in her hands, then picked it up again. "Mags, we're shooting our appeal for food today at the TV station. I want to look good."

"A hint of violet. Oh, she will be so beautiful." Carlotta loved anything involving color.

"And your Wranglers," Mags added.

"Bet Wentworth wears the relaxed size." Carlotta poofed. "My husband still wears the same size he did when we were married and he looks good."

Both Jeep and Mags smiled because a fellow with a tight butt did look divine in Wranglers. A girl could lose her composure way too fast.

"Should I wear a scarf to hide my wrinkled neck?" Jeep was now getting excited.

Carlotta shook her head vigorously. "No. Your silver necklace that the Navajo chief gave you years ago. The one with the square-cut lapis lazuli."

"Chief Eddie." Jeep beamed. "He would be proud of what I'm going to do."

Chief Eddie, gone to his reward, entertained Jeep many times and vice versa. She adored his outlook on life, his fantastic sense of balance and proportion, and she discovered Navajos can do a lot more than make gorgeous jewelry. Chief Eddie was a wonder in bed.

After seeing that nasty ad, Babs Gallagher picked up her cell and called Asa Chartris. "Asa."

"Babs."

"Did you just see Patrick Wentworth's ad?"

"Yes. Jennifer called me into the den to see it."

Jennifer was Asa's second wife, his first dying tragically young, many years ago.

"I had listings on many of those properties and as I recall when you all picked up the pieces of Truckee Amalgamated, you also picked up those foreclosed properties," Babs said.

"We did."

"Asa, you, Jeep, and I had a productive meeting about how to revive that area, which is good for me, good for you."

"I certainly thought so."

"Patrick Wentworth has just made this a lot harder. He should have stayed focused on Cracktown."

"Yes. I suppose he has."

"Pull your support," urged Babs. "Your bank has given Patrick Wentworth contributions, has it not? Cut the faucet and publicly disavow him."

While not brilliant, Asa was a man of above-average intelligence. He grappled with this. He did not want Reno Sagebrush dragged into this. Nor did he want to unduly upset his boss, the bank president.

"Babs, I think I can get the campaign funding cut off. A public disavowal might be more difficult. Let me talk to some folks."

After he hung up the phone he called his old mentor, Howie Norris, who had yet to see the incendiary ad. Asa explained it all as best he could.

Howie's reaction was clear. "Cut the cord, just like Babs suggests. Then do nothing. If the bank is publicly attacked for supporting Wentworth in the past, you respond that you support revitalization but believe he is going about it in the wrong way."

"Did I tell you the dead kid was a male prostitute?" Asa half mumbled.

"No. It won't make any difference if you think pulling campaign support will bring the wrath of the anti-gay people on your head. Furthermore, they rarely have enough personal funds to upset our assets, so to speak, should they boycott the bank."

"Right." Asa tried to sound bolder.

"Can you imagine, Asa, can you imagine being a kid, alone, and dying in a foreclosed house? I don't give a damn how you've had to scramble for a living."

"No, Howie, I can't imagine it."

"People like Wentworth make life more difficult for all of us. The Wentworths of the world love laws. They particularly like enforcing them no matter how specious those laws might be. Never, never forget the Volstead Act, which made drinking liquor illegal. What it cost our nation will never be fully known, but one thing it did cost is a loss of respect for government and law enforcement. It's like a fever that subsides and then flares up again."

Asa was not relishing a history lesson about Prohibition. He voiced his agreement, and he did agree up to a point. "Howie, I may need you again."

"Whatever it takes, Asa. I'll always be on the Reno Sagebrush team."

"Thank God," Asa said, then said goodbye.

As that conversation unfolded, so did a much shorter one. Having gotten hold of his personal cellphone number, Michelle Speransky called Patrick Wentworth.

If Patrick had been less arrogant he would have realized her nimbleness, her ability to pry open closed doors.

"Michelle."

"Patrick. A good politician does not fail to listen to good advice. You are going to lose this campaign."

"I've heard that before." He flipped her the bird with his free right hand as his left held the cell to his ear.

"I'm sure you have, but you haven't heard it from me before." She hung up.

The person whom this political ad affected the most was Bunny Matthews. Drinking coffee on his living room sofa, he watched it in horror.

"Twinkie." He'd phoned his workmate.

"Yeah." Twinkie knew an early call meant Bunny would be late or something was up.

"Cover for me at work. I'll be in as soon as possible. I'll explain when I get there."

"Consider your ass covered." Twinkie asked no questions. Why? Bunny was his friend. Twinkie considered questions needy. He wasn't a needy man.

Bunny hopped into his truck and tore down to Spring Street. Parking right in front of 141 Spring Street, he saw some people with cameras shooting the exterior of 230 Spring Street. He didn't know if they were newspaper people or gawkers. He didn't much care.

He knocked on the door. "Irene. Irene. It's Bunny."

Wrapped in a furry robe, she opened the door. CeCe shot past her to launch herself onto Bunny.

"Oh, Bunny. A man's been found dead," said Irene, face drained of color. She looked like fear itself.

"You're coming with me, Irene. This is no place for you and CeCe." Bunny walked inside, putting CeCe down.

He spoke to the child. "Get your things, honey." Then

he focused on Irene. "This isn't safe. I'm taking you where you'll be safe."

"Bunny, I can't pay you any rent. I have nothing."

"Leave that to me. I could never live with myself if something happened to you and my angel. Now come on. Tell me what to do and we'll be out of here."

They could hear CeCe's rapid footsteps as she gathered her meager belongings. She rushed out into the barren living room with her little sweater, coat, and some underpants in her arms.

"Uncle Bunny, don't forget my 'cycle."

"Oh, I won't forget that. You have to teach me how to ride it."

Squealing with delight, CeCe carefully placed her clothes at his feet, ran back into the kitchen, and rode her little tricycle out, ringing the bell.

"Irene, you're outnumbered." A big grin crossed Bunny's face. "Come on, what do I need to tote?"

Irene had about as much—or as little—as CeCe. They packed the truck and were off in fifteen minutes.

Bunny drove his "two ladies" to his apartment.

He opened the door, unloaded the truck.

"Honey, you'll be warm here." He smiled at CeCe.

The little girl ran through every room of the apartment, not a huge apartment but two bedrooms, a nice kitchen, and even a fireplace in a living room with a cathedral ceiling.

Irene looked around, not quite believing this.

Bunny quickly reassured her in a soft voice, "I don't expect anything, Irene. I just want you to be safe. I— I don't expect anything." Then with a sheepish grin, he added, "I'm losing my hair. I'm twenty pounds overweight, and well, I'm not much. I don't have the money right now to get you your own place but I don't want you to worry that I expect—well, you know."

Tears welled up in her eyes, then she sagged against

him, sobbing hard. "I'll be a burden. I'm not smart, Bunny. You fix things. You understand things. I can't even work a computer. I'm just dumb and now I can't even get a job at McDonald's."

His shirt soaked with her tears, Bunny was bewildered and flattered at the same time. "Now, don't you worry. You just settle in here. And I'll take computer classes with you. You'll see. You're brighter than you think. You've just had a hard go. It makes people lose their confidence." He patted her back, comforting her while enjoying the feel of a woman hanging on to him.

CeCe ran out into the living room, saw her mother sobbing.

"Mommy!" She ran and hugged her mother.

Irene let go of Bunny, hugged her child. "Tears of gratitude, CeCe. I'm not sad."

CeCe leaned against her mother. "I hate it when you cry, Momma. I don't want you to cry anymore."

Bunny was afraid he might start bawling, too. He cleared his throat. "I've got to get to work. You two girls just do, uh, girl stuff. Irene, I can't leave you the truck but we'll work something out. I'll be home about six."

By the time Bunny arrived home later that night, Reno Sagebrush had cut off all campaign funding for Patrick Wentworth. Also, Jeep had shot two electrifying commercials, which would begin airing in two days on all channels.

Howie Norris, still delighted by his piece of silver ingot, was doing his best pushing the Steering Committee to hire Donald Veigh and others for the upcoming school bus expo. He seemed quite unconcerned that he'd been shot. While others were debating, he was heard whistling, "Stars and Stripes Forever."

At day's end, Bunny stopped short as soon as he entered his apartment. The place sparkled. Flowers—granted, they were silk flowers he'd forgotten were in the closet—had been tastefully arranged on a living room side table. The aroma of pasta sauce filled the house.

CeCe ran out, arms held wide. He picked her up and spun her around. "Mommy says you have to clean up and then we'll have supper. Uncle Bunny, I'm all washed up, too."

Irene stuck her head out from the kitchen. "Found a few odds and ends to dress up the place. Hope you like it."

He kissed CeCe. "I won't be long."

In times to come, Bunny would look back on that simple evening of delicious food and good company as one of the happiest in his life.

CHAPTER TWENTY-EIGHT

Thursday, Mags peered at the computer screen in her small cubicle at Davidson and Fletcher. The information she was amassing about foreclosures in Nevada, and the nation, provided anything but assurance. Her function at the brokerage house was to identify any positive movement in the market with the focus on possible investment. Not every stock is a blue-chip one but identifying good-value start-up companies was vital to economic growth.

For decades there really had been blue-chip stocks. Mags no longer felt that that was true, but she kept it to herself. The U.S. government decided what to save and what to cast aside, making the entire concept of blue chips worthless. A company, if it is allowed to perform without undue restriction, lives or dies by the wisdom of its leadership. What appears to be saving a company by federal interference only assures that the incompetent leadership continues. Instead of getting the punishment only free market capitalism can deliver, such management feels unhampered to repeat their mistakes.

The research gave her information that might help her great-aunt, Babs Gallagher, and the others coming on board to save Spring Street.

Gathering up her papers, she walked down the deep-pile carpet of the hall to Greg Posner, a vice president who had earlier asked her to drop by.

Ever the gentleman, Greg stood when Mags entered the room.

"You look chipper this morning." The fifty-two-year-old man smiled. "Sit in the big chair. I'll sit in the ladderback. My back."

She smiled. "That's the price we pay for walking upright."

He sat down, offered her some peppermints. Greg would likely have a bag of peppermints in his coffin.

Mags took one and unwrapped it. "Whew."

"Knock your nylons off." Greg laughed. "My wife gets them from Germany. There are some things the Germans do better than us and peppermints is one of them. Boy, it's a beautiful country. Have you ever been there?"

"I have and I was overcome by its wealth." Mags had made many trips to Frankfurt back in the days she'd been wheeling and dealing in New York City.

Sitting quite upright, Greg dove in. "Any positives?"

"Mr. Posner—"

"Will you call me Greg? Mr. Posner is my father."

"Greg." She smiled. "Given the huge number of foreclosures, a million homes are now owned by banks and there are five-point-two million homes still in the foreclosure process. Also, what I saw Tuesday at the courthouse steps intensifies my aversion to recommending investing in banks."

"I see." He frowned. Knowing it was bad, hearing the most recent numbers made it all the worse.

"Banks have stopped foreclosure sales in some states as state attorneys examine, with prejudice I think, their loan practices. In my estimation, there is no way that in the next two years those banks can produce honest profits."

"You might want to leave off the word 'honest,' and therein lies a greater problem." Mags looked quizzically at Greg, who then continued. "If you can't trust your banker, who can you trust? The banker and the banks have always held a central, somber, and stabilizing position in the community. The bank president is a figure of great respect. With their image so tarnished, it's going to make it extremely difficult to advise clients to put their funds as shareholders in any bank. The bailouts have made them poison."

"There are a few bright spots and I would cautiously say that Reno Sagebrush United is one," said Mags. "Not now, but next year. They, too, have a lot of foreclosed homes on their books because of taking over Truckee Amalgamated. Truckee Amalgamated did take bailout funds. I can't yet pin down the dollar amount."

"Reno Sagebrush is still tarred by the same brush. The public doesn't know the difference between banks that took bailout funds and those that did not." Greg put his feet flat on the floor. He stood up, stretched his back, then sat down. "Sorry."

"I wish I could think of something to tell you to ease that pain."

"I've heard everything from papaya treatments to removing a disc to spinal fusions—well, maybe they're the same. I'm not doing it. I'm holding out for stem cell treatment. Sooner or later it will happen. Anyway, I got you off the track."

"Any investment in local banks would be ill advised, I'd say, until we know how long it will be before they can sell off those foreclosed homes on their books. My great-aunt and Babs Gallagher have come up with a small but good idea that could have larger applications concerning those toxic assets if, and I believe they are, ultimately, assets."

"Really?"

Mags told the vice president of the plan, the help already generated by the churches. She also told him the key, and most difficult part of this plan, would be bringing around the utilities to a reduced rate for the squatters with perhaps the banks picking up the percentage of the reduction to make it a full rate.

Greg was silent for a good two minutes. He rapped his knee with his right hand. "It has possibilities. The best part is that it pulls Reno together. The only way this can work is if those utilities, the banks, the casinos, and the supermarkets contribute. Well, you said the churches were already helping."

"They have been wonderful. The problem with Reno and indeed much of Nevada is that a huge number—perhaps forty percent—of the residents were not residents last election. Our turnover is astonishing. That doesn't help build community."

"You're right." He thought a bit. "I think the Spring Street plan has a chance. May I pass this on to Alfred?"

"Of course."

"You know, you have a real problem with Patrick Wentworth. Now with this young man being found yesterday, well"—he paused—"I heard your dogs found him."

"Yes, they did." Through Pete Mags had learned a bit more about Brad Heydt. "He was a runaway from Ukiah, California. His family refuses to claim the body."

Greg's face registered surprise. "No wonder he ran away."

"I have a friend in the sheriff's department. They contacted child services over there and I guess the boy had often gone to them for help, but as you know, children have a hard time convincing adults. With nowhere to go, he finally ran away at age fifteen. He'd been sexually abused by his uncle and there is some speculation that his father abused him."

"Shoot them." Greg's jaw tightened. "I'm sorry. I have no compassion for anyone who abuses a child. And if anyone touched my daughters—they're now twenty-eight and twenty-six—I'd still kill them. I wouldn't think twice."

"Greg, a lot of people feel that way. But as you said, Wentworth can create problems for us by identifying this area as unsavory."

"I guess things like this always happened. We just didn't know about them."

"Or if we did, we turned the other way. But then again, people took care of things in their own fashion, as you would. Right?"

"Right." He stood up, stretched again, remained standing.

Mags stood up. "One more item. This foreclosure mess is one domino hitting another. Reno can't collect property taxes from defaulters."

He put his palm in the small of his back. "That will affect services. A drop in tax revenue always does. And remind me again, five-point-two million homes still in foreclosure. Nationally?"

"Right. Most banks are terrible investments right now."

"Are any of the foreclosed homes occupied by the mortgagees, not the squatters?"

"Yes. No hard numbers. Some states, like New York and Florida, have tremendous legal roadblocks for the foreclosure process—not the least being the amount of time and legal fees it takes to actually evict a defaulted tenant."

"Here?"

"Mostly, people got upside down on their mortgages, handed the keys to Truckee Amalgamated or Western United, and walked away."

Greg's eyebrows shot upward. "I see. Well, thank you for your report. We're a long way from crawling out of this mess."

"In housing and banking we are, but I know the rest of the people here will find some companies to recommend."

He smiled. "That's our job. If people don't invest in America, we don't have America."

Mags left the office. While she deeply believed in American ingenuity and the ability of regular people to solve big problems nationally, she believed that faith in Wall Street and investing would be a long time returning. The big players would keep at it, millions would be made, but the crisis' real solution was a long way off.

More than anything, she hoped Aunt Jeep and Babs could restore three blocks in Reno. It could provide some hope, perhaps not a beacon of hope but even a burning match in darkness is precious light.

CHAPTER TWENTY-NINE

Jeep and Babs were driving south of Reno while Mags was meeting with Greg. This area of Reno had suffered its share of foreclosures, with much of the loans held by Western United.

The two wanted to personally contact every priest, minister, and rabbi they could to ask for help in the form of food but also assistance in lobbying the utilities, when that time came, which would be soon.

After five hours of face-to-face encounters with the God Squad, as Jeep called them, the two stopped for a quick lunch.

Gulping coffee, having been badly in need of caffeine, Jeep, once enlivened, said, "Babs, are you surprised at the response?"

"Yes. Only one preacher denied us today. I confess, Jeep, I go to church more out of a sense of duty, to see friends. Dogma leaves me cold. Thankfully, there's not much of it from our pulpit." Babs attended a Methodist church, with many movers and shakers as members.

"I trot down to Trinity Episcopal more for the organist than anything," said Jeep. "I've never been motivated by religion, although I've sure prayed hard when I've been in trouble. But I'm changing my mind." She took another swig.

"How so?"

"Since we've been doing this, we have had three

preachers turn us away, counting today's. Every other priest, preacher, and rabbi has offered help. Some worry they can't do as much as they'd like, but they'll try. I believe there really are people who do God's work. It's done quietly, without attention drawn to one's self. That pretty much applies to everyone we've talked to today. I'm humbled, really."

Perfectly coiffed as always, Babs smiled slowly. "A first."

Jeep laughed. "I deserve that, but you don't get anywhere if you don't believe in yourself first."

"I believe in both of us." Babs's voice rose slightly. "And I'm truly excited about tomorrow, when your appeal ads are aired. Friday was a smart move for the first day."

"I hope so, honey, I do. I figure the Wentworth campaign will slow down a bit over the weekend so we might catch that crew off guard, plus we'll give the residents of Reno a chance to think this over when they are with their families. Maybe they'll realize how lucky they are and be willing to help someone else."

"You were right not to go into that poor boy's death."

"It's an outrage, but we can't mix our messages." Jeep had told Babs what Pete had told both her and Mags concerning Brad Heydt's background. "It's funny, Babs, here I am daily singing 'Nearer, My God, to Thee' along with Howie as I roar through my eighties but I have more energy than ever and I think more focus. I was focused on the war. Then trying to survive after the war. Then mining. Then building the salvage business. But over the last twenty years I've relaxed. Look, it's been wonderful, don't get me wrong, but my engines are revved."

"Mine, too."

"Oh, honey, you aren't half old. Your engine doesn't need an overhaul."

They laughed as they picked through their large salads.

"I'm no spring chicken." Babs speared a seared scallop nestled among lettuce, mandarin oranges, almond slices, and other tidbits designed to caress the palate.

"That makes me a winter chicken." Jeep smiled.

They chatted about people they knew, people they remembered who had gone on, grandchildren, the up-and-coming baseball season (both were Aces fans), all the minutiae that tie people to one another and to a place.

Satisfied that she'd left room for dessert, Jeep ordered crème brûlée, always her test for any restaurant.

"I'll pass." Babs handed the dessert menu back to the waitress.

"You haven't a spare pound on you."

"That's why I'll pass."

Jeep nodded. "I'll give you a bite of crème brûlée."

"I've been thinking about our situation here in Reno, and Nevada in general." Babs folded her hands, leaning forward. "What we do here truly can affect the nation."

"How so?" Jeep leaned forward herself.

"If we can find solutions for Nevada, they might work elsewhere. Our idea—about restoring value to the foreclosed homes, restoring value to lives and getting people back to work—is small, granted, but it's a beginning."

Jeep nodded. "Right now, there's only one person who's actively working against us," she said, thinking of Patrick Wentworth, "but he can inflame others. Fear sells."

"Does it ever." Babs took interest as the crème brûlée, with three fresh raspberries and a mint leaf on the top for decoration, was placed in front of Jeep.

"Would you like the first bite?"

"No, that honor belongs to you, but I'll take the second." Babs held up her clean spoon.

After both sampled the crème brûlée their verdict was: delicious.

After the usual fight for who pays the bill, won by Jeep, the two headed back to Reno.

"Do you mind if I take a short detour?"

"Of course not."

"There's a development that started in 2006, nice homes, the two hundred-fifty-thousand-dollar range out here. Very well planned."

They cruised through two curving riverstone abutments, large wrought-iron gates swung wide open.

About one-fourth of the homes had inviting desert landscaping, which conserved water. No lawns here but a good use of local plants and the ever-present rock outcroppings.

However, many of the homes sat empty and an entire section of the development had abandoned houses still in various stages of construction.

A work truck, light yellow with a mountain outline on the side, announced Sanchez Construction. A dark blue BMW 6 series was parked alongside.

Babs slowed down as she approached the parked vehicles. She recognized Michelle Speransky talking to a man dressed in work clothes, both of them looking at blueprints as they stood in front of one unfinished house.

"Come on, let me introduce you to the senior loan portfolio manager at Reno Sagebrush," said Babs. "She was at our gathering at High Roller but you were surrounded by people. I don't think you met her. Mags did though."

As Babs parked, Michelle looked to the car, saw who was in it, and smiled. She said something to the good-looking man, perhaps in his midforties. They both walked over. Introductions were made.

"Where's your hard hat?" Babs teased Michelle.

"I'm hoping I'll be needing one in the future. I'm here to walk through this unfinished house and to check the condition of the foreclosed ones with Todd. Truckee made all the loans out here, as you probably know." She nodded to Babs.

"It's a lovely development. Close to good schools."

"I'm proud of it," Todd replied. "It's a terrible time for construction. Kind of like being on the Death Star, you know, but I wanted Michelle to see it. We need an extension of our line of credit. No one's lending." Todd Sanchez ran the business started by his father.

Babs looked at Michelle approvingly. "Most officers would just read the numbers on the reports, but you're here."

"Numbers can lie, Babs. I want to encourage business, not smother it, and it's an uphill battle to get money for something like construction, one of the hardest-hit industries. These homes have value, as you know. When the market turns, they'll be worth something again. We've got to restore confidence."

Dry tone to her voice, Jeep said to Michelle, "Your bank and every other has money."

Michelle responded straightforwardly, "Ms. Reed, we do. We also have the massive liability of Truckee Amalgamated's robo loans. And their bailout money, which at some point we must pay back, but here's the real problem: It's easier to make one loan for five hundred thousand dollars than ten loans for fifty thousand. Less paperwork, fewer personnel. The central problem, as I see it, is getting small business loans to the businesses that need them. Clearly, General Motors did not have this problem."

Jeep appreciated Michelle's candor and acumen.

Babs, too, liked Michelle's coming right out with it. "What are your chances of convincing the top brass? You wouldn't be here if that wasn't your intent."

"I have to step softly. Asa Chartris sees the problem,

but he's one officer among many. Bankers are scared, Babs, and they're vilified and, hey, people do have egos. I don't want to make someone feel belittled. Bankers are paralyzed by indecision. And the economy is paralyzed. I hasten to add, bankers aren't the root cause."

Jeep listened carefully. "The root cause, Ms. Speransky, is a generation that came to power, oh, say fifteen years ago with no direct experience of the Great Depression and who disregard the checks and balances in place from those who had suffered. Hubris. The gods always punish it."

"They've been spectacularly successful doing just that." Michelle smiled ruefully.

"Hey, you keep pushing," Todd Sanchez said. "That's what Dad says, and he's right. If one door is closed, knock on another."

"Todd," Babs asked, "would you mind showing us one of the unfinished houses?"

"With pleasure." Todd took Jeep's elbow, acting as an escort.

As they walked through the building, which had the roof on and siding up but nothing else, he pointed out the sturdiness of the frame, showing off joints and joists, even drawing attention to the type of nails used, screw types, and so forth. His knowledge was detailed and intimate. His pride in what his company produced was refreshing. He wasn't selling the building, he was boasting, in a nice fashion, of the company's workmanship.

After the tour, Babs, back at the car, turned to him. "You've created good housing at a good price. No shortcuts, unseasoned lumber, second-grade materials. I truly hope things work out for you and the company."

"Thank you, Ms. Gallagher."

"I do, too." Jeep then noted to Michelle, "You're wise to set aside the paperwork and see for yourself. I hope you can prevail on Reno Sagebrush's leadership."

"Thank you."

Driving back to Wings Ranch, the two talked about what they'd seen. Then Jeep put her forefinger to her lips for a moment.

"That means a pearl of wisdom is about to be tossed."

"Your eyes are supposed to be on the road."

"I have good peripheral vision," Babs shot back.

"I'm trying to understand fully Nevada's crisis and I had one of those errant thoughts that usually contain a bit of a new idea. We are really a two-industry state: mining and gambling."

"We are."

"Here's what just occurred to me: Those states with a plethora of different industries and with strong agriculture like New York, Illinois, and Georgia even—I know I'm leaving a lot out—they are subject to many different economic points of view by people who have built and run those companies."

"Ah." Babs got the point. "We are continually reduced to two streams of thought. They may be good, but they aren't enough."

"When you have a lot of different viewpoints from successful people on the table, I think that state has a better chance of finding solutions to their economic crisis than we do."

"What about California? They have everything."

"They were so rich for so long that their government over the last thirty years promised everything to everybody. They can't possibly pay the bill. But California, I believe, is still our most versatile state. Agriculture alone is amazing, three growing seasons! But you can't promise endless benefits to every Tom, Dick, and Harry. There's probably more to it than that, but that's what I see."

"No one will ever accuse Nevada of being versatile.

Seven inches of rain annually defines much of what we can and can't do."

"Which is why we've been so resourceful in the past," said Jeep. "Look, Babs, old Nevada folk were tough. Are we still tough?"

"You are."

CHAPTER THIRTY

"Hey, Mom, turn on Channel Two," Pete called out as he walked through the door of his parents' home at 6:15 P.M. Friday.

"You're late," Mrs. Meadows called out from the kitchen.

"I know, but I took a shower. Be grateful."

"That kind of day?"

"Yep. Where's Dad?"

"Right here," Whit Meadows said as he emerged from the bedroom. "Had to take a shower, too."

Father and son possessed the same powerful build and similar baritone voices. Pete took his mother's coloring—dark hair and eyes—while his two sisters took their father's sandy coloring along with their mother's curvaceous physique. Like all families, they were a mix of the genetic jackpot. Both of Pete's older sisters, well educated, lived on the East Coast. One was in Washington, D.C., and the other in Greenwich, Connecticut. Both girls married well. Despite being far-flung, they stayed emotionally close with Pete, who bore the brunt of his older sisters' teasing.

"Why Channel Two?" Rebecca walked out of the kitchen, her apron tied on.

"Mags said Jeep's ad is going to run during the six-thirty news."

"What ad?" Whit followed his wife into the kitchen.

"Something about the homeless."

"Is it something to do with that poor starved boy?"

"Yes," Pete answered his dad. "He was twenty."

"Starved." Whit repeated, shaking his head.

Rebecca refrained from comment as she put the finishing touches on her pot roast. Talking about starvation seemed like a jinx.

Pete set the kitchen table. Whit put out the glasses.

"Hon, do you want coffee?" Whit opened the cabinet containing cups and saucers.

"No, sweetie. Too late for me."

"Pete?"

"No, Dad."

"Well, I guess I don't want any, either."

A familiar voice brought their eyes to the small TV in the kitchen.

"Each year ninety-six billion pounds of food are wasted in America. Each day children and adults go hungry. These are hard, hard times. Don't be hardened by them. This is Jeep Reed asking you to help me help the hungry. Together we can end hunger in the biggest little city in America. Please visit www.nohunger.com to see how you can help. Thank you."

"Jesus!" Whit exclaimed because the opening shot was of Jeep standing next to an endless mountain of wasted food.

One pile was actual tossed food from the casinos. Special effects altered it, creating more piles of the same size to represent the pounds ruined.

That image was then followed by shots of clean, but not well-dressed children, bundled up, walking from Spring Street to school with their mothers. That shot was then followed by a long pan of foreclosed homes, which then cut to people standing in line at church soup kitchens. Next were people removing boxes of food from parked vehicles on Spring Street. Many of the vehicles carried church logos, others were private vehicles. A quick shot of a poor child, smiling as she ate a sandwich, preceded the final shot of Jeep.

"That much food?" Rebecca exclaimed. "That's a crime."

"Not yet." Pete smiled ruefully.

"I bet that ad cost her a pretty penny." Whit appreciated Jeep's effort. "She was damned good to us when we fell on hard times. Whatever Jeep wants, the Meadows will pitch in."

Pete spoke up. "Dad, I bet she'd be happy to hear from you and Mom. I know she and Mags threw this ad together very fast and knowing it reached you two would make it worth the cost."

"Ninety-six billion pounds." Whit couldn't get over it.

"The sight of all that wasted food ought to get people fired up," Rebecca said as she passed the peas.

It did.

Patrick Wentworth happened to be home when his wife frantically called him into the den.

"Damn her!" he muttered as he watched the images.

His wife remained silent.

Patrick looked for his cellphone, cursing as he rummaged through the den.

Phillipa walked out into the hall, plucked it off the hall table, walked back into the den, and handed it to him.

He snatched it from her hand and dialed his campaign manager and brother.

"Norton, did you see Jeep Reed's bullshit on Channel Two?"

"No."

Patrick then went on to explain it as best he could, given his angry state.

"Calm down."

Patrick fumed. "Calm down. I've built my campaign on cleaning up this city, on cleaning up this congressional district. That old rich bitch goes right down to Spring Street where that little faggot was found and asks for food? I'll kill her."

Norton replied wryly, "Not a good idea."

"Don't get smug, jackass. If I lose, you lose. I really will kill her."

Watching the ad quite by accident was Michelle Speransky, who was working late at the office. A large computer monitor on her desk was always scrolling the stock market quotes while other windows displayed news sites. She wanted to be up to the minute on what other bank stocks were trading for as well as anything she thought might affect banking in general. Since the market had closed, she watched the local six-thirty news.

She was amazed at the mountains of wasted food. As the message unfolded, she stepped closer to the screen. When the ad closed out, she said out loud, "Wonder what this will really do to those house values?"

It's one thing to see reportage of yet another disaster in Haiti, quite another thing to see something unsettling in your own backyard.

The appeal for help hit Reno like a bombshell. The website got twenty thousand hits in the hour right after the airing.

Jonas Forloines, the advertising director at CBS, had given Jeep good advice: Find the defining image. She had.

Even Zippy noticed the ad because Howie about fell off his chair when he viewed it.

A small group of people whom those images also affected worked at the topless bar on Fourth Street. Business, tepid at seven, would heat up at ten and stay wild until closing time.

Sitting at the bar, watching the lust of his life, Lark, Teton Benson called the girls over.

The girls watched, a flurry of comments and surprise coming from all of them.

Lark, her arm around Tu'Lia, stomped the floor with one high-heeled foot. "That's terrible."

Teton shrugged. "What can we do?"

"You go to the computer and go to the website. That will tell us." Lark had grown accustomed to giving the besotted ex-addict orders. He was one of those guys in his late thirties who, given a choice, would usually make the wrong one.

Lark was actually helping him.

He'd been in love with her for over a year, finally making progress before last Christmas.

Lark tended to react to everything she encountered with emotion. Only later could she take a step back and think more about it.

The manager of the club let Teton use the computer. When he came out of the office, he told the girls the appeal was to organize a food caravan.

"We can do that," Tu'Lia said enthusiastically as the others agreed.

It was to be a caravan with unintended consequences.

CHAPTER THIRTY-ONE

Friday night, eleven P.M., with a comforter pulled up to her waist and a shawl around her shoulders, Jeep sat in bed reading.

Sound asleep in a sheepskin-lined bed was Toothpick. He'd been to the vet, was washed and spruced up. Poor little guy weighed half of a standard Manchester terrier's eighteen pounds.

He'd slept downstairs his first two nights, but Jeep eventually let the dog follow her to bed.

The vet estimated his age to be two, a bit younger than Baxter. Apart from needing more meat on his bones, the vet was certain Toothpick would bounce back. She told Jeep that this breed of dog usually does not get along with other pets, but Toothpick liked everyone fine, disproving the stereotype.

King sprawled on the rug on the other side of the bed from Toothpick.

Jeep read the same paragraph on page fourteen of Diane Rehm's *Life with Maxie* over and over. Her mind kept wandering.

The nightstand supported a stack of books, most of them concerning war through the ages. She placed *Life with Maxie,* a book about love, atop all those others. She'd delighted in love in her life, she just never thought much about it, hence the decision to read *Life with Maxie;*

love for an animal was easier for her to understand than Romeo and Juliet.

Silver frames on a beautiful, graceful round table by the window caught the thin light from the lamp by the bed. She rose, put her feet in shearling slippers, and walked over to visit those she loved and who loved her who had gone before.

King raised his head off his paws, yawned, and got up to be with her.

She stopped at the table and picked up the frames one by one.

Dot's big smile looked back at her. She was thirty-two in that photo, in her prime, wearing a stunning Dior gown for the Cattleman's Ball. Gorgeous Dot did the gown justice. Danny, twenty-four, wearing his Army uniform, smiled at her from his frame. She picked up a photo of her mother and father, longing to once again hear their voices. Relatives, old friends, her copilot, Laura, their arms around each other, a P-47 behind them. Her first horse, Queenie, a quarter horse, who patiently endured her learning to ride as a child. Then the first horse she bought once she made money, Pedro, a sleek, fast animal. Oh, how she loved to fly along with him! She laughed looking at the photo of Thor, her goose who would attack people. She had a photo of the Ford brothers and their wives, the ranch's original settlers and an old photo of the spread when they started it. Strong people with a dream had made Wings Ranch and made Nevada, too. Last, she ran her forefinger over the top of the frame of King's grandmother, Nellie Melba, so named since she could sing.

"I loved your grandmother and mother, King. See, you look just like them." She took a photo of each generation to show the dog, who dutifully put his nose on the glass.

Jeep just as dutifully wiped the moisture off. "King,

I never really told the people in my life that I loved them. One didn't in my day. If you cared for someone, you did for them. It's all different now. People are more expressive. I try but somehow it doesn't quite get out of my mouth. The old ways die hard." Then she looked into his deep brown eyes, "But I always told your grandmother and mother that I loved them."

"I love you, Mom." He wagged his tail slightly.

"And I've really tried to tell Enrique, Carlotta, the grandchildren. Still, it just doesn't come easily." She sat in the chintz-covered deep chair with the big arms. "I can't sleep."

"If you can't, I can't."

"I'm tired but I can't shut off my mind. So many people have called to help and when I checked in with the kids running the website and the little phone bank I set up downtown, I couldn't believe the responses. We are making our first big run after church on Sunday. Seems appropriate. That's only one day's notice but it will help us understand what we have to do to really organize. Babs, that smarty, has called the city councilmen, the Sheriff's Department, the *Reno Gazette-Journal,* the weekly paper, and all the television stations, only to alert them not to direct them. And God bless him, Enrique has organized his old soccer buddies. Mags is working hard, too. My family and my friends have been wonderful."

"They love you," King murmured.

Shifting in the chair, she tucked her feet up under her while she gave King the eye not to pick up her shearling slippers. King's weakness for slippers had her buying a pair once a month, sometimes twice.

"You know what else I can't get out of my mind? Now, King, this is really stupid. Here, I've bought the seed for the one thousand acres that will be irrigated. I've got to put up new fencing for the red Angus that

Enrique is having shipped here, plus I really think I'd better build another good cattle shed. All that. It's a big project, this feeding idea of mine, but you know what I can't get out of my mind?" She leaned over a bit to speak directly to her attentive German shepherd mix. "The half silver ingot found on Howie Norris's ranch. King, that stuff is buried somewhere on that ranch like the old gossips surmised. Where? I know Howie and Ronnie, God rest her soul, looked for it over the decades. But where?"

"Zippy will find it if anyone can."

She heard the little grunt and leaned over farther to pet the glossy head. "I have got to get to sleep. Maybe if I turn the light out."

She crawled back into bed, cut the light.

King waited a few minutes, then he jumped up on the bed.

"You're not supposed to be up here."

"The next two days will be big days. You need your sleep."

Jeep, intending to tell King to get off, rolled over, put her arm around the big boy, and fell fast asleep.

CHAPTER THIRTY-TWO

As Jeep finally slept, Zippy at Peterson Ranch woke up, lifting her head. She strained, ears forward, hearing the calls of coyote. She thought she heard a car motor cut off in the far distance. Jumping off the bed she hurried to the back door, slipping through the dog door.

Howie and Tito, even awake in their separate rooms, couldn't have heard the faint motor noise. They might have caught the coyote calls.

Zippy trotted to the first cattle shed, stood still, and listened intently.

One coyote called to another, *"Stay out of your den for now. Keep the puppies with you."*

Wisps of clouds high in the sky and brilliant stars presided over a cold high-desert night.

Moving in the direction of the coyote call, Zippy headed toward the ridge where Howie had been shot. As she drew closer she saw out of the corner of her eye the mother coyote playing with her pups on a higher ridge beyond that. From time to time, the slender gray animal looked down to her den.

As Zippy approached the crest of the first ridge, the wind shifted and she caught scent of a human male. Dropping low, she moved quickly, stopping at the crest. To her left, a few feet below the crest, reaching into the coyote den was a man perhaps in his thirties.

Zippy could smell the crepe soles on his boots, soles that wouldn't leave a track in this terrain unless there happened to be snow. Wearing a short heavy coat and a lumberjack cap, he used a pole with a hook. Whatever he was trying to recover proved difficult. Finally, he snagged a saddlebag, pulling it out.

On his left hip, he wore a revolver with a long barrel. Zippy heard him breathing hard as he fished around for another bag. Finally, he snagged that one too.

With effort he slung one saddlebag over each shoulder. The heavy contents slowed him as he headed east, sliding down the back side of the second ridge. The mother coyote observed him with as keen an interest as Zippy, who rose to follow him at a distance.

The Australian kelpie, highly intelligent, shadowed him just out of range. Each time he'd stop to take a breath, putting down the heavy saddlebags, she laid down flat, head on her paws. He would have probably missed her in daylight but at night she looked like a small rock outcropping. Zippy marveled that he couldn't smell her. Humans' dulled senses never failed to amaze the dog. Much as she loved Howie, she couldn't believe what he missed about his environment, about other people.

The longer the man carried his bounty, the more exhausted he became, stumbling at times. Finally, reaching the bottom of the second ridge, he sat for about five minutes. On his feet again, he crossed the flatter land to an old Jeep truck that he'd parked off the old access road. No one used that road since no one lived back there. The road occasionally was used by someone from the Bureau of Land Management.

Whoever this man was, he knew his way around. Zippy heard the door of the old truck creak as he opened it. Heaving one saddlebag in at a time, then himself, he slumped over the wheel for a moment. Somewhat restored, he cranked the motor, slowly driving away in the direction of a better unpaved road that would lead to Red Rock Road.

Zippy watched until she heard the wheels crunch as he turned onto the other road. Then she turned and flew back to the den.

She stopped short of the opening for she smelled the coyote and heard her pups.

"That's mine," one yelled.

"Prove it," another little voice yipped.

"That's enough," the mother admonished her children.

A silence followed, then the mother wriggled out of the small den opening. *"What are you doing here?"*

"I heard the truck motor, came out, and found that human taking two bags out of your den."

"This is the third time he's been back, the pain in the ass. He was nearly spotted the second time. That's when he shot at your human, the one you work with."

"How'z 'at?" Zippy was becoming more and more curious about this.

"Your old man came along unexpectedly. This idiot thought he wasn't around. He slunk down behind the ridge, made a big circle and then under cover, what cover there is, took a shot. Whenever I smell him, I stay away or he'd likely shoot me, too. He's obsessed with the junk in here."

"May I look inside?" Zippy inquired politely.

"Well"—the mother, on her haunches, rose, then turned—*"for a minute. The puppies have bones everywhere."*

Zippy squeezed into the den behind her. Once inside, he saw that it was large with tunnels leading to other exits.

"Who are you?" a small, bright-eyed puppy asked.

"Zippy. I live in the ranch house."

"Well, what are you doing here?" The bold little fellow sniffed the dog.

"Bats, go lie down. We have business." She then said to Zippy, "I call him Bats because he drives me batty."

"It's huge in here." Zippy marveled.

"The human who made it created rooms. They're full of these saddlebags and boxes. I can't move them. They're very heavy."

Zippy grabbed the strap of a saddlebag and pulled, only to drop it. "I'll say."

"He might get the saddlebags but he'll never get the boxes out. They're filled with metal. Why would anyone want metal?"

Zippy shook her head. "I don't know. Humans desire so many things that aren't useful. Even Howie—and I love him, I truly do—can get excited about dumb stuff. He'll open his wife's jewelry box, pull stuff out, and tell me how great it is, how beautiful Ronnie looked wearing it. I mean, you can't eat it, and it doesn't keep you warm."

"Strange animals."

"Thank you for letting me come inside. Do you think you'll be safe from that man?" Zippy asked.

"I think so. He smells strong. And like tonight, my friends warned me while the children and I were out not to come back."

"Heard them. He smells like lemons. Cologne, I guess."

"Could be worse." The mother smiled as she walked Zippy to the entrance.

"I'll bring a bone and put it nearby tomorrow. Thank you again." Zippy then trotted toward home.

Small stones rolled downward as she descended the lower ridge. Careful though she was, the freezing and thawing had loosened the rocks.

Zippy thought about what Howie, being a cattleman,

had told her. He said that so much commercial feed is loaded with hormones, some even with antibiotics, that it changed the taste of meat and it changed hides. That had occurred to her as she tugged at the old saddlebag. The leather was tough, thick. The bags were made before hormones were introduced into feed. Were they more recent, they would have partially disintegrated.

She understood then that the well-disguised den hid the Garthwaite treasure.

CHAPTER THIRTY-THREE

Sunday at one o'clock, sun shining brightly, Jeep, Mags, King, and Baxter turned onto Spring Street. They had left Toothpick at the ranch, fearing he might become upset returning to his former home. Babs's organizing ability shone as brightly as the sun on a day that felt like true spring. Cars were parked along the curb. People, many coming from church services, unloaded food, clothing, and games for children. Some even unloaded books in case anyone liked to read. All three television stations had newscasters there, as did the daily and weekly papers. The sheriff's department, as well as the sheriff himself, helped.

"That's interesting," Mags noted.

"Means our good sheriff talked to the city council."

As Jeep parked, Pete, who'd been watching out for them, left his parents, and sprinted over.

Opening the door, he kissed Mags on the cheek as she disembarked.

"Weak mind, strong back," he said. "Give me orders."

Jeep, now outside herself, opened the door for the dogs. "Pete, isn't this something?"

"Powerful ad." He kissed Jeep on the cheek. "Powerful lady."

She smiled. "All I did was give the people of Reno a chance to show their goodness."

"Mom and Dad are here," Pete informed Jeep.

"Wonderful. I'll get over to them as soon as I check in with Babs."

"Aunt Jeep, let Pete escort you. People will stop you every step of the way. I can unload the truck."

"I'll protect her." King lifted his ruff.

"I'll protect my lady, too." Baxter set his jaw, which made his moustache even more prominent.

Hand on Jeep's elbow, Pete guided her toward Babs, who was standing on the bed of a truck, quietly dispensing orders.

Some of the neighborhood's impoverished residents, now emboldened, emerged from the houses. Other remained sequestered, especially the illegal immigrants. Donald Veigh acted as a runner between groups of people.

Down the block, Howie Norris was chatting with Asa Chartris.

"How'd you swing it?" Howie asked.

"I went to the board and said two words: 'Do it.' I mentioned that banks currently are reviled. We need to help people as best we can without harming shareholders."

"Resistance?"

"A little. Michelle Speransky brought up a good point, which is that nowhere in the city ordinances does the word 'squatter' appear. Homeless is the word used for street people. These people here are considered trespassers, which breaks the law."

"Kind of like Bill Clinton's lesson in semantics?" Howie stuck his hands into his pockets.

"Yeah, well this won't cost the taxpayer seven million dollars."

"How'd you get around it?"

"We didn't. I called the sheriff and he went over to

City Hall. They all decided on the humane approach. What good does it do to throw people out on the street, especially children? What good does it do when all of them are up for election next year? They chose the rational course and so did we."

"Your jackets are nifty." Howie liked the maroon jackets with white lettering: RENO SAGEBRUSH UNITED.

Asa laughed, sweeping his hand outward. "We aren't the only ones advertising our goodness."

Howie laughed, too, as many groups wore armbands or light jackets since the temperature hovered at about 53°F—pleasant but not T-shirt weather.

Zippy smelled King before she saw him. She lifted her head, then ran over as King and Jeep reached Babs.

"Hey, someone brought meat loaf."

King, tail upright, walked over to the bounding Zippy. *"We won't get any."*

"But it smells so good." Zippy wagged her tail. *"Where's the sawed-off shotgun?"*

"Back with Mags."

Donald, returning for more orders, helped Jeep up into the bed of the truck. "Thank you for this, Miss Reed."

"It's my pleasure, really. Just look at all these people."

Moving slowly down the block bustling with activity were Patrick Wentworth and Reggie Wilcox, with his camera rolling.

Lorraine, Pete's ex-wife, was interviewing the sheriff. She had just finished when Patrick Wentworth approached.

"Sheriff."

The sheriff waved him off. "Patrick, I'm a public employee. I can't endorse a candidate."

"I'm not asking you to endorse me," Patrick replied evenly.

Lorraine whispered, "Get this," to her cameraman.

As Patrick pursued the sheriff, he was intercepted by Pete, who simply put a hand on his shoulder.

"Who the hell are you?" Patrick snarled.

"Deputy Pete Meadows, off duty."

"Take your hand off me."

Pete dropped his hand. The brief delay allowed the sheriff to walk into the middle of the Lutheran church group and start lifting out a few boxes.

"I recognize you from TV," said Patrick. "You're the guy who found the murdered man."

"In the line of duty." Pete weighed his words.

"What are you doing down here now?"

"Trying to help out. I thought you might want to see the inside of one of these foreclosed homes." Pete cleverly held out the bait, which might get Patrick out of hardworking people's way, at least for a little while.

Reggie muttered. "That's a good idea."

The three walked toward a house Pete knew was vacant. The sheriff watched him go, grateful that he had an officer who could think on his feet politically as well as physically.

Just then a minivan pulled onto the street, filled with food and clothing, as well as the beauties from the Black Box. Within minutes, the girls, in tight pants and boots, spilled out. Giggling and tossing their hair out of the way as they unloaded boxes, they brought with them a gust of youth, energy, and unconventionality.

Babs noticed, as did Jeep.

Babs leaned down to Donald and said, "Tell the girls they can drop food at the houses midblock. You can judge how much food they have and see if they need extra hands."

"I guess that ad did reach a lot of people." Jeep smiled broadly.

Teton, reluctant to come out from behind the wheel,

was finally coaxed out by Lark. At the back of the mini-van, she pointed to boxes.

SSRM also had people there. Twinkie carried boxes. Bunny helped out, as did Irene and CeCe. Irene was nervous but Bunny, busy, didn't notice.

Mags, never having seen Lorraine in person, watched her with curiosity. Lorraine was conventionally beautiful, made up for the camera. Mags neither liked nor disliked her. Pete said that Lorraine wanted a big career. He wanted to stay in Reno.

Enrique, Carlotta, and their friends, thanks to Carlotta's knowledge of Spanish, found the homes wherein illegal immigrants hid. They left food and clothing at the back doors.

"This is my big-break day," Tu'Lia told Lark breathlessly as they delivered goods.

"Whatever you say." Lark was accustomed to Tu'Lia's boundless optimism.

"I mean it. You, too. Look at all the cameras. I'm going to get interviewed. Just watch."

"Tu'Lia, let's empty out the van first. You can get ready for your close-up once we're done."

"I want to be filmed carrying food. Come on, girl, this is our big chance."

Lark just nodded.

On Lark's side, farthest away from cameras and people, Teton bent his head. "Tets, honey, no one is going to give you grief," she said.

"Yeah, well, whenever cops are around I like to make myself scarce."

"Depends on how cute they are." Tu'Lia giggled.

"Uh, none of them are cute to me, Tu."

Tu'Lia wrinkled her pert nose. "Why do men always have to say something like that? I mean, are you really afraid someone will think you're gay? It's so stupid."

Teton kept his mouth shut.

"It's a guy thing. Just forget it." Lark set the heavy box down on a house's doorstep and knocked on the front door.

Tu'Lia, pushing her chest out to the maximum, saucily said, "No man refuses me."

Just then a little boy opened the door a crack. Lark smacked Tu'Lia in the midriff so she stood up straight without pushing out her bosoms.

"Honey, this is for you and your Mommy." Lark knelt down.

The child, thumb in his mouth, stared up at her, then ran toward the back calling, "Mommy."

After a few words with a harried mother, the two girls and Teton headed back to the van. As they did so, Pete, Patrick, and Reggie emerged from the empty house.

Teton groaned upon seeing Pete.

Grin in place, Lark waved to Pete, then said to Teton, "You're here for a good reason. Get over it."

Tu'Lia recognized Patrick Wentworth about the same time he recognized her.

"Reggie, get footage," he said. "I can really use this."

"How?" Reggie had a bad feeling.

"Show disreputable elements. The first sign that things are going from bad to worse. Get those girls on camera!" Patrick lunged forward.

Tu'Lia did also, breasts more than prominent.

"Uh-oh." Lark hurried after her.

Teton hurried back to the van.

Lorraine ran toward the potential collision. Her cameraman ran after her. They stopped ten feet away.

Seeing people run, King and Zippy naturally ran after them. What's more fun than running after a person or running with them?

Tu'Lia threw her arms around Patrick, giving him a big kiss. She rubbed her breasts on him.

"O-o-h," Tu'Lia squealed suggestively.

Patrick pulled her hands from behind his neck, threw her on the ground, then kicked her.

Pete immediately put himself between Patrick and Tu'Lia, who curled up on the ground. Lark knelt down to help up the foolish girl.

Tears ran down Tu'Lia's face. Lorraine was getting all of it.

"Are you all right, honey?" Lark asked.

"He kicked me, he kicked me right in the tits. It hurts," Tu'Lia wailed.

Now alert to the situation, the sheriff walked over slowly. Pete had it in hand, but the sight of a uniform can work magic.

Lark walked off with Tu'Lia, who had her head on Lark's shoulder.

King snarled at Patrick Wentworth.

"Get that vicious dog away from me," Patrick spat.

Now in front of Patrick, the sheriff said quietly, "That dog saved a woman's life this year. You'd best be moving along, Mr. Wentworth, before you're charged with assault."

Anger abating finally, Patrick noticed all three network cameras rolling.

He leaned toward the sheriff. "I am going to be your next representative to Congress. You're going to have to deal with me."

"That's up to the people of Washoe County." The sheriff threw his shoulders back. "I advise you to leave. Now."

As the other networks shot Patrick skulking away, Lorraine walked over to the van where Tu'Lia was wiping her tears. True to form, the stripper gave her one hell of an interview.

Tu'Lia's wish came true. She was all over the TV news that night.

CHAPTER THIRTY-FOUR

By Monday, April 18, Patrick Wentworth had cobbled together an ad that he hoped would muffle the damage of the news footage of him kicking Tu'Lia when she was down.

His ads ran on the morning news and again at night. People unloading boxes from vans were seen in the background, but the foreground was of Tu'Lia and Lark at the open doors of the minivan. A quick cut of Tu'Lia exiting the Black Box in the cold—the footage shown in his ad six weeks ago, breasts blurred so as not to offend those bothered by the sight of a good-looking woman's breasts. She was identified as a "so-called exotic dancer." He then slammed Jeep as a woman rich enough to buy Reno, buying favors from the people on Spring Street, and on he ranted, also including a shot of King snarling. His point was that Spring Street was headed for the skids, bad elements were moving in.

Both his mother and his brother tried to talk him out of such an incendiary attack.

"We're running out of money," his brother warned, but even that didn't dissuade him.

"All three stations are run by liberal flunkies. I'm going to win!" He banged his mother's kitchen table with his fist.

Bad as it was kicking Tu'Lia and then trying to weasel out of it by saying she attacked him, his real mistake was in sliming the sheriff and the city council. In his new ad, he quoted the ordinances concerning trespassing and declared that he would bring suit against the city council for ignoring their own laws, and against the sheriff for same.

The next day, Tuesday, city council members on the steps of the county offices, along with the sheriff in full uniform, read a statement: "The economic crisis of our city has created unexpected suffering among adults and children. Removing those devastated by our nation's economic downturn, casting them into the streets, is not in the interests of this city. We refuse to do this.

"What we promise is to do everything in our power to find employment for the people out of work wherever they might be. Nor will we allow children to go hungry in our city."

The head of city council then unfolded a sensible plan so children could get one hot meal—their school lunch. He gave a website address so residents could examine the details and costs of this plan.

He then ended with: "Reno is the biggest little city in America. We have the biggest hearts, too."

Airing this as a public service ad during prime time was unusual, but no news director had ever remembered public servants making such a statement.

The news directors, all three of them men, also realized that few heterosexual males in Washoe County would be offended by Tu'Lia's assets even if they were blurred. They were left intact on the screen. Those males in adolescence, although they could access porn faster than their parents, were entranced because they could watch this as news with their parents.

As for the women of the county, for most of them it was the usual shrug and wry smile. It's difficult for women to comprehend how mammary glands imprison male minds and body parts. Not that women were complaining. You take what God gives you and make the most of it, or in Tu'Lia and Lark's case, you take what God gives you and add to it.

The news directors milked Sunday's events for two days. Tu'Lia, not in her work clothes, gave humorous, lengthy interviews. Lark had coached her.

After the last microphone walked out the door, she clapped her hands. That night, at work, the place was packed with men chanting her name.

She sidled up to Lark. "I told you Sunday was my lucky day. This is just the beginning."

Lark put her arm around Tu'Lia's waist and whispered, "I hope so, Tu, I really do."

On his barstool, Teton listened to the men, observed Tu'Lia's radiant face. In the doghouse for bailing on them Sunday, he wondered how to right himself in Lark's eyes. The last thing he wanted was for his face to be seen on TV. She knew that.

She also knew that when her friend Tu'Lia had been hurt she could have used a hand getting her back to the minivan. Lark, an average student in school, while not a reader or much of a thinker, was reasonably intelligent. America values book learning, but Lark had common sense once her emotions calmed down. She knew her days were numbered at the Black Box. She'd never found what she wanted to do in life, but she knew she didn't want to serve in a topless bar forever. She also knew the first wrinkle would demote her. Tu'Lia's need to be the center of attention, which was part of the performer's personality, wasn't hers. Lark just wanted to make a decent living and knew she could make a lot more money serving drinks in a spare costume than she could as a clerk at Walmart.

Lark had hoped Teton would grow up and accept responsibility, and some of that responsibility included her. His behavior on Sunday shook that hope.

She smiled as Tu'Lia ran from table to table, her excitement enlivening the patrons.

She is on her way up, Lark thought. *Where am I heading?*

On Wednesday night, Mags was working in her great-aunt's den, going over some papers from her part-time job. Great-aunt and great-niece discussed fully all that had transpired. She punched in more requests, numbers, etc., then sat and stared at the computer screen for a long, long time.

Baxter was asleep in front of the fireplace. Toothpick was curled next to him, lifting his head when King, claws clicking, crossed the hardwood floor, then also settled on the carpet. Jeep followed.

"Sweetie, you're going to ruin your eyes," Mags's great-aunt said.

She smiled at this person she loved so much. "Guess I have been at it too long."

"Wrap it up. I'll fix us both a drink. Let's sit in front of the fire. You know the snow's still on the top of Peavine Mountain so we'll have fires in the fireplace at night for a bit more."

"Right." Mags nodded, then shut down the computer.

Jeep fixed herself a stiff bourbon, and for Mags, a scotch and water with two ice cubes from the small bar in the den.

The two women sat down, each gratefully taking a sip. It had been a long day.

"Aunt Jeep, the more I investigate bank stocks for Davidson and Fletcher, the more I realize that clearing up those foreclosed homes on Spring Street or wherever they occur will be extremely complicated."

"Will this be any more complicated than usual?"

"The government doesn't know what it's doing. There are too many government agencies with oversight all blaming each other for the catastrophe. Listen to this: Loans are supposed to go to a secure trust when sold. But the banks were selling so fast at such volume, they cut every corner they could, even using robosigners and people who rubber-stamped all loans without investigating the creditworthiness of the applicant. The banks, to save time and make more and more money, just assigned the loan *blank*. They decided to fill in the paperwork later."

At this unbelievable fact, Jeep's eyes popped open wide. "You're kidding. Mags, if the American public ever truly understands how it has been robbed and duped I believe there will be widescale violence. Blood." Jeep inhaled deeply.

"In a small way, there already has been. Pete told me Robert Dalrymple was a robosigner."

"Ah." Jeep looked at the three dogs fast asleep and peaceful. "It's like when I flew in the fog and I was approaching mountains. I couldn't see them but I knew if I didn't climb, I'd be dead."

"Well, that's the question. Can we climb? There are government officials and bankers swearing we're not in a fog and there are no mountains."

"Yes." The ice cubes tinkled in the cut-crystal glass, another of Dot's lovely purchases for Jeep who would have been happy with an old paper cup.

"What we don't know can hurt us individually because, Aunt Jeep, we've drawn attention to a huge foreclosed area, as has Patrick Wentworth. I have this sensation, like a bug crawling on my back that I can't reach, that we've both brought scrutiny to areas that some people would wish we hadn't."

"Oh, I think we're safe enough."

"Aunt Jeep, why would a middling former bank employee have his throat slashed? It can't be because he made bad loans or there'd be thousands dead all over America."

Jeep leveled her eyes on her beautiful niece's lustrous ones. "Point taken."

CHAPTER THIRTY-FIVE

That Thursday, April 21, Jeep drove over to Howie's to walk through his cattle. Her hidden agenda was to check up on him. Tito was on the tractor putting out large hay bales.

Zippy ran beside the two humans along with King and Baxter and Toothpick, who wore a knitted sweater as he didn't have a lot of fur or fat.

"Hard winter. Spent an extra four thousand on hay." Howie stood admiring his herd of Baldies.

A blush of green on the creek bed gave hope that winter was over.

"Money well spent. They look good. Should bring a good return."

"Anything can happen, but I hope you're right. An outbreak of cattle disease in Britain can scare off people here. They stop eating beef. You and I have seen the damnedest things."

"That we have." She pointed to an especially well-made heifer. "You're not selling her, are you?"

"Nope. She's what I'm aiming for but I really have to buy another bull and tell you what, my neighboring goddess, those costs have spiked. Saw in St. Joseph, Missouri, where a bull went at private sale for forty-five thousand dollars."

Jeep put her hand to her face and stroked her chin for a moment. "Well, that's a hell of a lot of bull." She smiled. "But if you do artificial insemination, sell those semen straws, you can make that purchase price back. How long it will take, I don't know."

"If I were younger I'd do it. But I'm not collecting semen at my age and besides, I'd need a special place to store the semen and I'd need a centrifuge, too, to separate the semen from the fluid. It's a bit of work and a whole lot of know-how. I'm not hiring anyone to help me with my operation. Christ, the payroll taxes, the paperwork. Do you realize how much productivity is lost because of this crap?"

"Yes, I do." This subject so depressed the old woman that she returned to the health of the herd. "You do a wonderful job all by yourself."

Beaming from the praise, Howie shrugged. "Takes a cattleman to know a cattleman. And thank you again for sending Tito after I got out of the hospital. I resisted but I forgot what it's like to have someone in the house. He's a good worker. I owe you for his labor."

"You owe me nothing. You've gotten jobs for some of the Spring Street people for the school bus expo. That more than covers it."

As the humans talked cattle, prices, and chances for a better hay year on irrigated acres, the four dogs skirted the cattle.

One momma cow, coat gleaming, eyed them suspiciously. *"Come near my baby and I'll stomp you to death."*

"Marlene, these are my friends. We aren't going to molest your beautiful calf." Zippy trotted around her followed by King, Baxter, and Toothpick.

"What's that little hairy thing?" Marlene indicated Baxter.

Stung, the intrepid wire-haired dachshund asserted, *"I kill vermin. I don't herd. You got a rodent problem, you call on me. I'll go right down their hole. I'll get them!"*

Marlene appeared unconvinced.

"Come on, Baxter, before her two brain cells fry," the energetic Zippy prodded.

Taking one more look over his shoulder at the large lady, Baxter picked up speed to catch up.

The four dogs ran over one ridge, then climbed half-way up another, very near where Howie had been found.

Toothpick, thrilled to be outside, to have friends, whirled around once out of happiness.

The humans turned to go back to the house.

Howie put his fingers in his mouth and whistled for Zippy.

"Damn." Zippy pouted.

"Practice selective hearing," King counseled.

"I will but only for a little bit. He gets so upset. He worries me. I mean he's okay but he's still not a young fellow," Zippy stated.

"Yeah, I know what you mean," King agreed.

"Jeep's got my mom. She'll take care of her." Baxter stuck his chest out.

"Come on, let's take a peek then race back before they start bitching and moaning." Zippy ducked behind the big rock outcropping. *"Here."*

The odor of coyote filled the air.

"A den all right. Clever. Very clever." King stood in front of one opening, other camouflaged openings dotted the hill a short distance from this one.

The coyote female had dug out under the big rock. Given the other rocks jutting around it—the opening faced away from the west, the Peterson range—it afforded protection and was not visible until one came right up on it. Even then, it could be missed.

"Vermin!" Baxter wriggled right in only to face a snarling mother with her pups.

Toothpick, terrier blood up, stood behind Baxter. *"Let me help."*

King heard the growl as did Zippy.

Baxter barked, "*I will tear your throat out.*"

The coyote opened wide her jaws, "*You haven't a chance.*"

"*Toothpick, get out of the way,*" King ordered.

Hearing that, Zippy, smaller than King, put her head in the den and grabbed Baxter's tail, pulling the enraged dachshund out of danger.

"*I can handle it.*" Baxter fumed.

"*Me, too,*" Toothpick declared.

"*She's bigger and she's defending her cubs. Don't be stupid, you two. Even I wouldn't take her on alone and not in her den. Toothpick, you're still skinny and weak. Don't be brainless,*" King said emphatically.

A shrill whistle pierced the air.

"*Come on. If we go back we might get treats.*" Zippy flew back down, little rocks flying up behind her paws. "*If we don't, no goodies.*"

The three now ran alongside Zippy.

"*Look happy. He likes it when you look happy when you come to him.*"

"*He can't see that far. He's a quarter mile away or more.*" King laughed.

"*Doesn't hurt to practice,*" the wise dog replied.

"*There's stuff in that den,*" Baxter, recovering from his encounter, sang out.

"*I saw numbers on the boxes,*" Toothpick added.

King, a bit ahead, called back, "*Must be more than one coyote.*"

"*Sure there's nothing we can eat? She's stashed food. They always do,*" Zippy asked hopefully.

"*No food.*"

"*Well, then the hell with it.*" Zippy reached Howie and jumped straight up in the air but not on him. "*He loves this.*"

As it turned out, Jeep and Howie had been discussing food.

"They say they're willing to do it but their owners aren't. Liability." Jeep told him about her efforts to get more food from the casinos. "I did get a little cooperation from some of the local owners who saw the TV coverage of our Sunday food deliveries. The casinos owned by out-of-city companies are the most cautious."

"Lawsuits. It's the biggest waste in our country, not food. These guys are worried about lawsuits."

"Time, money, emotion." Jeep shrugged. "Mags has been researching foreclosure information. I've been researching foodstuff. The Emerson Good Samaritan Food Donation Act, passed by the Congress and Senate, protects restaurants, orchards, and the like from liability. But they're all scared. One thing stuck in my mind. I've been investigating state to state and our next-door neighbor, California, is estimated to have ninety thousand restaurants. Only a thousand of them donate food. I'm having a devil of a time getting information for Nevada."

"It's hard to believe there can be so much waste. Well, it's everything, isn't it? Paper, rubber, steel. I mean even something like old bed frames tossed in the dump, all those things can be refashioned."

"I guess our worst waste is people. We toss them aside if they can't fit into our competitive society the way we want. I'm no Goody Two-shoes, I think you have to work for a living, but when people tell you you aren't good enough or demote your skills, such as viewing a carpenter as not as valuable as a computer whiz, that's harmful."

The two drank cups of coffee together. Tito walked in through the back door. "Boss." He tipped his worn Stetson to Jeep, then turned to Howie. "Sir, another heifer gone."

"Dammit!" Howie grimaced. "Wonder if I put up those motion-sensitive cameras if we'll see who does it."

"If they pass by the camera, you will," Jeep replied. "But it's a big spread, Howie. My advice is you and Tito carry a sidearm. You know I usually do."

"You're right," Howie grumbled.

Jeep looked at Tito. "Come on by later. I have an extra revolver. You'll need a holster, but that long barrel sure helps the accuracy."

Driving back to Wings Ranch, Jeep thought the chances of actually catching someone rustling one heifer to be small. Still, given events at Peterson Ranch, Howie should be armed. It bothered her that Pete and Lonnie hadn't come up with anything. She knew they were good officers. Whoever was sneaking around on Howie's ranch was either very smart or very lucky.

King, in the passenger seat along with Baxter and Toothpick, said, *"I think Mom would like to know what's in that coyote den."*

"How will we ever get her up there?"

"I don't know. And how will we ever get the coyote out?"

"I'll do it," the thin black and tan dog piped up.

CHAPTER THIRTY-SIX

"Think UNR will sign that kid from Ely?" Lonnie asked Pete as they drove toward Reno from the south.

"Be great if they did. But a lot of other schools are looking at him, too. Be pretty tempting to go to Auburn or Oregon. Someplace far away."

The kid in question led the nation in pass receptions and was being courted heavily by many schools. He would soon have to make a decision. This would be much publicized, with TV footage of the young man putting on the hat of the college as well as holding up a football jersey or T-shirt. Beaming smiles would fill the screen. Secretly, the coach would pray the kid would hold up through four years of football, not rape any coed or get caught stealing a computer, or take a car as a gift from an agent already scouting for the pros. Fortunately, most college players possessed enough sense to avoid these splashy scandals.

"Ever wish you'd gone into the pros?" Lonnie rubbed a quarter between his thumb and forefinger, feeling the outline of a cattle skull, for the back was emblazoned with an image of Montana.

"Sometimes. And I play league ball here. I never want to leave Reno."

"I would. If a job opened up somewhere, a lot more

money and a promotion, I would. Given the economy, that's not going to happen."

"Yep." Pete considered Lonnie's thoughts. "Do you want to work in a bigger city?"

"Well, if I got paid more. I mean, working on the Phoenix force would mean a lot more action than Reno. If it weren't for your delightful company, I'd get bored."

"Oh, geez."

The dispatcher broke up this conversation with an immediate directive to Yolanda Street.

"You might regret using the word 'bored.'" Pete hit the siren. They roared through traffic.

"The address is right next door to where we found Robert Dalrymple," Lonnie noted.

"Yep."

They screeched in front of the foreclosed home, windows broken. Yolanda Street seemed even more forlorn than when they had made their last call here.

Waiting at the front door was a worried but calm young man with the bad teeth that often indicated a meth addiction. "I didn't do nothing."

"No one's accusing you." Pete nudged the door, which was ajar, open with his foot.

Other sirens pierced the afternoon calm. Pete was glad for backup.

"You stay here," Pete told the young man.

Lonnie followed.

Pete walked around Patrick Wentworth's body. His throat had been slit. Blood covered the wooden floor. His fly was unzipped, his genitals exposed.

"Same M.O., sort of," said Lonnie.

Next to him, stabbed through the heart, lay Tu'Lia, blood still oozing out of a deep wound. She wore provocative clothing: a shiny blouse, opened, and a miniskirt pulled up. Her panties had been thrown across the room.

"Son of a bitch." Lonnie could never accustom himself to the sight of a murdered young woman. It invariably aroused anger and pity.

"Bring that kid in here," Pete ordered.

Seconds later, Lonnie brought in the young man.

"Your name?"

"Bill Sandobar. I didn't do this."

"Mr. Sandobar, tell me how you found the bodies."

Nervously, Bill, his black curls already dampening with sweat, spoke, words tumbling out. "I was looking for a place to stay. Just for little while. I checked out some houses down the street, but they were too close to dealers. So I walked this way. The place looked okay, I mean, the broken windows are bad, but the upstairs windows ain't broken. I tried the door. It was open. There they were."

"Quite a shock," Lonnie murmured sympathetically.

"Yeah, but I used to work in the morgue. No sense of smell. Do they stink?"

"No," Pete replied. "They haven't been dead long enough. Why'd you leave the morgue?"

"Laid off. And there hasn't been a lot of work. When summer comes the murder rate pops up, old people die in the heat. I'm hoping I get hired back."

"Good luck, I think. You've seen people with their throats slit before?"

"Mostly gunshot wounds, but I've seen a few. There are worse things to see."

"It doesn't appear they defended themselves." Pete spoke to Lonnie. "Doesn't compute."

"Does if he was on top of her," Lonnie said. "The killer could just pull his head back, cut, then stab her through the heart. Here's the thing, partner, we're supposed to think they were having sex. Maybe they were. The real question is if they were, why would this woman consent, even for money, after what happened at Spring

Street? She wasn't a female Einstein, but I don't think she was that stupid."

"Possible but like I said, strange. Same with Dalrymple. No struggle."

Backup arrived. This team involved a woman officer. She blurted out upon seeing Patrick Wentworth: "That lying sack of shit."

This attitude permeated Reno when the story of the double murders hit the six-thirty news.

At her locker at the Black Box, Lark was pulling out her costume when one of the other girls screamed in the main room.

Lark ran into the main room. When she heard the news about Tu'Lia, she sat on a barstool, put her head in her hands, and sobbed.

Soon all the girls were crying, some louder than others. Tu'Lia, although childish in her desperation to be a star, meant no harm to anyone. The owner, also shocked, had the tact to close business for the night.

Lark called Teton on his cell. This was the first communication initiated by her since he'd bailed on Spring Street.

"I'll be right down."

She ran to him when he came through the door.

"Come on, honey," he said. "Come on home. I'll make you a cup of the tea you like. You know, citrus mint."

After collecting her things, she walked up to his apartment, drank the tea, and cried. He wound up crying, too.

"What an awful death," Lark said over and over again.

"Try not to concentrate on that. At least she wasn't tortured and it was fast."

* * *

Jeep, in the kitchen with Carlotta, watched the news.

"Mags," she called out.

When no answer came, Jeep grumbled something.

"I'll find her," Carlotta offered.

"You've got flour all over your hands. I'll find her."

"That's some news." Carlotta sprinkled out more flour.

"Stunning." Jeep hurried down the hall, King behind her, Toothpick behind King.

"*Baxter,*" King called out.

"*Upstairs.*"

King headed up the stairs. Jeep followed him, knowing his senses were better than hers.

"*Mags!*"

Towel wrapped around her, Mags walked out of her room. "Aunt Jeep, what's the matter?"

Jeep repeated the news story almost verbatim.

Listening with surprise bordering on disbelief, Mags said, "Aunt Jeep, do you mind if Pete comes over for supper? If he's free? He's had a rough day."

"Of course."

Pete readily accepted the invitation. No one brought up the murders while eating but afterward, in the den, they discussed them.

"And you think this is connected to that other fellow's death?" Jeep raised her eyebrows.

"I do, though I don't yet know why. But I'll find out. Well, that's my job, isn't it?" He patted Baxter, who sat on his lap. "Your orphan has put on a pound or two."

"*Suck-up.*" King sniffed on the floor next to Jeep.

"*No one wants to hold you, you're too big,*" Baxter said.

"*Says you.*" King curled his upper lip.

"*You're too big to sit on anyone's lap.*"

"You can be a real pissant." King curled back his upper lip more.

Toothpick jumped on Mags's lap, smiling down at King, now completely disgusted.

Baxter traded places with Toothpick. He wasn't ready to share Mags.

"I don't feel sorry for Wentworth. He showed his true colors when he kicked that poor girl. I feel sorry for his wife," Mags said.

"First, she finds out he's dead. Then she finds out he's lying next to a young woman, both of them in a compromising situation. Poor woman, I wonder if she knew what he was when she married him?"

"Does anyone?" Mags fired back, then looked at Pete. "Regardless of gender."

"Yeah, well, I guess marriage is one long journey of discovery. If you're lucky, it's a pleasant one." Pete shrugged. "I'll have more to go on when we get the toxicology report, plus the report on whether they'd had sex."

"He barked up the wrong tree." Baxter shrewdly assessed the situation.

"Yeah, but whose tree?" King wondered.

"I'm glad he's dead." Toothpick's whiskers swept forward. *"Every now and then, he'd drive down our street. Brad would hide. Everyone would hide. He didn't find what he was looking for so he'd drive off."* Toothpick sighed. *"My dead master was a good person. He was just scared all the time."*

Baxter reached over and licked Toothpick's forehead. *"You don't have to be scared. You're safe here."*

CHAPTER THIRTY-SEVEN

Everywhere throughout Reno—from gas stations to supermarkets, even at elementary schools—the town buzzed about the spectacular demise of Patrick Wentworth and Tu'Lia. Some laughed derisively.

His mother, brother, and wife were not laughing, but even among his family there was a sense that he brought some of this on himself. Murder seemed outrageous, but Patrick's stubborn persistence had whittled away those who might have supported him.

Emma Logan, Robert Dalrymple's girlfriend, didn't laugh, either. She called Pete. He and Lonnie drove over to see her at her job at Dr. Marahbal's office.

Waiting in the plush office, a huge flat-screen TV tuned to the Discovery Channel, Emma came out and greeted them in her nurse's uniform.

"Come on back, please. Dr. Marahbal says we can use the small visiting room."

As they walked down the spotless corridor, they noticed that every examining room door was closed. There were beautiful underwater photos on the walls. It was obvious that the doctor had built a thriving practice, as well as an office that minimized the fear and distaste in seeing one's physician. His specialty was respiratory diseases. Given the lack of humidity and an annual rainfall of seven inches, many patients suffering from allergies moved to Nevada. Most of them immediately felt relief, a few did not, and Dr. Marahbal treated them. All too often the persistence of allergy-like symptoms signaled something more serious.

Emma led them back to a cozy room, which was painted in high-desert colors. A comfortable couch and three equally comfortable chairs surrounded a gorgeous coffee table, inlaid with beautiful tiles.

"Can I get you two anything?"

"No." Pete sat as she indicated the sofa.

Lonnie sat next to him and took out his notebook.

"When you visited me, I told you that Robert had gone to Patrick Wentworth's campaign office to offer his services."

"Yes, you did."

"Well, I thought of something else. I guess it was Wentworth's death that jarred it loose. Robert tried to interest him in the business side of those abandoned homes, but the guy just blew him off. All he cared about was drugs, sex, that stuff." She paused. "Robert said Patrick Wentworth had no sense of money and didn't care. Every now and then, Robert hinted that fortunes would still be made in the housing blowout."

"Did he say how he thought this would happen?"

"No. He said loans had been rubber-stamped and the same thing was happening with foreclosures. The computer spits out names, addresses, and numbers and no one actually looks at their owners, their earning potential, their past credit reports. They just foreclose. *Boom.*"

"And he tried to tell Patrick Wentworth this?"

"Yes. He said the now-stalled foreclosure process would prove a gold mine for people who know how to work the system, especially those within the system. Again, Patrick wasn't interested in that sort of corruption. So Robert left."

"Do you think he tried to tell other people this?"

"I don't know. He might have talked about it with his brother. They were close."

"I see." Pete glanced over at Lonnie, who smiled back.

"There is one other thing. Patrick Wentworth asked Robert if he knew of any sex scandals in his old bank or among any government employees. I think this took Robert back a little. He wasn't interested in that sort of thing. Robert's policy was it's better not to know, even if you know. But the really weird thing is the guy offered to pay Robert for information."

Lonnie shook his head, but said nothing.

"Of course, Robert didn't take the offer." She smiled tightly. "Do you have any more leads about his death?"

"Miss Logan, given the manner of Patrick Wentworth's death, a carbon copy of Robert's, I'd say we're getting closer. So often all it takes is one slipup on the part of the murderer, one person who walks by and remembers a car or license plate near the crime scene."

"What about the girl?"

"She wasn't having a secret affair with him, we know that. We've interviewed everyone who worked with her. I know the stereotype of women in that line of work isn't a nice one but, Miss Logan, you'd be surprised how many people in personal entertainment are good people, and I include prostitutes. Some have drug problems, others were mistreated as children, but a lot of them are there for one reason, they need the money."

"I can understand that. I remembered one more thing. At one point, Robert said he thought he had a partner for his new business. He never said who it was."

"Someone on Yolanda Street?" Lonnie asked.

Emma replied quickly, "No. He wouldn't do that. I know his murder looks like he was involved with those criminals down on Yolanda Street. All he said was this was someone who understood the business, had lots of contacts."

CHAPTER THIRTY-EIGHT

"Have you ever noticed when a government agency or a corporation has not distinguished themselves"—a slight smile crossed Michelle's lips—"they issue statements from a woman spokesperson?"

Asa Chartris, sitting across the table at a high-priced restaurant for lunch, nodded. "People trust women more than men."

Michelle shrugged. "For now. That will last until the public figures out you lie for whoever is paying you. I kind of hate to see it, really."

"I do, too, perhaps for different reasons." Asa dipped into his rich barley soup. "My mother used to make this. I love barley."

"Me, too. What are your different reasons?"

"I'm a good twenty-some years older than you and try as I might, I still harbor many of the things I was taught about women. I thought women inhabited a higher emotional and spiritual realm. Men dealt with the rough-and-tumble of the world. Women were to lift us above it, not engage in it." He put his spoon on the plate that sat under the bowl. "There's something about fighting, grubbing in the business world that lowers a person, and I include myself."

"You seem upstanding to me."

"Oh, I don't mean my ethics have crashed and burned, but these days I look at the world with a jaundiced eye, which is how I look at the statement from a Fannie Mae and Freddie Mac spokesperson you just mentioned." He smiled ruefully when he said "spokesperson."

Michelle, who read *The Wall Street Journal* on her Kindle, plucked the device out of her purse, turned it on, and began rolling up copy. "Here it is. 'Our decision was motivated by several factors, including the protection of buyers with title insurance, the negative impact lingering on foreclosed properties has on the neighborhoods, and the cost burden that is placed on taxpayers when bank-owned sales are suspended.'" She looked up at a grim Asa. "Sounds reasonable." Glancing back down at the small screen, she said, "November 27, 2010."

"At least we weren't blamed for stopping the foreclosures." He sighed, returning to his delicious soup. "Reno Sagebrush is fortunate in some ways. Set aside housing for a moment, most banks' loan portfolios carry about forty percent in commercial property and that's not going anywhere, for years. The vacancy rates are through the roof, it's about seventeen-point-five percent nationally, and worse here."

"Everything's worse here."

"Well, yes, except for the people. And I can't fault many of those businesses that are in trouble. They surfed a big wave and then it finally dumped them. We're in pretty good shape, even with the debts we took on when we bought out Truckee Amalgamated." He finished the last of his soup. "When they went under, they didn't use a spokeswoman."

"They always were one step behind." She speared a hard-boiled egg in her salad.

"We need to divest ourselves of the foreclosed homes. Sooner or later it will dawn on all of us to forget about the document problems, the robolending, and get the hell out."

"Yes, until more state attorneys general get into it," Michelle grumbled.

"But not here. How can we intelligently unload what we have without causing undue concern and too much negative publicity?"

"We might be able to repackage debts for places like Spring Street, but the Yolanda area is a total loss."

"We're thinking along the same lines," said Asa. "Do you believe at some point we can sell those foreclosed homes to a larger institution?"

"Not now. Three hundred billion dollars in loans must be rolled over in the next five years. People are going to come up short and there will be more properties on the market, both residential and commercial. There's no speedy way out of this and I'm starting to wonder if there's any way out of this without the government squeezing every penny out of the taxpayers to cover these astronomical debts."

"I don't know if that will work anymore."

"One bright spot. The food and job program for Spring Street is both good PR and good business. It will restore some value down there—unless there are more starved or murdered bodies found." Michelle sounded hopeful.

"Don't even say that." Asa blanched. "My mother used to say, 'Talk of old troubles brings on new.' I believe that."

Twinkie and Bunny cruised down Spring Street.

Passing Irene's old house, Bunny spotted two men knocking on her door.

"New tenants," Bunny noted.

"The good news is we don't have to turn off water anymore. The bad news is we aren't turning it back on."

"Yep." Bunny brightened. "CeCe drew me a truck."

He laughed. "She's so bright. Picks up everything the first time you show it to her, and she loves my truck."

"They're like sponges at that age."

"Irene's settling in. She was so nervous at first. She's been through a lot." He paused. "She's a good mother. Good cook, too."

"Bunny, the right woman is pure heaven. The wrong woman is pure hell."

"I didn't say anything about the right woman." Bunny bristled.

"I know." Twinkie chuckled and changed the subject. "Howie Norris bought me a GPS system for my old truck."

"No kidding."

"He said he owed it to me for giving him that ingot." Twinkie shook his head. "He's straight up."

"Yeah, he is." Bunny swayed as Twinkie took a sharp turn in the SSRM truck. "There's got to be more where that came from."

"I bet it's right under everyone's noses. Ever notice that? Sometimes something is right in front of you and you can't see it."

"Yep."

"Makes me wonder what I miss."

If Twinkie and Bunny and others had noses as powerful as dogs, they might have discovered things sooner. But being human, they'd stumble on treasures or horrors in their own good time.

CHAPTER THIRTY-NINE

"Never." Norton Wentworth's jaw stuck out. "He would never be involved with a woman like that."

Pete, sitting in the small conference room at Patrick Wentworth's campaign headquarters, said quietly, "I'm glad to hear that."

Next to Pete, Lonnie leaned forward and looked at Sophia Wentworth, Patrick's beautiful mother. He decided not to ask the question that was on his mind. Instead, he peered intently at his notebook.

"He was set up. Given the hypocrisy of so many mendacious politicians, who will believe us about my son?" She was composed, despite her distress.

"Threats?"

Norton snorted. "I kept a nutcase file." He tapped a manila file folder in front of him. "Nothing but threats. I've made copies for you."

"Thank you. Do you feel any of them could have been made by the killer?" Pete accepted the folder containing the copies.

"Who knows? I always thought that people who make threats don't carry them out. That killers just strike. But let me tell you, there's stuff in there that makes you wonder. I mean, here's one." He flipped open the folder and took a typed letter off the top. "Mr. Wentworth, you have incorrectly identified the source of Reno's ills. They are caused by those miners killed, angry over lax practices. They are all reincarnated at this time and seek revenge. Signed, Harvey S. Enright."

"I think we can dismiss the idea that Patrick was murdered by vengeful spirits." Sophia, elbow on the desk, cupped one hand under her head.

"Vengeful, yes. Spirit, no." Norton nodded. "Mom, he pissed off a lot of people."

"But is there anyone you felt was personally affronted?" Pete asked. "All politicians rub someone the wrong way, but not many people running for public office are murdered. Can you think of someone who followed him from speech to speech?"

Lonnie added, "Sometimes people who are fans turn against their star. You know, they feel slighted in some way. Unrequited love?"

Sophia's even voice replied, "Patrick didn't seem to inspire such devotion. Maybe because he stuck to the issues that meant the most to him."

"His words or actions could have been misinterpreted," said Lonnie. "To someone who's unbalanced, just making eye contact can be loaded with meaning."

Norton ran his hand through his thick hair. "God knows there are enough whack jobs out there."

"We see them." Pete half smiled. "I don't think your brother was killed by a whack job. The manner of death, the place where the bodies were found, that points to what Mrs. Wentworth said, that this act was done to discredit him. Can you identify any special interests he might have jeopardized?"

Both mother and surviving son sat for a moment, looked at each other, then Sophia leaned forward.

"The drug lords. The people running illegal prostitute rings. After all, he was found in their territory."

Pete nodded. "Do you know whether any such person ever called or threatened him personally?"

"They absolutely did not," Norton answered vehemently. "Probably because they didn't believe he could really harm their profits. It's always about money."

"Ninety percent of the time," Pete agreed readily. "Were there more-legitimate business interests that he might have upset?"

Norton threw up his hands. "No." Then he added, "We got generous contributions from businesses."

"How generous? Were the contributions large?" Pete asked.

"None more than one thousand dollars. It's early in the campaign. I have that information for you here, too." He pushed another folder across the table.

"What about individuals?"

"Only a few. They're in there." Norton pointed to the folder.

Lonnie scribbled in his notebook.

"Norton, would you give me the name of the campaign's legal counsel?"

"We didn't have one. Patrick didn't want to spend the money this early along. It was a bone of contention between us."

Pete looked at Sophia. "I appreciate you coming down here. I'm sorry your son's wife wasn't up to it, but that's understandable. I will need to question her at some point."

"Give her a few more days," Sophia answered.

"Did you ever think he might be physically harmed?"

Sophia looked straight at Pete. "Yes. I told him to tone it down. Norton told him to tone it down. But he wouldn't listen. He kept saying *the people need to be stirred up*. He could tone it down later, but right now he needed to get their attention." She smiled sadly. "He was a bright child, a bright man, but he could miss emotional nuances."

Pete liked her. "Yes, ma'am, I'm afraid we all can."

Back in the squad car, Pete drove a few blocks before

pulling over and parking. He took the folder with the dollar sign on it from Lonnie. Flipping through the pages, he then handed it back to Lonnie.

"Look at the contributions."

Lonnie did. "Yeah."

"You see that each week the money has been added up?"

"Right."

"Lonnie, a month before he was killed the best week's contributions came to five thousand something."

Lonnie flipped through the pages backward. "Right."

"The cost of Wentworth's TV ads alone are way beyond that. Mags showed me the ad rate schedule."

"Yeah?" Lonnie's eyebrows rose. He didn't know where this was going.

"Wentworth had ads at news time and also prime time. Thirty seconds on Monday night between nine and ten P.M. costs fifteen hundred dollars. He ran ads throughout the week. Not every night, but he ran them during high-cost times. Fifteen hundred dollars for thirty seconds. Norton Wentworth is lying about their contributors."

Lonnie read the figures again. "Think the old lady is?"

"She wouldn't be the first mother to lie for her son. But Norton sure is lying."

"So why would he give us the campaign contributions? Maybe he doesn't know."

"Clearly Norton Wentworth thinks we're stupid. It's insulting, but we can use it to our advantage. Likely it would never occur to him that we'd know or even look at the cost of TV ads."

"How we gonna get it out of him? The real contributors?"

"I don't know. The last thing I want to do is give him time to tip off whoever was funneling funds to his brother's campaign. If we could figure out what was truly at stake, we'll be that much closer."

"You've completely discounted personal hatred or revenge?"

"Well, you can never discount that. The guy rubbed a lot of people the wrong way. You can't discount someone who's crazy. I remember when I was studying law enforcement I read about a case in Ralph, Alabama. A kid there had taken so much LSD he scrambled his brains and thought he had been appointed by Archangel Michael to see that everyone wore a cross. If they weren't wearing one he'd cut one onto their chest. He sliced two people before they apprehended him. That kind of perp, you have to struggle mightily to see the world as they do. But Wentworth's grandstanding was economically useful to other people. Hey, even one of these large evangelical churches could make money off of him. There are lots of ways that Wentworth could make a buck for others as well as himself."

"We just have to find it."

"Right, and we also must understand how this is linked to Dalrymple's death. But first I have to hold Norton's feet to the fire." Pete glanced at Lonnie. "Notice there were no computers in the office?"

Lonnie, surprised that he had missed this, said, "No."

"By the time we request them, they'll be scrubbed clean."

CHAPTER FORTY

They sat in the small room at the indoor firing range. Pete had been teaching Mags to use a sidearm. Her hand-eye coordination was exceptional, plus she liked it. Built to be soundproof, the room was filled with coin-operated machines dispensing a lot of junk you wouldn't want to eat, plus sugary drinks. They were the only ones there. For whatever reason, it was a slow night.

"How about trying sporting clays once it warms up and we can go outside?" Pete raised his eyebrows expectantly.

"What gauge shotgun?" Mags replied.

"Depends on how much recoil you can stand. I use a .28, even though I can take the .12. But after an hour, a half hour even, it's punishment. There are gel pads you can put on your shoulder. Oh, and you need really good ear protectors."

"I'm game. I can get all that together and I'm sure Aunt Jeep will lend me her .28. Her rifles and shotguns are works of art." Mags exhaled and leaned back in the cheap chair. "Maybe what I should do is ask for the least expensive shotgun."

"Your aunt has beautiful stuff. My fave vehicle of hers is that old Jeep," Pete said.

"That will be your fave until you're in the passenger seat. It's bad enough when she drives the truck, but when she slides behind the wheel of that old World War II

Jeep and flips the windshield down, she drives like it's still wartime. Her crazy driving was how she got her nickname."

He laughed. "Bet it makes her feel young again."

"What's making her feel young is her Spring Street project, that and irrigating the thousand acres. Her whole focus now is feeding people. She and Babs are together all the time." She looked at her father's thin Jaeger-LeCoultre watch. "They're down there now."

He looked up at the round wall clock. "It's almost eight."

"Well, she thinks she can talk to some new people at night. They won't be as worried about police patrols, immigration sweeps. By now most neighborhood residents recognize the two of them, even if they haven't talked to them."

"Patrols drive along but we aren't picking anyone up. As for immigration"—he shrugged—"Crummy job. Send them back, they just cross over again. Whoever gives them instant citizenship will have that vote for the rest of the century. Kind of like the South always voting Democratic until LBJ signed the Voter Rights Act. That's what Dad says."

"I hate politics."

"Most of us do, but we're stuck with it."

"Hey, speaking of that, how is it going with the Wentworth case and the other murder?"

He leaned forward. "Mags, it's strange. I feel so close sometimes, then it slips away."

"Close how?" She leaned forward, too.

"Motivation. Lonnie and I have questioned at least forty people by now and we'll question more. We've gone back to high school friends. Wentworth was the type who would never make the football team, any team. So he'd run for student government. We've all seen the type. First, they want attention. Then they want power."

"What about the other guy? The bank guy?"

"Joe Average." Pete took the cap off the thermos. "Want some?"

"What is it?"

"Yerba maté. My oldest sister got me hooked on it. It's great when you need a pick-me-up. I can only drink so much coffee."

"Me, too." She held out a cup. "He had to be a little kinky, off-center, your Joe Average, I mean."

"Either that or he just put his foot in it. Well, that's where I am. Frustrated. The department is under pressure. I'm getting my fair share. But I knew that when I took this job. Well, you know and you don't know. I will crack this damned thing."

"I'm sure you will."

"How's your work at Davidson and Fletcher going?"

Her eyes brightened. "Pretty good. I mean, what I'm digging up is fascinating. For instance, China has a Global Credit Rating System. They just lowered our country's credit rating. I've memorized his statement, that's how much it hit me." She put down her cup. " 'The serious defects in the U.S. economic development and management model will lead to the long-term recession of its national economy, fundamentally lowering the national solvency.' " She slapped her hand on the table. "What a sock in the kisser but if you want to know the truth, look to your enemies or competitors."

" 'Fundamentally lowering the national solvency.' " He whistled. "Even I can understand that."

"So then," she held up her hand. "Stop me if this gets tedious. I get really excited. Well, anyway, back to my work. I decided I'd better look at the Great Depression, even though everyone else is. Between 1926 and 1933, the housing market dove steeper than an osprey after a fish. No construction hardly, no houses being sold. Just a complete and total wipeout."

"Watched a documentary about those times on the History Channel. Looks like we forgot the lessons."

"Big-time. The true signal of recovery is always housing. It was then and it will be now. We can pile up the reasons, but since my work research is focused on the value of bank shares—in other words, do we suggest to our clients to buy stock?—well anyway, here's where we are. Nothing has happened since our nosedive began. Nothing. In fact, Pete, fifteen million Americans owe seven hundred seventy-one billion dollars more on their homes than they are worth. I'm not even talking about foreclosures, which are beyond belief."

"I'm missing something. Honey, I'm not as smart as you." He smiled broadly at her.

"Pete, you're smarter. I couldn't solve a crime, plus I blew my life up on Wall Street."

"You're flattering me, I like it, but go on."

"Oh." She threw her hands up excitedly. "Basically, it means people who are living in their homes and making payments are royally screwed. The homes aren't worth it. So the banks are holding overvalued mortgage assets, seven hundred seventy-one billion dollars overvalued. Right? Therefore, how can anyone believe the balance sheets of any bank anywhere? Actually, Mr. Jianzhong understated his analysis. He could have simply said, 'They're screwed and they don't know how to fix it.'"

"What about all the foreclosed homes?"

"If some value can't be restored to them, the losses will be even more catastrophic than they are, which might provoke some people who are paying their mortgages to just stop, reevaluate the current worth, and pay the real value."

"No one has the guts to do that."

"Not individually, but if there were a national movement, think of what could happen."

"But what about all the money that the government has pumped into the banks?"

"Do you see it being spread around the local economy?"

"Uh, no."

"I rest my case. Actually, I don't. If the banks issued new mortgages with lower principal amounts they would take short-term losses. However, this could send a message to investors that the bank balance sheets are truthful. It would sure help the balance sheets of home owners. The other tactic along with that, get those foreclosed homes back on the market at true valuation. Again, this would entail more short-term severe losses, but it's the only way out, that I see anyway. As I said, all recovery begins with the housing market, whether it's the 1930s or now."

"And we're the worst-hit state."

"So our banks should take the lead. I sure give Babs Gallagher credit. She's doing her damnedest to restore equilibrium to the foreclosed homes. Oh, before I forget, Howie Norris has gotten jobs for some of the people for the school bus expo. It's the end of April, they start next week. Who knows about after the expo, but it is a start."

Pete smiled at her, appreciating her enthusiasm, her acumen, and naturally, her beauty. "Do you ever think suffering cleanses people?"

A silence followed this. "It did me. But I think most people run away from pain so it keeps coming back in different forms. Or they desperately scan the horizon, seeking someone to blame."

"I learned from my mistakes," said Pete, thinking of Lorraine. "Hey, it's not the same as the crisis you're talking about, but either you learn or you fail. I've reached a point where I don't have compassion for people who don't learn. Know what I mean?"

"Yes, I do. Let me go back to banking and to Wall Street," said Mags, still on a roll. "Isn't the foundation of all transactions trust?" He nodded, she continued. "And some professions, critical professions, must have individuals who are upright—some more than others. Police is one. Banking is one. So the more I study all the facts, the numbers, the elaborate explanations, *poof!* Comes down to trust. Until trust is restored, we aren't going anywhere." She saw a shadow cross Pete's face. "Did I upset you?" she asked. "I'm sorry."

"No. The murders, I think they come down to trust. Someone broke their word."

She reached over to put her hand on his forearm. "All relationships come down to trust. It's so simple. My relationship with Baxter is built on trust. Human, animal, institution—trust is the glue that holds everyone together."

He put his hand over hers. "True."

She squeezed his muscled forearm. "You know what else puzzles me? Howie getting shot. For no reason anyone can remotely discern."

"Something's going on out there, for sure. He called and reported another heifer missing. Lonnie and I drove out. We walked the back enclosure and when we got down to the old farm road, sure enough, there were the tracks."

"What about a trailer? If people haul cattle don't they load them on the livestock trailers?"

"You can put a couple of cows on the bed of a pickup if you have pipe rails or wooden rails. Walk them up a ramp." He thought for a moment. "But I don't think Howie was shot at because of his cattle." He threw up his hands. "Though I couldn't give a reason why."

"You'll figure it out. I trust that big brain of yours and that big heart." She leaned closer and kissed him on the cheek.

On Spring Street, Jeep, Babs, King, Baxter, and Toothpick, who was in a sweater, made house calls.

His house still cold, Donald Veigh greeted them with a smile, happy with news of a temporary job working the expo.

The two ladies then stopped over to see the two brothers. Milton answered the door, his back to Mike who was warming himself by the fireplace.

"He's going to have a fit," Tookie called to the other dogs.

Mike's eyes rolled back.

Tookie barked. *"Milton!"*

Milton turned around and ran to his brother. He pulled a tongue depressor out of his pocket, always carried for this purpose. He held his brother down and put the flat piece of plastic in Mike's mouth crossways.

Babs and Jeep knelt down with him.

"What can I do?" Babs asked.

Tookie kept licking Mike's face. The other three dogs sat behind him, concerned for Tookie's distress.

"He'll settle down and then I can give him his Dilantin."

Within forty-five seconds, Mike's seizure ended. He sat up with Milton's help, Tookie now licking his hands.

There were no chairs so Mike tottered upright, supported by his brother, then slid down, his back to the wall.

Finally Mike looked up at the two concerned women. "I charge extra for entertainment."

Jeep laughed. Babs smiled, kneeling to pet Tookie and be on eye level with Mike.

Milton walked into the kitchen and returned with a bottle of water and a bottle of pills, fetching one for his brother. "Open your cakehole."

Mike opened his mouth, Milton popped in the pill, twisted off the cap on the water. Mike downed the pill with a big swallow.

"Cakehole?" Babs inquired.

"That's what our ma used to say." Mike's light voice was steady now.

Tookie informed the other dogs. *"He warms up a little. Once you know the smell, you can tell. Some things set him off. Some lights, like flashing lights. Some kinds of music. Excites him. Other times, I don't know. He just falls down. Sometimes he's slow for an hour or so after his fit. Other times he bounces right back."*

Breathing deeply, Milton pleaded with the two women. "Don't tell anybody about this, please. We just got hired to work the expo. They need welders. We'll be down in the pits. The garage stuff. Sometimes Mike can't get hired. Know what I mean?"

"We won't say a word." Babs stood up.

After making sure all was well, the two women left with the dogs. Tookie called goodbye to the others. She liked being with dogs as much as she liked Mike and Milton.

"Jeep, I can't stand this anymore," said Babs. "No water. No heat. You know the list. I'm calling Lolly Johnson. Okay with you?"

"Okay with me."

They walked companionably back to Babs's SUV. They saw stray cats and dogs nudging around the houses, looking for any scrap.

"Dear God!" Jeep exclaimed upon seeing a bony dog rush behind a house.

"First the people, Jeep, then the animals." Babs put her arm around the old woman. "I see your little hobo has a sweater."

"He's put on two and a half pounds."

"Carlotta's magic."

"I know. I have to be careful myself."

"Food and love," Toothpick said to the humans.

CHAPTER FORTY-ONE

Two rooms, about fourteen by fourteen each, comprised Reggie Wilcox's business. A steel locker, tall and deep, was against one wall. Stills from various commercials and documentaries that Reggie had worked on were framed neatly in marine blue and covered the walls.

A well-worn sofa rested under a series of shots of a man on a motorcycle jumping cars. In front of that, a coffee table was wiped clean. The place was tidy. Reggie sat in a director's chair, as did Pete and Lonnie. The cameraman had been telling them the story of getting the footage of the motorcycle jump.

He tilted his hand at an angle, palm downward. "Line up, build a ramp on each side. If they really want to advertise the school bus expo, that would be the way to attract attention: a motorcycle jump."

"It would attract mine." Lonnie stared again at the motorcycle shots, the color was so deep.

"Even if you hit it right, the landing must be a jolt." Pete grimaced.

"Those guys are held together by pins, duct tape, and bailing twine. They can't stop," Reggie noted.

"Evel Knievel was the greatest." Lonnie remembered the daring man from his childhood.

So did his mother. When Lonnie had tried to jump

three trash cans laid side by side with his two-wheel bicycle, he didn't make it.

"Danger—the ultimate high," Reggie stated simply.

"There are all kinds of dangers. You worked with Patrick Wentworth, who seemed to court danger."

Reggie looked disbelievingly at Pete for a moment. "Chickenshit. What a total chickenshit. All I can say for the guy is, he could run. He'd drag me down to some pretty grungy places. I'd shoot over his shoulder. The split second anyone took a step toward him, he'd take off running, leaving me in the dust with all my equipment. What he courted were votes. He thought the public was apathetic. Juice 'em up. What's better than sex, drugs, and rock and roll?"

"Given the manner of his death, maybe he juiced them up too much." Outside the window, Pete noticed clouds swooping in.

Reggie turned to look. "That front must be coming in. At least it's not freezing anymore."

"Were you surprised at Mr. Wentworth's death?" asked Pete.

Reggie sighed, looked at the floor, then at Pete. "Sure, I was surprised, especially at how he was killed. I worried that he'd push some Yolanda Street kingpin too far, but I don't think I ever actually believed he'd be murdered."

"Did he sleep with women other than his wife? Men running for office or who are in office often say one thing and do another."

"Nah. He never talked about sex except to point out how disgusting the streetwalkers were, the higher-priced call girls. He was kinda weird that way. His wife seemed nice enough and he talked about her a bit. He seemed to care a lot about her, but he was just weird about sex. He couldn't stand that other people didn't share his outrage over our moral decay."

"Do you think he was a repressed homosexual? You shot his ad about the boy found starved who was a rent boy."

Reggie's lip curled slightly. "That was low. I told him not to do it. Especially blaming the kid's death on AIDS. He had no proof, no nothing. He just figured it would stir people up. But repressed homosexual? I don't know. He hated the gays, but then he hated whores. He hated that woman he was killed with, and she wasn't a whore. She just showed off her body. Like I said, he was a bit off about sex."

"Did you like him?"

"No," came the direct, swift reply.

"Did you agree with his other ads?"

"No."

"But you worked for him?" Pete probed.

"Deputy Meadows, there's a depression on. I'd work for the Devil if he paid on time."

"And Wentworth did?"

"Yep. Never late."

"Did he discuss where he got the money?"

"Campaign funds."

"Did he discuss those funds? You know, who was supporting his candidacy?"

Reggie's eyebrows lifted. "He said that a few private individuals believed in him, his family, and some businesses, a couple of car dealers, one of the banks—nothing huge, but enough to keep him going."

"Did he ever say how he raised this money?"

"He didn't say too much about that. He credited his brother, Norton, with being good at fund-raising. He was cynical about it. He said banks, ad agencies, construction companies—any kind of business—usually gave a bit to both parties. Hedging their bets."

"He was critical?" Pete continued.

"Not so critical he didn't take their contributions. He was an ideologue. They're the worst."

"Got that right," Lonnie piped up.

"You never met any of the contributors?"

"No, but I know he was being very careful not to piss off the casinos in any way. That made me wonder. It wasn't because he liked them. He didn't. Thought they had girls on call when needed. We'd pass a casino and he'd go off on yet another tirade about how sex was available for someone who knew how to ask for it and knew what palm needed greasing."

"Did he ever discuss anyone pulling back their support? Cutting off funding?"

"Yeah. He lost a bank. I don't know when. Pat didn't always tell you something when it happened. But I do know one of the banks cut their support and then when he made that idiotic ad about Brad Heydt, the kid who starved, more funding dried up. We're all damn lucky he didn't get elected. I didn't think he would, though. I figured he'd get dumped at the polls."

"He got thumped," said Lonnie.

"Did he ever seem afraid to you?"

Reggie's voice rose. "He'd troll Yolanda Street and there are some serious people down there. I wonder if one of them wiped him out. He was bad for business."

"You're right," said Pete. "We just don't know what business."

Reggie lowered his voice, said confidingly, "Some of those boys down there carry thousands in cash. A few of them have to be worth big bucks. Pat could only see the hookers. But Yolanda Street purveys other, finer products."

"Coke and smack?" Lonnie asked.

"You'd know better than I."

Pete smiled. "Don't know that we do. No one down there is going to volunteer information to us."

"We know Yolanda Street is a market for all kinds of illegal substances and activities," Lonnie said. "Myself, personally, I think that's where the big guys offload lesser products. The good stuff is sold quietly to the rich or well connected."

"Pat focused on the Walmart of such activities," Reggie replied sarcastically.

At this, both law enforcement officers laughed.

"Ever run into any of those bad guys while you were shooting?" Pete inquired genially.

"No. I don't even know if they live in Reno. Probably some do. What I'd see were, I guess, the version of the store manager. Never saw the owners." He patted his shirt pocket, pulled out a pack of cigarettes. "Smoke?"

"No," both men replied in unison.

"Mind if I do?"

"It's your studio." Pete smiled.

"Yeah, but some people are really aggressive about this."

"I'm not," Pete replied.

"Me neither." Lonnie seconded the thought.

Reggie fished matches out of his pocket, then pulled a large ashtray toward him. He lit up an unfiltered Camel.

"You don't fool around." Pete blinked.

"You're in as much danger from the tiny particles in filters as you are from tobacco. Might be bad for my health but I want pure tobacco."

"When did you start to smoke?"

"Two years ago."

This surprised Pete and Lonnie.

Reggie continued. "Work dried up. I'd worked at the NBC affiliate, did a little moonlighting on the side. *Bam!*" He emitted a puff of smoke. "Over. I wasn't the only one out of work. There isn't a lot of work freelancing, but that was my only option unless I wanted to change careers. Smoking took the edge off. I don't drink.

Can't handle it." He inhaled deeply. "I never smoked around Pat. To him, it would have been a sure sign that I engaged in nefarious activities. He dealt in stereotypes. A lot of people do. Maybe he would have been more successful at the polls than I thought."

"Maybe."

"Did you talk to his wife yet?" Reggie inquired.

"Yesterday. She was still very upset. Will be for a long time. It took us a while to be able to question her because she was so sedated," Pete responded. "In a way, she still can't believe he's gone."

"Well, I only met her a few times. Thought she was nice enough. Good-looking. Couldn't imagine what she'd want with a guy like that."

"We'll never understand the mysteries of attraction," Pete quipped.

"Hey, can I get you guys a beer?"

"No. Can't drink on duty."

"Like I said, I don't drink but I always have beer. Sometimes when someone comes in to look at my reel, that beer helps. I have soda, tea, that stuff."

"No thanks. Let me ask the obvious question. Can you think of anyone who would kill Patrick Wentworth?"

"No, I mean, not other than all the people we discussed."

CHAPTER FORTY-TWO

At noon on this particular day, the sun shone brightly on the courthouse steps. Finally released from a series of temporary laws devised to halt foreclosure sales, Reno Sagebrush put twenty-nine small holdings up for auction. Although this was but a small portion of what they took on when they bought out Truckee Amalgamated, it was a start.

Babs, Mags, and Jeep congregated at the base of the steps. A few other real estate agents were also there.

Nate Thornton, Reno Sagebrush's resell head, was there along with Michelle Speransky and Asa Chartris.

The same official who had offered the Western United foreclosed homes now appeared on the top step.

After the usual brief explanation of protocol, she then read out the first property. "1990 Harvey Street." She looked at every person at the foot of the steps. "1990 Harvey Street." A pause followed. "Is there anyone for 1990 Harvey Street?" She put a small mark behind that address on her clipboard. "1996 Harvey."

The same dismal silence followed 1996 Harvey and the ensuing properties.

"Did you expect this?" Babs asked Riley.

"We'd hoped for a few bids."

Upon reaching the end of the list, the official turned around and walked back into the courthouse.

Jeep said to Mags, "I've never seen anything like this."

"Aunt Jeep, this is the way it is all over America. You can't give these houses away."

Babs rejoined them. "The only good thing I can say is this gives us more time to prepare Spring Street and perhaps other areas."

Hands in her silk coat pockets, Jeep shook her head. "What a nightmare."

"Yes, indeed. And the tragedy is that there is worth in these properties! And my God, what a bargain." Babs sounded stalwartly upbeat.

"It's only a bargain if one has the funds." Mags pointed out the obvious. "Your ideas are such good ones, for the homeless in those places, for the banks, for the country, but who has ready cash?"

"The banks are sitting on billions." Babs felt her anger rising.

"As are corporations. But no one knows what's going to happen with taxes, personal property, you name it. Banks will sit tight until they know who's coming to power in November 2012. So will everyone else. Why take a chance on anything? No one can do anything until then anyway, not really."

Babs exhaled. "If only I had more money, I'd buy up blocks. I saw how real estate turned around in Denver and Houston after the recession in the early eighties. Those who bought blocks of abandoned homes at the bottom made millions upon millions."

"They did." Jeep put her hand on Babs's elbow. "I could buy some of these properties but Babs, I've never been one for city investments. Right now my energy is directed toward growing food. I may be throwing money away, but it's worth a try. And there's not much profit, I know that. Like you, I believe there's profit in these properties, just not for me."

* * *

As the three women left the courthouse, Norton Wentworth unlocked the door and entered his brother's campaign headquarters. Empty, no phones ringing, he stood there for a moment before closing the door behind him.

He'd need to call a cleaning service. He'd already had the phones disconnected. He'd given the landlord notice. A couple of desks, file cabinets, chairs. Wouldn't take long to empty out the space.

His footsteps reverberated as he walked to his small desk.

Sitting down, he scanned the room. The impact of his brother's death felt darker here than at home, with Patrick's widow or their mother. Here his grisly end was almost palpable.

Norton looked down at his desk surface, where a sealed envelope, white but spattered with bloodstains, had been laid. Opening his desk drawer he pulled out an old, thin wooden letter opener.

Hands shaking slightly, he slit open the envelope, pulled out an 8½ x 11 piece of white paper. A hundred-dollar bill stuck to the paper. Soaked in blood, Ben Franklin's eyes had been neatly cut out.

CHAPTER FORTY-THREE

Babs walked with Lolly Johnson down Spring Street in the morning. After a shared breakfast at Lolly's country club, for both were early risers, they arrived at Spring Street just in time to see Donald, Melvin, Tookie on a leash, and some other local residents leaving for temporary work at the expo. A few people already stood at the bus stop. No one had a car.

Donald had told Babs she could show Lolly around his house.

Lolly stood in the empty living room, the chimenea in the fireplace still emitting some warmth. Mornings remained cool.

As Babs walked with her from room to room, Lolly commented, "He keeps it clean."

"Most of them do." Babs, making light of it said, "There's not much to get dirty."

Wisely, the real estate agent refrained from pointing out the difficulties. Lolly, an intelligent woman, would figure it out for herself. Why insult her by pointing out the obvious?

Back on the sidewalk, Babs walked Lolly farther down the block. "Mothers with preschoolers stay home. Their plight is the worst because they can't work. And, of course, no men."

Furrowing her brow, Lolly remarked, "I will never believe America and Americans truly love children until we have child-care facilities on a par with libraries. Of course, library funding is being slashed but still the library is a treasure of the community. All are welcome. That's what I mean."

"It will never happen, Lolly. The hypocrisy runs too deep, plus children are seen as one man or woman's possession. God, when my two were little there were times when John and I would have gladly given them away." Babs grinned.

"I remember one time when Karen was fourteen, Darryl looked at me, pointing a finger, 'She's just like your side of the family.' Then he stopped and added, 'but when she's good, she's like mine.' Wouldn't you do it all over again?"

"In a heartbeat."

Spying a famished kitten studying them intently from behind an upturned garbage can, Lolly knelt down. "Kitty, kitty."

The curious little one trotted over. From her coat pocket, Lolly pulled out a little dog biscuit and broke it, but the kitten's teeth weren't up to the hard biscuit.

Lolly, loving her dogs, always carried treats.

"They're all over, cats and dogs, abandoned. No one has dumped their children." Babs sighed.

Lolly scooped up the orange tabby. Placing it partially inside her coat, she was rewarded with very large purrs from such a tiny thing. "What's one more cat?" She looked at Babs. "I will get the water turned on one way or another."

"God bless you, Lolly."

"He'd better because I don't know if anyone else will."

They laughed and returned to Babs's car, where she whisked Lolly over to her vet. The kitty needed a checkup.

That evening after a wonderful dinner, Lolly sat in the

den with Darryl, telling him what she'd seen and why SSRM must take the lead in giving people a leg up. All the while, Hobo, the newly named kitten, slept on Darryl's lap. He loved cats and Hobo took right to him.

"Honey, this is a big order. George W. spoke to me about it, too. I've sounded out the board. You can imagine their response."

"Yes, honey, I can. And I know you can bring them around. Darryl, we must do something."

Like many successful men, he had married successfully, too, and trusted his wife's judgment. "All right."

"If SSRM does this and the public knows, the other utilities will be shamed into it. I just know it."

"Someone has to make up the shortfall. We can't supply services for less or for free."

"Oh, I know. Babs and I talked about that and it's the banks that have to come through on the difference. She said Jeep thought so, too, and even some people inside the banks feel some responsibility for all this."

"Well, they aren't responsible for the squatters." He then added, "I wonder if any of those people worked at banks that have gone under. One can fall out of the middle class very fast."

"I have a plan. Let me give it a shot and then I'll tell you." She looked at Hobo: warm, full, probably happy for the first time in her short life. "She loves you already. Females always do."

He stroked the kitten. "Mrs. Johnson, you're working up to something, don't be coy."

She smiled. "I'm not. But sometimes I think about all the years, how we met, how you built up the business, how we raised our kids and I am reminded again of why I love you. You love other people and so many people with drive don't, I think."

"They don't have a wife like you, who reminds me of

what's truly important. The rest of it, while exciting, is"—he waved his hand—"just stuff."

T hat same evening Pete and Lonnie were at Emma Logan's apartment. It had occurred to Pete that Robert Dalrymple might have used Emma's computer. The personal computer found at his apartment had been damaged and the sheriff's department couldn't repair it. Pete asked if he and Lonnie could look through her files and she readily agreed. She said that indeed Robert had used her laptop when his had started to fail.

Velcro sat at Emma's feet as the three of them huddled around her Mac.

"Do you two always work this late?" she asked.

Lonnie, about Emma's age, replied, "Sometimes Pete gets a lightbulb moment. I always pay attention when he does."

"Right." Pete rolled his eyes as he sat next to Emma.

For whatever reason, Emma loved her mouse, which she had decorated as a mouse. She moved it about while they ran searches for files using specific key words.

"Try mortgages."

She typed that in. Nothing came up.

The three of them threw out words involving loans, mortgages, foreclosures, Fannie Mae, Freddie Mac. Everything they could think of, but nothing worked.

"Let's try auditing," Emma offered. "He said every bank has an auditing department but given the mess, they are overwhelmed. He said if you wanted to steal from a bank that this was the best time." She then added, "Not like Dillinger, but from inside."

"No kidding." Lonnie was surprised.

"Someone good with a computer, who knows the routine, can move money around quickly then replace it, they can hide it, too. He said given the chaos, especially when one bank buys another, it can be done. Also, Truckee took government money. In theory, management knows what's on the books, but they might not know where it is. And he said, each bank had its own computer system. Meshing those systems would take months and there still will be glitches."

"Think he did that, took money and replaced it?" Pete asked.

"No. He was like a big kid. If he'd outsmarted Big Daddy, I don't think he could have kept it to himself."

"Emma, what if someone else outsmarted Big Daddy and he knew about it?" Pete inquired insightfully. "Do you think he'd inform the bank?"

She looked from the screen to him. "No, never. He'd watch them take the hit. After all, they shoved him out," she said with some feeling.

After forty-five minutes of searching through various file folders of documents, they had found exactly nothing.

"May I use the bathroom?" Lonnie asked.

"Sure. Down the hall, first door to your right."

"Don't forget to hitch up your skates." Pete teased him.

"I never heard that before," Emma said.

"My father says it. He always instructs me to zip up, wash my hands, and leave everything as clean as I found it. Still says it to me."

"Hitch up your skates. I'll remember that." She sat up straight, feeling energized, and typed in "Big Guy. Here we go."

Lonnie rejoined them just as financial information filled the screen.

"Foreclosed homes." Lonnie whistled.

"And what he believed their actual value to be." Pete allowed himself a tingle of hope.

Emma scrolled through as the number of foreclosures

from Truckee Amalgamated numbered over two thousand. A simple asterisk in front of some of the addresses identified those properties Robert felt had the best resale value.

Emma ran more searches.

"Try resell officers," Pete said.

A list of bank resell officers for each bank filled the screen. Their assistants were also listed, as well as what Robert thought their special interest might be, and which parts of Washoe County that person favored.

They tried loan officers. The same type of information filled the screen.

"He really was trying. He was sure he could put real estate people, realtors, buyers, and loan officers together." Her eyes misted over. "It's such a shame."

Pete gently placed his hand on her forearm. "It is. Obviously, Robert put a great deal of effort into this." He paused. "Try elected officials."

She typed that in and the names that appeared were state and county officials, including Patrick Wentworth.

Without being told, she clicked on Patrick's name. Information came up about his seat in Carson City, as well as his campaign for a congressional seat and his focus. His address and various phone numbers were listed, as well as email.

When she clicked on other officials, similar information came up.

Lonnie, hand dangling down, felt Velcro sniff it. "Emma, try Norton Wentworth."

"He's not on the official list."

"Run a search. See if his name pops up anywhere," Lonnie urged.

When she did, a page appeared with foreclosure information. There was also the dollar valuation of various homes that might be acquired should they fail to sell on the courthouse steps.

What riveted all three of them was a single line: "Potential funding available for items identified with asterisk in this list: five-point-five million dollars."

"What?" Emma exclaimed.

"Emma, thank you. We've got to get to Norton Wentworth right now." Pete was already heading for the door.

Lonnie was also on his feet. "Emma, how'd you find it?"

"It was all in a file password-protected with Big Guy."

He put his forefinger to his forehead as a salute and hurried to follow his partner.

n the squad car Pete tore out of the underground parking, tires squealing. He hit the lights and sirens. They pulled up at Norton Wentworth's fifteen minutes later.

Pete had the presence of mind to cut the lights and siren two blocks from Norton's house.

Knocking on the door, they were greeted by Norton's wife.

After identifying themselves, they asked to see Norton.

"He's not here. He left for Las Vegas yesterday."

"Did he say how long he'd be gone?" Pete asked.

"No, he said not too long."

"Has he called you today?"

"He called earlier to say it was warmer down there than here."

"Would you mind giving me his cellphone number? It's important."

She grabbed a notepad off the hall table and scribbled a number.

"Thank you."

Back in the squad car, Lonnie punched in the numbers as Pete pulled away. No one picked up so Lonnie left a message with his name, not identifying himself as a police officer, and asking for a callback.

"You're getting smart." Pete smiled.

"No point tipping him off. Of course, if he calls his wife again, she'll tell him we were there. We can hope he doesn't call."

"He's scared."

"And maybe guilty."

"Maybe both."

"You think he killed his brother?"

"I don't know. But I'm willing to bet he has a good idea who did. I'm also willing to bet the murderer is smart enough to find him."

CHAPTER FORTY-FOUR

"This is the day in the Middle Ages that people felt Noah left the ark. Land ho." Jeep slipped her arm through Howie's. "I bet the ark wasn't as big as that giant school bus."

Howie, feeling like a kid, spouted statistics. "That's a Type D, the biggest of the buses. Has a weight of over thirty-six thousand pounds. Some are lighter but I tell you what, this is a beast. The body mounts on a separate chassis—unique among all these school buses." He swept his arm over the assembled vehicles. Many were still rolling in. "The entrance door is mounted forward of the front axle."

"How do you remember all that?"

Beaming, for he loved praise as do we all, Howie said, "How do you remember the cockpit of those cargo planes you flew, the D-Threes or the P-Forty-seven fighters? You remember what gets in your blood."

"*Bones.*" Zippy glanced up at her human.

"*Full of rich marrow.*" King sighed. "*They don't like it. How can they get excited over school buses? Big ugly metal things. They're yellow, too, which is so awful.*"

"*Easy to see,*" Baxter pointed out.

Fascinated by all the activity at the large parking area, Toothpick commented to Zippy, "*Does he always get excited like this?*"

"*Poppy loves to make things happen. This is the twen-*

tieth year for his expo. He tells everyone. It brings money to town. Poppy cares about that."

The huge lot just north of town near many of the warehouses was owned by the Peterbilt Motors company. A large garage in a steel Quonset hut gleamed. All the hydraulic lifts, the tires hanging on the wall, the tools, everything gleamed. Oil stained the concrete floors, but those floors were as clean as possible.

Peterbilt, known for its reliable engines and sumptuous cabs, was owned by an old friend of Howie's. Well, now it was owned by his daughter.

Originally, twenty years ago, Howie wanted to gather the buses before the parade in the large parking lot where the Washoe County school buses were kept. The education department, at that time, thought this unwise. They couldn't completely protect the buses from vandalism, a problem then because neighborhood urchins would crawl over the fence and graffiti the buses. And one county commissioner feared that if all the locals saw all those shining buses next to theirs, they'd want new ones. He kept a tight rein on the budget, which for the most part was a good thing.

Howie looked elsewhere and found the perfect place. At Peterbilt, the school bus manufacturers, bus drivers, and the salesman hit it off, all of them kindred spirits. The gearheads popped hoods, including those of the Peterbilts.

Jeep liked engines well enough, but her passion was plane engines—the kind before jets. Still, she could appreciate excellence and wondered what the history of the world would be without the invention of the diesel engine.

"How many people can the D carry?" Jeep looked at the long bus with its flat face.

"Anywhere from fifty-four to ninety, depending on how big," Howie answered. This was a passion of his, clearly. "You see the Cs over there, again, depending on size and engine, they can haul thirty-six to seventy-eight. When most folks think of a school bus, that's what they think of: that boxy nose. It's versatile. We don't think about it, but school enrollment fluctuates. Counties have to consider that when they purchase anything. Just think what it was like about ten years after the war. All those kids. Guess we'll never see numbers like that again."

"Will we ever see confidence and hope like that again?"

"Maybe. Maybe not," Howie said. "Well, it's always easier to be pessimistic, isn't it? If you go around claiming doom and gloom, you can always say you saw the hard times ahead." He playfully punched her with his right fist. "Not you."

"Never. Well, is there anything I can do down here?"

"No, I just wanted you to see the big boys rolling in. Parade's tomorrow. And those crazy guys from High Point, North Carolina, are going to decorate their buses."

"How?"

"They aren't saying but, of course, word leaked out to the other manufacturers that they're up to something, so now everyone's on a beautification program. Indiana, Illinois, right next door in California, New York, Ohio, all of them are cooking up something."

"Can't wait."

Puffing out his chest, he said, "You tell me what other city has a school bus parade."

"If they do, they're copying us."

"Right." Howie looked over at Mike and Milton on the other side of the garage. "Those two already look better. I see they brought the dog."

"So did we."

"We love getting out of the house but the diesel smell is awful." King complained.

"Even they can smell it," Baxter noted.

Although he was fattening up, Toothpick still had to

wear his deep turquoise sweater when outside. Each day the handsome dog's spirits improved, too, but he still missed Brad. He probably always would.

"Wonder how Tookie stands it?" Toothpick said.

"He has to stick near the one who has fits." King felt a slight breeze pick up his heavy ruff.

While Jeep, Howie, and the dogs observed the activity at the Peterbilt lot, Darryl Johnson announced to the media, the gas company, and the electric company, that SSRM would be turning water back on in those occupied homes on Spring Street. He made clear that the fees for that water would be paid by "a consortium of concerned citizens" for one month until, and if, the other utilities followed suit, and the banks made up the difference when a reduced rate was announced. SSRM's reduced rate would be sixty percent of the normal rate. He emphasized that this was not free water, those paying the full rate were not being taken for granted.

Darryl knew that some residents would try to get the reduced rate, which is why SSRM was doing this for one month, to see how it would work.

The "concerned citizens" had been organized in one night by Lolly after she learned the approximate service cost for water from Darryl. Given that only thirty-eight families had been identified as possible benefactors to the policy, this turned out to be relatively modest.

The wives of the bank presidents, the utility presidents, the heads of all the charities that happened to be women—the ladies who got things done in this and every other city—enthusiastically got on board, meaning they opened their purses.

It wouldn't be long until their husbands followed suit although the process, thanks to boards, reports, arguments, and counterarguments, would take longer.

And the argument that this was for one month carried weight. The effort to find employment stepped up.

The bus expo had been a godsend for their project.

Phone calls and text messages about the Spring Street initiative flew all over Washoe County. No one had ever seen anything like this before and mostly people felt pride that their county and city was actually doing something substantive. Then again, the history of Nevada was the history of overcoming hardship.

One call being made was to Norton Wentworth.

"You should come home. Good things are happening. Really good things."

"I'm not that stupid." Unlike Patrick, Norton realized the cleverness of the person on the other cellphone.

Soothing, reasonable, the voice almost crooned, "I don't know why you ran. What are you afraid of?"

"That you'll kill me."

"Why would I do that?"

"Why did you send me a one-hundred-dollar bill soaked in blood with Ben Franklin's eyes cut out?"

A long silence followed this. "When did you get that?"

"The day before I left."

"Why would I be so stupid as to warn you if I wanted to kill you? It doesn't make any sense. Your brother and his campaign offended many people. The entire episode with him kicking that topless waitress probably set off somebody."

"Maybe, but I still have no reason to trust you," Norton said.

"You have no reason not to. The longer you stay away, the less convincing your business meeting excuse is, the more you look like a suspect yourself. Norton, your brother was about to blow the millions we've been working for. We're so close. That man was an idiot."

Angry but knowing this was so, Norton grunted. "He was still my brother."

"A brother who would cost you the future—just like that idiot Robert Dalrymple. Stupid people are more dangerous than intelligent ones."

"I never thought Dalrymple was stupid."

"Up to a point. When he wanted a bigger percentage, that was stupid."

Norton replied, "He didn't threaten us."

"He didn't have to, Norton. The threat was implicit: more money or I talk."

Another long pause before he mentioned his wife. "Two men from the sheriff's department visited Dory."

"And?"

"And nothing. She doesn't know anything."

"You'd better come back to Reno for a lot of reasons. Right now everyone is distracted. The school bus expo is here, the big parade's tomorrow. And here's the fabulous news, better than I had hoped: SSRM is turning the water back on. I'll give you the details later, but Spring Street looks good. So I'll be buying all those foreclosed homes while everyone is looking somewhere else. Within a year, that area and some others will be climbing back up. Maybe not to their former values, but up. And we'll own them."

"Let me think about it."

"I didn't have to make this call, you know. I could have let you run and kept all the money for myself. But you've kept your word, worked for our project. But, hey, if you want to walk away from it. I'm not paying out if you do."

"If I come back, how do I know I won't be picked up?"

"Why should you be? Fly in tonight, go home like everything is normal. If they come by, so what? You haven't done a thing and, really, you haven't. Yet."

Late that same night, the humans asleep, Ruff came back on the porch, scrounging for bones and scraps.

King smelled the coyote, ran downstairs, and blasted out of the dog door. Within a minute, Baxter followed, as did Toothpick.

"*Another one?*" Ruff examined the Manchester terrier. "*You need groceries.*"

Toothpick bared his teeth. "*Get out.*"

King took over. "*Tooth, it's okay. We know him.*" He then said to the coyote, "*I left my bones in the barn. You can have them if you do something for us.*"

Baxter edged closer to King, wondering what King wanted. Whatever it was, he'd back up his friend.

"*I can take the bones anyway,*" the handsome young coyote bragged.

"*Don't be an asshole,*" Baxter growled. "*King's really smart. If he offers a deal, you should listen.*"

Amazed that King and Baxter talked to this clever predator, Toothpick sat next to Baxter, his black ears forward, his eyes wide open.

"*All right.*" Ruff lowered his head slightly, then raised it. "*What's the deal?*"

King, his voice deep and low so as not to wake any humans, said, "*Peterson Ranch has a gyp with three cubs. You know where that is, north of here about two miles if you go straight back up over that ridge.*"

"*Tell me more about it.*" Ruff's curiosity rose.

"*Old house, lots of Baldie cattle and an old man who runs them. He has an Australian kelpie, kind of your size but more squat, Zippy. She's a good cattle dog, she told us about the gyp and about her strange den. Zippy's kind of friends with the gyp. She said she carries bones out for her but the coyote needs lots of food,*" King informed him.

"*Oh, I know the place.*"

"*The coyote has no mate. We sniffed all around her den—*"

"*I stuck my head in!*" Baxter bristled.

"That was stupid." Ruff chuckled undiplomatically.

"That's what I told him but back to the female. No male. We would have smelled him so she's alone, has to feed her pups. They're about seven weeks old. If you help her, bring her food, she might be yours."

"How does that help you?" Ruff wondered.

"Find her another den. Move her and the cubs. If she trusts you, she'll do it and she'll trust you if you feed her. So go to the barn, take my bones and whatever else you find, and go to Peterson Ranch."

Baxter, appreciating King's plan, added, *"She's pretty. We want to show the humans the den, what's in the den. If they know she's there, they'll kill all of them. They think the coyotes will kill the newborn calves."*

"That's only true if there's nothing else to eat," Ruff confessed.

"There's lots to eat. We'll make sure Zippy always leaves stuff out," King promised.

"What's in the den?" Ruff's golden eyes brightened.

"Wooden boxes and old leather saddlebags." King shrugged. *"Junk, but it will make our human and the old human there so happy."*

Baxter said, *"Really happy."*

"Why do you care?" This puzzled Ruff.

"We love them." King smiled.

"They saved me," Toothpick spoke up.

Ruff thought a bit. *"I don't know if humans are worth loving but you all have been fair to me and if I can win a mate doing this, I'll be happy so I'll try to do what you ask."*

After Ruff left the porch, the three dogs slipped back into the house through the dog door, which flapped behind them until the magnetic strips on the bottom caught.

Glad to be inside since it was still cold at night, Toothpick said, *"When I was a stray, his kind ate a lot of us."*

King nodded. "*Coyotes would, especially when in packs.*"

"*If we traveled together, we'd be pretty safe but then the humans would get us and haul us to the pound. Either way someone ended up dead.*" Toothpick said this matter-of-factly.

"*How'd you survive?*" Baxter nuzzled the still-skinny fellow.

"*I had hiding places too small for the coyotes to squeeze in. Had them everywhere. Sometimes I'd duck in and there'd be a cat or two in there and we'd all huddle up. Brad let me sleep with him at night. We tried to keep each other warm.*" Then Toothpick added, "*At the end, I think he wanted to die. He'd given up hope. He was so hungry he really couldn't think. I miss him but I am glad to be here and I am learning to trust the two ladies. Still, I think about Brad not wanting to live. I want to live!*"

"*I don't understand it,*" King said.

"*I can understand going off to die or knowing it was my time but I can't imagine wanting to die.*" Baxter pondered this. "*When Mom's career ended, her friends, not a lot, but people she knew took poison, jumped out of windows, some hung themselves. Over money. Mom said they couldn't live with the shame, with failure.*"

"*I'm glad I'm a dog.*" Toothpick smiled.

"*Me, too,*" Baxter agreed, with warmth.

"*I love my human, I'd die for my human.*" King mused. "*But I wouldn't want to be a human.*"

CHAPTER FORTY-FIVE

The high-desert sun bathed Reno, the mercury stuck at 57°F at noon. The pale blue sky completed a perfect day.

The route of the buses would be from the Peterbilt lot, past the casinos, and down the main drag.

Crowds lined the streets as much to wave on the school buses as to celebrate a spring day. The Fourth of July might be the city's best annual parade but Reno's inhabitants needed scant excuse for a public celebration: a motorcycle convention, Hot August Nights—when restored cars and hot rods trolled the streets—St. Patrick's Day, of course. They were all celebrated events enjoyed by many. If the city council had their wits about them, they would formulate a bash to honor St. Rita, the saint of impossible causes, surely the patron saint of gamblers. Sooner or later, someone would suggest it. A full moon was as good a reason as any to mingle with others. A school bus experience served a municipal purpose: let it rip and have a good time. The sight of all those parading school buses was so goofy that Reno's residents wouldn't miss it.

The buses lined up by size, so the first bus was a Type A, a cutaway—the little squirt bus. This particular bus, manufactured in Conway, Arkansas, was festooned with garlands. Each bus sported some decoration, be it homage to its home state, to spring, or to the casinos.

Those on the sidelines cheered at the adornments. The drivers rolled along with the doors open, eyes on the road, hands on the wheel. Every now and then, they waved. Someone would be in the doorway, holding on to the rail and throwing out candy, key chains, and tiny flashlights. The goodies kept people alert. Sometimes this dispenser of largesse was a handsome fellow. A few were shirtless, exposing pecs delightful to the ladies. More, however, were clothed ladies exposing pecs buoyed by glorious nonmuscular tissue. These lovelies were greeted with whistles, catcalls, and deep appreciation. They smiled and tossed out treats. One even threw out little teddy bears, the mascot of the company. Big toothy smiles accompanied all this.

After the cutaways came the Type-B buses, larger with a sloping hood. The engine rumble, louder now, was masked by some of the Type Bs blaring music from loudspeakers mounted on the roofs. A few of the buses had people inside dancing.

Not one bus, so far, carried children.

Jeep and Howie, along with the city council members and the county commissioners, sat on a dais near the end of the parade. King sat next to Jeep and Zippy lay under Howie's chair. Mags, Pete, and Lonnie stood in a cordoned-off area just below the main dais but the area was raised slightly. Amelia Owen accompanied Lonnie. Held by Mags, Baxter observed the whole spectacle, though he kept sneezing because of the exhaust.

Toothpick sat in Jeep's lap. Today he wore a little sweater with a safety patrol cross on it. Carlotta had made it. Everyone commented on it.

Howie and Jeep waved to the people in the buses, who waved back. Jeep caught a teddy bear.

Howie checked his watch. "Making good time. The Cs ought to show up in about fifteen minutes."

"Howie, this is the biggest expo yet. How'd you do

it?" Jeep, nominally on the committee since she had started this with Howie, no longer attended meetings because her agriculture projects took up most of her time.

"Can't take any credit." Howie nodded toward the city council people and the county commissioners. "They made it very inviting, as did the casinos. Big break on hotel costs, special activities if people brought their families. The casinos gave everyone some free chips, I mean, they knocked themselves out. The Peterbilt people are a big draw, too. It's the best garage and this is now the biggest expo of its type in North America. Nothing like it. Anything that brings people to Reno is good for Reno."

Down at the lower level, Mags handed Baxter to Pete for a moment.

"You're heavier than I thought." Pete put the dachshund over his shoulder.

"It's Carlotta's fault," came the reply.

"I still can't believe Norton called you at midnight," Mags said to Lonnie.

"I'd left my cell number. He apologized for not immediately returning my call. He knew who I was because his wife told him. I was so groggy I didn't ask him anything."

Amelia ducked as a shower of gold foil–wrapped candy rained upon them. "Poor thing. You're just worn out."

"Uh"—Lonnie thought for a moment—"Well, I was, but I said we'd like to see him in the next day or two."

"Hey, there's Michelle and Asa and the Reno Sagebrush gang." Mags waved as the bus sponsored by the bank passed.

Most of the buses now rolling by were sponsored by local businesses. The buses put banners on their side if those businesses gave to charity. Their charity of choice was also promoted on the side of the bus. While the manufacturers wished to display their wares and sell fleets of them across the nation, if they could also do a good turn, why not? A lot of people needed a lift these days.

A cheer erupted from a block away. That C bus, filled with ladies, clad, but with strategic areas still very much on display, sent bystanders into the street running after the bus. The girls leaned out the windows to wondrous effect. The driver crept along at a slow pace and the ladies tossed out pens that glowed when you pressed the end.

By the time the girls reached the dais, the noise was deafening. The dogs watched, fascinated by the human uproar.

Zippy yelled over to King, *"Why are they excited about pens?"*

"I don't know." King was mystified.

Even Jeep let out a whoop of approval.

The girls added that extra something and it was cheeky fun.

Toothpick stared as the bus slowed slightly for by now young men were running alongside of it. Some reached up and the girls touched their hands. One fellow shook his hand as though it burned.

"Mental. They're all mental," the Manchester terrier decreed.

The Reno Sagebrush bus, two buses ahead, slowed because the line was bunching up.

Pete looked in that direction and noticed Bunny—pockets full of flashlights, candy, printed neckerchiefs—walking with CeCe clutching her little teddy bear. Irene walked on the other side of CeCe. He didn't know Irene or her daughter, but Bunny sure looked happy, which registered with Pete.

Country music blared from one of the buses.

"Pete." Lonnie pointed to their right where the buses were waiting.

Pete handed Baxter back to Mags. "Honey, I'll be back."

Though off duty, the two men hurried toward Norton Wentworth making his way through the crowd in the opposite direction toward the Reno Sagebrush bus.

Michelle had seen him, too. She stepped off the bus along with a few others.

She bumped shoulders and squeezed through people as she hurried through the crowd.

Pete and Lonnie tried to move faster as they rushed Norton's way.

Mags observed all this with apprehension. "Amelia, I'll be right back."

"What's going on?"

"I don't know. I don't know." Carrying Baxter, Mags hurried down the steps in the direction of the Reno Sagebrush bus.

"*I can walk.*" Baxter wiggled.

"Be still." Mags's voice was sharp.

Still pushing through all the people, Michelle called out to Norton. He stopped for a second, then a look of terror crossed his face. He turned, ran through the crowd out onto the road, and began running alongside the buses, showers of goodies falling on his head and shoulders as he passed each bus.

"Dammit!" Pete literally pried people apart. Some moved aside quickly, others cussed him out. Lonnie did the same a little farther down. Soon both men were running alongside the buses on the same side as Norton.

At five foot nine, Mags could see over some of the heads but not all of them. She, too, managed to get out onto the street.

Just ahead of Pete and Lonnie, Michelle scooted between two buses. Wearing cowboy boots and a skirt, she ran after Norton. She was in better shape than he was.

"What's the matter with you?" she screamed over the din.

Head down, Norton kept running, slipping on some of the bounty still on the street. As Michelle caught up with him, he whirled around and backhanded her. This stunned her for a moment, knocked her back. He tried to get away, but she was on him again.

Baxter pulled his leash out of Mags's hand and ran ahead with Pete and Lonnie. Mags was gaining on everyone, though. If there was one thing Mags could do, it was run.

Norton tried to hit Michelle again, but she ducked under the blow. He reached up and grabbed her throat, choking her.

Pete and Lonnie reached them, but before they could collar Norton he released Michelle, holding up his hands in surrender. She took off, coughing as she ran toward the front of the parade line.

"She killed my brother." Norton was shaking, his hands held over his head.

Pete hesitated for a moment. If he believed him and ran after Michelle, Norton would get away. If he didn't, Michelle would get away.

"Take him," he told Lonnie, then ran after Michelle.

Mags caught up with Lonnie, reached down, and grabbed Baxter's leash. "Does Pete have his gun?"

"No."

Mags left them, Baxter running with her, heading toward the front of the cutaway buses that were moving at about fifteen miles an hour.

Reaching the first bus, Michelle hopped in. She pulled out a gun, and gave orders to the driver. The greeter on that bus was shoved out, rolling onto the street. The double doors shut with a whoosh just as Pete reached the tail of the small bus, which picked up speed.

He hurried to the second bus just as Mags caught up to him.

"Stay here, Mags."

"No." She hopped up with him, Baxter in tow.

Pete called out to the people on the bus who'd been tossing out small flashlights. "Please leave the bus now. I'm a deputy for Washoe County Sheriff's Department. I need this bus now." As they hurried off, Pete said to the driver, "You can go."

"I can't leave this bus."

"All right then. Follow the bus that just took off."

Lonnie called for help. He flipped shut his cellphone as he walked with Norton to the street parallel to the main drag. Within seconds, a sheriff's patrol car was there.

Shoving Norton into the back, Lonnie hopped in with the driver, thirty-one-year-old Frances "Francie" Shelton.

"Stay on this road until you get to the Truckee, turn left and get out on the main drag. We're following two school buses."

Francie did as she was told, hitting the siren and lights.

In the first bus, Michelle had a slim chance of escaping. She was heading for the parking lot at Reno Sagebrush. Other employees and she had left their cars there to pile into two vans that took them out to the Peterbilt lot. She knew it wouldn't be long before a report went out to pick her up. She needed to get to her car, drive a few blocks, ditch it, and run to Yolanda Street. It would be easier to hide there until she could clear out of town.

The bus rolled a bit at speed. The driver was sweating at the sight of a gun pointed right at him. He did what he was told. He screeched into the parking lot. Michelle vaulted out of the bus just as the second bus pulled up.

Pete flew out of the bus, followed by Mags and Baxter. *"Let me off this leash, I can get her!"*

Fast as both Pete and Mags were, Michelle was already in her car. She turned the key and roared out the exit.

"Goddammit!" Pete cursed just as Francie and Lonnie, with Norton in the back of the squad car, barreled to the front of the bank. The two school buses slowly made their way through the parking lot, the police cruiser right behind them now.

"BMW 6 Series. Dark blue. 'FIN'—couldn't get the rest of the plate." Pete opened the back door as Francie pulled up.

"You're not leaving me here." Mags slid into the backseat, slamming Norton up against the door as Pete heaved himself in.

Francie headed east. "She drove this way." A beat. "Hello back there. Best school bus expo ever."

"Magdalene Rogers, Baxter's my dog."

"Hello, hello." Francie floored it.

"Jesus, these things are awful in the back." Pete smashed into Mags who smashed into Norton.

"So Norton, you were buying up foreclosed properties. How'd you do it?"

Lonnie turned around. "Mags."

"I'm in finance, remember? There was just too much attention on Spring Street, Yolanda Street, the subdivisions south of town."

The siren wailed.

Francie kept her eyes on the road but her ears were wide open. "Why bother?"

"Even if those houses never return to their full value, if you buy them now, eventually you'll sell them and it will be for a lot more than you paid. And if you're getting them for free, it's pure profit." Mags tried to plant her feet on the floor to steady herself. Didn't work.

"Free?" Pete swayed into the door this time.

"The bank was buying its own properties—right, Norton?"

"We'd tried a few as a trial balloon over in Sparks."

"And you were ready to really buy big?" Mags grabbed Pete with her right hand, holding on to Baxter with her left.

"She drives worse than Aunt Jeep," the dog observed.

"How could we not know?" Pete knew all this had to do with the properties but he couldn't understand how they'd slip it under their noses.

"Because the funds were moved around inside the bank," Mags explained. "It's chaos in the auditing department, everywhere, not just in this bank. All they had to do was buy, shift money out of one department, replace the money as they sold others. No bank money was lost—and Michelle took title. Really slick. Michelle could cover it up, she's the senior loan portfolio manager. When the time was right they could make a big killing."

"Actually, initially we used campaign funds. Patrick amassed a war chest from the religious right. Some drug lords also chipped in. You'd be surprised at how often those two groups want the same thing without ever knowing one another. We hadn't used the bank's money yet."

"You were going on with this scheme even after Michelle killed your brother?" Mags was incredulous.

"He was going to take us all down. He began to believe in his bogus campaign and what he was spouting. He got careless. Hell, he wanted to take his portion of the money to fund a *bigger* campaign. I could only hide so much as campaign contributions. He wouldn't listen to reason. He really would have taken us all down."

"You're down now, Norton," Lonnie said as the squad car skidded to a halt.

"Shit, shit, shit." Francie let fly.

The sleek dark blue 6 series was parked on a curb. No Michelle in sight.

They sat there.

"She can't be far," Lonnie posited.

"No. But she's got a gun and she'd hit us before we knew where she was. I have great faith in her ability to administer pain." Pete blew out his cheeks, then turned to Mags.

Before she could say anything Norton played his last card. "If I tell you where she is and I'm right, will you go easy on me? I'm not an accessory to a murder. All I did was illegally spend campaign funds. I might have had big plans but as you can see, they're not going to happen."

Pete nodded. "I'll do what I can but I can't do as much as a good lawyer."

"Don't throw the book at me. Really, all I did was hide and spend campaign funds."

"A great American tradition." Francie smirked. "Well, boys, what do I do, sit here as useless as a hooker who's found Jesus or do we do something?"

"I will do all I can, Norton, but if you don't tell us, she'll probably slip away." Pete reached across Mags and Baxter to shake Norton's hand.

"Go to 93356 Yolanda Street. Where you found Robert Dalrymple."

"Francie, don't hit the siren, and park a block away," Lonnie cautioned.

"You got an extra piece in here?" Pete leaned forward.

"Only my baton."

As they drove along, keeping to the speed limit as they were approaching Cracktown, Pete said, "For some reason, why I couldn't say, I'm always more frightened of a woman with a gun than a man."

"I'd be frightened of Michelle if she had only a dinner fork. She knows a lot of these houses," Norton warned.

"She knows which ones have basements, small half basements, attics, all that stuff. She traded information and told the guys making drugs which houses were safer than others. Where they could hide and where they should keep moving. She said all these houses were assets and she made a point of knowing the area. She traded this information for cash from the drug guys."

They reached the block before 93356 and parked the car.

"Mags, swear to God, you stay here," Pete commanded.

"All right, but take Baxter. He can smell her. He's a hound, remember, he'll follow his nose."

Pete dubiously looked at the intrepid animal.

Francie was out of the car, gun drawn. She handed Pete the baton and said, "She's got a point."

Pete, Lonnie, and Francie quietly walked toward the house in which Robert Dalrymple had been murdered.

Norton and Mags sat on opposite sides of the backseat, finally with enough room.

"Don't try to run, Norton. I'll catch you." Mags smiled as she said that.

"I won't, I came back. Well, I had to, really, she convinced me it was all right. And I believed her for a minute, until I saw her. Then I knew I was next. And if I didn't come back, she would have framed me for Patrick's murder." Tears welled in his eyes. "How can I face my mother?"

"I don't know."

Pete stood with Francie at the back door. Used properly the baton he held could be lethal but not as lethal as a gun. He'd have to get close.

Baxter sniffed the back door, wagged his tail, stood on his hind legs, and put his paws on Pete's knee.

Pete touched Francie's elbow, nodded at the door. She was in there.

Lonnie knocked on the front door. No answer, so he kicked it open, still standing to the side. With no gun, he hoped to divert Michelle so Francie could move in and get her.

As he did so, Pete and Francie flattened themselves to the side of the back door, out of sight.

Lonnie still didn't go inside. He heard a light footfall moving away from the front door. The houses had a similar floor plan, he hoped he knew the layout. Michelle had two places to protect herself and nail him if he stepped in.

He waited, sweat running down his back.

Pete and Francie waited, too. Baxter's keen ears pricked up. The little dog moved toward the back door.

Pete noticed, signaling Francie.

The door opened a crack. Michelle couldn't see the two officers, but she knew one officer wouldn't be out there alone. She stepped out, turned right, and fired, just missing Francie.

Baxter leapt forward, sinking his considerable fangs into her calf. Michelle hadn't seen Pete on her left who rushed up and clubbed her hard. The crack was loud. She went down, Baxter still hanging on to her leg.

Running through the house, Lonnie came up on Michelle.

Francie and Pete knelt over her.

"She's dead," Pete said. "And I'm off duty."

Francie handed Pete her gun, taking the baton from him. "I hit her," she declared. "We good?"

"Yeah," Lonnie agreed.

"Francie, they'll drag you through an inquiry," Pete half protested.

"And I'll be cleared. Do it my way."

* * *

Walking back from the parade, Bunny held CeCe's hand. Both he and Irene carried all the treats.

Coming in the opposite direction, slightly tight, walked a white man, fortyish. Irene couldn't hide but she ducked her head.

"Hey, don't act like you don't know me," he said swaying slightly on his feet, then he looked up at Bunny. "Best blow jobs in Reno, but you already know that." He affectionately tapped Irene on the shoulder as he walked away.

Bunny dropped CeCe's hand, turning to run after him and knock his teeth down his throat.

Irene slid to her knees, holding Bunny's knees. "I didn't know what to do. We had nothing to eat. I'm sorry. I'm so sorry."

Seeing her mother sob, CeCe put her arms around her. "Don't cry, Mommy. Don't cry."

Oblivious to the people walking around them, Bunny sank to his knees and held Irene. "It doesn't matter. I don't care. You're safe now."

Sunday's paper, May 1, carried an article about Officer Frances Shelton killing Michelle Speransky, a suspect in three murders, in the line of duty.

Norton cooperated, telling Pete and Lonnie that Robert Dalrymple and he had set up a corporation in the name of two old ladies: Robert's and Norton's maternal aunts. The old women readily signed the paperwork in exchange for five thousand dollars apiece. When the time was right, the corporation would buy the fore-closed houses for a song.

Knowing how a bank operated, Dalrymple was smarter than anyone thought and had figured out Mi-

chelle's plan. After getting in on the action though, Dalrymple decided he wanted a bigger cut, which proved fatal. It was easy for Michelle to lure him to an abandoned house in a neighborhood they hoped would become profitable. That same murderous strategy worked for Patrick, too. Norton didn't know how Michelle got Tu'Lia to go with her.

It had been the best school bus expo ever.

CHAPTER FORTY-SIX

A week had passed since the school bus parade. Congratulations rained on Howie for the affair. The car chase and the yellow bus leaving the route hurtling down the avenue was seen by some bystanders. All agreed it was the most exciting school bus parade yet. Howie accepted the accolades, but would smile and say he thought it might not be possible to guarantee a similar episode next year.

Howie had sent Tito back to Wings. He felt he prevailed long enough on Jeep's goodwill in using the young, strong worker on his ranch.

The sun setting behind the Peterson range cast a few long slanting rays between the ridges.

Jeep and Howie moved in from his back porch as the temperature always plummeted with the sun in the high desert.

Jeep noticed the tiny dust particles reflecting the last of the light as she carried in the salad bowl.

The two, dogs in attendance, had been gorging on Carlotta's chicken barbeque, not too spicy, not too bland, no one made it like Carlotta. Jeep threw together the salad once she arrived at Howie's and the two dear friends ate out on the porch for the temperature, then in the middle sixties, invited being semi-outdoors.

She set the big salad bowl on the table as Howie, gloves on, put the barbeque on a trivet. He then walked back out for their drinks—a whiskey sour for him, straight bourbon with a tonic water chaser, lime on the side, for Jeep.

King, ears forward, mouth slightly open in a smile, sat next to Jeep.

Baxter, allowed by Mags to go with his friends, observed this. *"She's not going to give you any."*

"Doesn't hurt to try." King never took his eyes off the barbeque.

Zippy, not as large as King, couldn't see the top of the table, but she could certainly smell the tantalizing aromas. Commercial dog food was okay, but nothing compared to food off the table.

Toothpick, happy to be in a kitchen, any kitchen, sat next to King.

Jeep felt King's breath on her thigh. "Move away a bit, buddy."

Doing as he was told, King grumbled, *"All I want is one big mouthful of Carlotta's barbeque."*

Zippy piped up. *"King, barbeque is sloppy. The only way we're going to get any is if they put it in bowls and from the way those two are shoving it in their mouths, I don't think so."*

Howie played with the stem on the cherry in his drink. "Ronnie made the best damn whiskey sours. I can't quite match it." He laughed. "I wouldn't drink a cocktail or mixed drink when I was young. Thought it was too girly. But one night to please her, I drank one of her whiskey sours. You know, they're really good."

"Soon it will be time for gin and tonics, vodka tonics. I'm not much for mixed drinks, either." She stopped to look at Howie with a devilish glint in her eye. "Too butch, you know, but I do love those gin and tonics in the summer."

Howie smiled. "Jeep, you're a beautiful woman. Always were, always will be. I don't care if sometimes you're more a man than I am."

They both laughed uproariously.

"You remember my sister, Catherine? She was the great beauty."

"In a different way, Mags's sister looks a lot like her. 'Course the dye job in the hair ruins it. Hear much from Catherine the Second?"

"No news is good news."

"Well, she hasn't made any more movies. I always go to Susie's to look for her."

Jeep put her fork down in feigned shock. "Howie Norris, you go to the sex shop? I am horrified."

He dropped his eyes, a little grin on his lips, then looked up at his oldest friend. "It's been a while since I've seen you there."

They laughed again.

"Hey, did I tell you the Japanese are making porn movies for older people? No joke. They're using good-looking golden oldies. Just think, Howie, new careers for us."

"I could never do it. I have such a good life here. That would just destroy my privacy. I mean, all those sixty-year-old-plus women knocking on my door."

"Of course, I forgot about that." She speared an artichoke heart in her salad.

After finishing their supper, as well as exhausting the endlessly fascinating subject of sex, the two, no room for dessert, did the dishes. She washed. He dried.

Jeep peered out the window over the sink. "Clouds coming in. Can't see the stars. I don't think it's going to rain. Hey, did I tell you I planted alfalfa, corn, strawberries—the list goes on—and I irrigated those thousand acres for the first time?"

"Big project."

"Yeah, it is, but I can't sit around."

"Jeep, when have you ever sat around? You've got the cattle, your business interests, and every now and then you roll that old plane out of the hangar and take 'er up."

"What's the point of sitting on your butt?"

"Don't know, but millions seem to do it."

"Howie, we ate so much—let's walk it off."

"Good idea. How about we check the fence line the boys repaired? So far the cattle have stayed in. They're putting on weight fast." He glanced down at Toothpick. "So is your rat terrier. He's a handsome thing."

As Howie got their coats, Jeep knelt down to pull on Toothpick's sweater. "It's colder than you think, squirt."

"Anyone ever tell you how fetching you look in turquoise?" Baxter teased the Manchester terrier.

"Anyone ever tell you your moustache droops every time you drink and you drop water all over the place?" Toothpick replied.

Once outside, the crisp air encouraged walking. Howie opened the gate near the house and they walked through the first lower pasture, then began the climb up the first low ridge.

"This is our chance to get them to the treasure," Zippy called out to her buddies.

"Let's do it." King's deep voice rang out.

As the two humans pushed up the low ridge the dogs pranced, twirled around, and called out encouragement.

"Somebody's got their knickers in a twist." Howie smiled, for he loved to see animals happy, especially Zippy.

"Come on." Zippy ran back and took his hand in her mouth.

Howie looked down at the bright eyes. "What do you want?"

Dropping his hand, Zippy stated simply, *"Follow me."*

King likewise encouraged Jeep.

"They know something we don't." She fell in with the dogs.

"Usually do." Howie stepped over a prominent rock. "Maybe I should have brought a flashlight but I like walking in the dark, then turning for the lights of home. Just feels so good."

"Does. Anyway, we can see a bit."

He added, "I've got a mess of coyotes out here but they haven't been much of a problem."

"Because I leave out treats." Zippy knew he didn't understand but she had to say it anyway.

"Good foraging right now." Jeep put her hand in her pocket, feeling the Glock she usually carried somewhere on her person or in her purse.

Jeep favored revolvers, but in the service she was issued a pistol to carry as a sidearm, easier to pack than a revolver, which required a true holster. A pistol she could jam in her flight jacket or even her belt. But she still carried a revolver when she rode her cow pony and there was one in the old World War II–issue Jeep. Jeep thought guns and rifles small works of art.

The two humans stopped, considered walking up toward the second ridge, but Zippy wouldn't have it. She blocked Howie, grabbed his hand again.

"She has a mission." Jeep laughed.

With patience, the dogs prodded, pulled, and bumped the two humans to the den. The female coyote had left it to go to a den higher up with Ruff.

King, eyebrows knitted together, pushed Jeep. *"Come on, Mom. Just a few more steps."*

Finally in front of the den, Zippy, voice calm and low, as though encouraging a puppy, said to Howie, *"Watch me."*

She wiggled into the opening.

"Me, too." Baxter followed while Toothpick stood at the entrance.

"All right, you guys. Come on out," Howie said.

Inside Zippy grumbled. *"He's so stupid!"*

"Is there anything we can take outside? They might get the message then," Baxter suggested.

They could smell the leather in the dark, smell the dried-out wood of the boxes.

The two tugged on a saddlebag but it wouldn't budge.

King, nose to the air, said, *"Lemons. I smell lemons."*

"Shit. It's him." Zippy shot out of the den as did Baxter.

"Who?" Toothpick asked.

"The man stealing this metal. The man who shot Daddy." Zippy looked toward where she knew the access road was but her eyes weren't that great. She could smell him coming, though.

High on the second ridge, Ruff with the mother and four pups, looked down at the dogs and two humans in the distance, and observed the lone young man coming up at the bottom of the ridge where the old den was. He had a pole with a hook on it strapped to his back.

"Watch out. He's climbing up!" Ruff called out in his clear, eerie voice.

"Make a racket." The house dogs began barking at King's command.

Howie's voice carried. "That's enough."

The thief heard Howie's voice, knew he was old, and figured he could easily dispose of him.

He spotted Howie on the ridge, perhaps one hundred and fifty yards away, but he didn't see Jeep. Running to get within firing range, he fired once.

The bullet passed over Howie's head.

The two humans dropped to the ground. The dogs, quietly, so as not to attract attention, filed down the side of the ridge out of the man's sightline. They intended to circle behind him.

On the high ridge, Ruff called out, *"He's moving up."*

Jeep reached in her pocket for her gun. "Howie, where's your gun?"

"Don't have it on me."

"Goddammit, I told you to carry a sidearm." Then she whispered, "You're as useless as tits on a boar hog." She crawled on her stomach to get behind the rock outcropping that housed the den.

Howie peeped over the rocks. "You could hit him now."

Voice soft, Jeep replied, "No. If he knows I'm armed, he might turn tail and run. This is the bastard that shot at you. We need to know who he is and hopefully bring him down."

Howie ducked back down. "Right."

"I could kill you for not carrying your gun, except he might kill you first."

Enlivened by danger, Howie grinned, "It's so nice to be wanted."

Jeep could hear him now, hear the roll of the stones under his boots. She picked up a baseball-sized rock and threw it over the den. He fired at it instantly. Pleased, for now she knew he was jumpy and impulsive, she waited coolly.

Howie started to pop his head up. Jeep tugged him down. The minutes ticked by from the sound of his footfall, clear now, Jeep figured he was maybe thirty yards away. He knew they were there for he had heard Jeep's voice when she said "Goddammit." If she jumped up, there was every chance he'd fire first. If she fired and missed, well, that was not a good thought.

Ruff sang out, *"Zippy, he's closing in."*

Zippy, hearing this, tore around the side of the low ridge, King right by her side, Baxter and Toothpick on their heels.

"Bark now!" Zippy hollered.

The four dogs growled furiously as they closed in on the man, turning now to meet these attackers, thinking all he had to do was pull the trigger on his long-barreled revolver then go forward to finish off Howie and Jeep.

Jeep stood up as the dogs barked. He turned to fire at the dogs, and that fast she got off three shots, each finding their mark. He went down with an *oomph*, crumpling on the pole and hook strapped to his back.

Zippy immediately pounced on him as King grabbed his gun hand, fangs sinking deep into the flesh. Baxter and Toothpick leapt onto him, too.

Jeep strode down to the figure. "Howie, it's safe. He's dead. Leave it," she ordered the dogs, rolling him over with her boot.

Howie, sliding down beside her, exclaimed, "Ben Huxley, the Bureau of Land Management agent. Thank God you had your gun, Jeep. I can't believe what a fool I was."

"I can." She smiled at him, relieved this was over.

Howie knelt down, feeling Ben's pockets. As he pulled out a map, he looked up at Jeep. "There'll be a big to-do now. You killed a man."

"This was self-defense."

"Cool as a cuke. Always were," he said admiringly to Jeep as he stood up with a map in his hand.

"I don't know about that, but I do know how the world really works. And if he were lying there groaning in pain, I'd put him out of his misery. He tried to kill one of my best friends. Life's not really that complicated. You take care of your own." She knelt down and patted each of the dogs. "They know that. If they hadn't distracted this joker, well, maybe we'd have gotten off unscathed and then again maybe we'd have some lead in us."

"I'll protect you, Mom, always and ever." King licked her hand.

Howie fished out a tiny keychain with an LED light on it, shining it on the map. "Jeep, he has this spot marked, this spot right here." He handed the map to Jeep as he followed Zippy to the den's entrance.

"*Zippy, thank God for you.*" It was dawning on Howie that his dog very well may have saved his life.

Zippy squeezed into the den, followed by Baxter and Toothpick.

Jeep, folding the map, watched Howie get down on all fours, butt in the air. She bit her tongue as a rude remark was on the tip of it.

Howie pinched the tiny keychain and saw what was in there. Rising, he handed her the little keychain. Kneeling down she saw the reflection of three pairs of eyes, then she saw the saddlebags, the wooden boxes. On some of the saddlebags the Sunrise brand was clear, others bore the double back-to-back *F*s for the Ford brothers.

"Sweet Jesus." She got back up. "The Garthwaite treasure. Some of that's mine." She laughed out loud. "And I owe you a heifer."

The two fell into each other's arms, laughing and crying.

Finally, Howie wiped his eyes. "You know what I'd really like?"

"Name it."

"Two things really. You have a photo of you and Ronnie moving cattle. I'd like a copy in a silver frame and"—he looked at the dogs, for the three in the den had wiggled out—"a silver-framed photo of our best friends."

"Yours." Then Jeep looked at the dogs. "I don't think you all want photographs but I bet we can make sure you get steak a couple of times a week."

"*Now they're talking sense.*" King sighed.

High on the ridge Ruff called out, echoed by his new mate and the puppies. "*Okay?*"

"*All's well,*" King answered in his basso profundo, then said to Zippy, "*Steak for them, too.*"

"*That will take some doing but I'll figure it out.*"

Gun back in her pocket, little keychain in Howie's, the two walked, skidded, down the low ridge arm in arm.

"And you're a rich man, Howie."

"And you're even richer, Jeep."

"Know something?" She pulled him closer. "Even when we were kids and our folks didn't have a pot to piss in, we were rich. We've always been rich. The money's just a bonus."

"Got that right." He stopped, kissed her on the cheek, then they picked their way home to the welcoming lights, remembered laughter and more laughter to come.

Dear Reader,

The statistics in this novel were current as of February 3, 2011.

Some of the technical information concerning our housing problems was removed by my editors. Their assessment was that you all didn't want to plow through all that, and I expect they were right. As it was, and this is true for most any novel, ninety percent of the research doesn't show up in the text. But one needs to study to reach the other ten percent, clarified like a broth, that does.

If you have a greater interest, I can point you toward some information. Look up MERS: Mortgage Electronic Registration System. MERS holds sixty-four million loans, and the issue is, can they foreclose or not? The Supreme Courts of Kansas, Arkansas, and Maine have ruled that MERS cannot foreclose on behalf of the banks because they are merely a placeholder and possess no authority. The banks created the MERS system to avoid paying recording fees.

A bellwether for you is when the number of homes and commercial properties on the market exceeds a six-month supply. Cities you might not think about like Jacksonville, Florida, are over that six-month supply period. For Las Vegas, God only knows. It's a disaster.

To learn more about economic ratios, you might take

a look at the February 24, 2011 issue of *Forbes* magazine, where Rich Karlgaard wrote an excellent column entitled "Wealth and Fitness Secret." It's simple and clear. There are also many books on the market trying to explain what has happened, why it happened, and when will it end. Most of these nonfiction books are quite well written. It's not like fighting your way through Adam Smith, Marx, Keynes, or Schumpeter, which I have done.

Good as these popular books are, the real problem is moral. It's not about complicated financial interests. When the drive for profit and power overwhelm the concern for the national good, we have a serious problem. Whether it's many of the people in the financial institutions or the people in government, all bear responsibility. It comes down to people and their decisions. It always does.

Which means it comes down to you and me. If we tolerate this, it will continue despite assurances to the contrary. If we don't, it won't.

Speaking of tolerance, God bless Cynthia Marsteller, vice president of the Marsteller Bradshaw Group. She patiently read this manuscript, made corrections, and helped me comprehend the financial meltdown. She is also a sister foxhunter and a good one, too. (We don't kill the fox. We just chase him. It's different here than in England for those of you recoiling at the thought that two women chase foxes while riding on beautiful horses.) Cindy refuses all compensation for a big job well done. I don't know what I am going to do to get even but I thank her and will continue to thank her.

Mark Catron, vice president and financial advisor of SunTrust Bank here in central Virginia, also endured discussions. A clarinet player in Charlotte for the North Carolina Philharmonic Orchestra, he now lives and foxhunts in Virginia. (You meet the most incredible people hunting.) He has the distinction of being First Shotgun for the Waynesboro Symphony Orchestra for his part in Johann Strauss's "Auf der Jagd." Incidentally, he is also the 2010 Canadian and Royal National Champion Road Horse to Bike. Actually, his horse, Cookie Monster, is the real champion, according to Cookie. As an aside, the first place ribbon at the Royal held in Toronto is red for the red of the Canadian flag.

Carol Lloyd of Reno was invaluable as my researcher. She fielded last-minute requests—some voiced with desperation—with uncommon good humor, plus she's really smart. Many thanks.

As always, the house dogs, the foxhounds, the bassets, even the horses with whom I share the best part of my life pitched in. The cats did not. They are appalled that there are no cats in this book.

May you be well and I hope you have some four-footed friends to make you laugh, to take you for walks.

Always and ever,

Rita Mae

Turn the page for an exciting preview of
Rita Mae Brown's next "Sister" Jane
foxhunting mystery

Fox Tracks

Available in paperback and eBook from Ballantine

Brilliant strings of moving rubies rolled away in the snow. At least that's how it looked to Jane Arnold, "Sister," as she peered out the window of her hotel room at The Pierre. The taillights of all those cars crawling down Manhattan's Fifth Avenue sparkled in the dark like rubies. When she was young, she would have seen parallel lines of headlights like diamonds coming toward her as well. Those days were long gone.

"Do you remember when the streets were two-way?" she asked her boyfriend, Gray Lorillard, who was carefully removing items from his Gladstone bag.

"Uh-huh."

"Do you think creating one-way streets in 1966 really made New York traffic move faster?"

"I do not," he answered this with conviction, his handsome brow furrowed as he once more reviewed his close items.

"Close" meant small clothing: undershirts, underwear, folded good shirts, and his Dopp kit, as well as a beautiful calfskin jewelry case although men never called it that.

"I don't think it helped, either," she said, turning from the view, "but there were fewer cars then."

"Fewer people," he mumbled, searching for something in his bag. "Goddammit."

"Is this male PMS I'm observing?" she asked, half smirking at him.

He rolled his eyes. "Men don't have mood swings."

At this, the elegant seventy-one-year-old woman with the incredible silver hair let out a whoop.

Younger by perhaps seven years, the year of his birth had a habit of sliding forward. Gray, taller than Sister who was six feet, brushed his steel gray military moustache while looking in the mirror above the desk. "Well, I don't have them—it's well known that I'm even keeled."

"Honey, you are smoking opium. You're a lot moodier than I am."

Looking at the beautiful woman who never made the slightest attempt to look younger than she was—perhaps one of the reasons she was so striking—Gray shrugged. "Janie, we're all moodier than you. I've never known such a cool customer."

"I don't know if that's compliment or an insult." She crossed the plush carpet and put her arm around his waist. "What's the problem here?"

"I'm missing one of my studs."

"Oh no, the chased gold fox head ones with the ruby eyes?"

"I know I put it in here. I did. You know how meticulous I am."

"I do." She bit her tongue because she wanted to say *and sometimes I wish you were not*. "Maybe it slid behind the lining. Your bag has some years on it."

"Buy the best. Then you only weep once." He sat on the side of the bed, taking a deep breath, "I am not going to panic."

She sat beside him. "Neither am I. Those were your Christmas present three years ago. I bought them from Marion at Horse Country." The proprietor had sneaked Jane the elegant studs when they'd driven up to buy tack for the staff.

As Master of the Jefferson Hunt, Sister and her joint-Master of three years, Dr. Walter Lungrun, were responsible for "the furnishings," as horse equipment was properly termed, as well as for the paid staff, which consisted of one huntsman and one whipper-in. Newly added to the payroll, Betty Franklin had served as an honorary, which means amateur, whipper-in for decades.

Betty and her husband faced tightened financial conditions thanks to the sinking economy and the fact that they owned a printing press. Few people patronized true presses anymore so after much discussion, Sister and Walter had worked out the necessary details to give Betty a salary of $25,000. The good woman wept at the offer, tried to refuse, but the two masters insisted. That $25,000 kept the wolf from the Franklins' door.

"Sugar, if you truly have lost it, I will buy you another," said Jane.

"I didn't," he insisted. "It has to be here."

"Go back over the last time you saw it."

"Did that." He rose, kissed her on the cheek, patted his chest pocket. "Dammit."

"Your language is going to Hell."

Her cursing as well made them both laugh.

"My mother would wash my mouth out with soap." He smiled at the memory of the formidable, late LuAnne Lorillard, a power in the African American community long before integration. Nobody messed with LuAnne without ample opportunity to repent later.

"Well, humor me," said Jane.

"All right. I was back home the last time I saw the studs. I went to my dresser after packing my clothing in this bag. I opened the top drawer, lifted out my personal case, carried it to the safe behind the painting that Daddy did, opened it and took out my studs. I opened the little green leather case, counted them, closed it and put it in my Gladstone bag."

"Why don't men say jewelry case?" Jane interrupted.

"How many years were you married? As I recall, it was twenty-eight. Did you ever ask Raymond?"

"No, but I didn't talk to Raymond as openly as I talk to you," she said.

"Really?" he asked, smiling, liking the compliment.

"Really. I loved him in my fashion, but it was a different time. Ray had a bombastic streak which meant he had a difficult time dealing with anything that didn't emanate from him."

"I lived in D.C. for most of your marriage, but Ray did not strike me as the sensitive or introspective type. How could you stand it?"

"I had a son, remember?" This was said in an upbeat tone. Any memory Sister recalled of her son, who died in a tractor accident in 1974, still brought her happiness.

She loved Raymond, Jr. beyond reason, but then doesn't every parent feel that way? Jane long ago came to terms with his death at age fourteen, growing determined to live each day with joy. Her son would have wanted that for her, not a lifetime of grieving and anger.

"It's not that I forget," Gray quickly replied. "It's only that I don't associate you with sorrows. You're a force of nature."

"You know, that may be the most wonderful thing you ever said to me. Now back to your studs."

"That's the chain of events until now." His hand went to his left pec again.

"Do I need to buy you a man bra?"

"No." He laughed. "I'm out of cigarettes."

"You can't smoke in hotel rooms anymore, at least not in this town. Actually, Gray, you can't smoke in public parks, the list goes on. If the mayor sees you smoking, he will assume you are a low-life, possibly a cheap criminal. It never occurs to these health nuts the damage they do to others."

"You mean the loss of jobs in our state, North Carolina, and Kentucky? Devastation."

"That, too, but I was thinking about the people who love laws that inhibit other people's choices. Is smoking a good thing to do? No. But those sanctimonious rulemakers live rather luxurious lives. They aren't working on an assembly line or in scorching sun outside. If your job is repetitive and boring or dangerous, sometimes that little hit of nicotine takes the edge off. The people that make the laws go get prescriptions for Prozac and how does anyone know the long-term effects of all that crap?"

He blinked as he hadn't heard her that impassioned in months, in fact, not since a person blundered and turned the fox back toward the hounds at a hunt in November. Fortunately, the fox escaped.

Sister and Gray, this January 27, had traveled from central Virginia to attend the Masters' Ball, an annual extravaganza under the aegis of the Master of Foxhounds Association of America. For forty years, Sister had attended the annual ball, always at the end of January. She loved to dance, loved to catch up with old friends scattered across the U.S. and Canada.

Over the last ten years, oftentimes when she spoke to city dwellers or suburbanites about foxhunting, she would notice the concern or distaste in their faces, so she invariably hastened to add that in the New World, foxes were chased, not killed. Usually, that opened up a torrent of quite intelligent questions and Sister would once again be reminded of how far most people lived from nature.

The last thing Jane Arnold ever wanted to do was kill a fox. She wouldn't mind dispatching a few humans, though, one of whom would be at this very ball. She wondered, could you kill a man with a butter knife?

Gray couldn't find a cigarette. "I am hooked and that's that." He came and sat down again, forlornly gazing into his opened Gladstone bag as though it would croak an answer concerning his stud. "I have stopped many times. Then pressure gets to me and I light up. I hate being controlled by an outside substance."

"I can't say that I understand. I don't have an addictive personality. I wish you could stop if only to suit yourself. However, smoking doesn't make you crazy, you don't lose your teeth like those pathetic meth people and it isn't illegal. And although you say you aren't moody, honey, there are times when I would happily shove a cigarette in your chiseled lips."

"You say."

"Look, you search for your stud. We have three hours until the Ball. I'll pop around the corner to Madison Avenue. As I recall, there's a beautiful little tobacco shop there that sells gorgeous small humidors, cigarette lighters, cases from as early as World War One and, of course, tobacco."

"It's snowing out there. I'll go."

"Gray, that stud is more important than a little snow on my nose. We hunt in weather worse than this."

"Yes, but you don't hunt in high heels."

"I'll start a fad. I've got my pull-on rain boots. My skirt is wool and my sweater is glorious cashmere. You look on your 'Droid to make sure it's still operating and I'll ring up the girls. They can come along to keep me company."

The girls were two young women, freshmen at Princeton, who hunted with Sister while attending an exclusive girls' school, Custis Hall, in central Virginia. They and quite a few other young women hunted with her for the duration of their secondary school education. Some of the faculty hunted, too, always swearing it made environmental studies more exciting for students.

Within minutes, Sister had rounded up one of the girls, Anne Harris who was called "Tootie." Using his phone, Gray verified the store was still in business.

"You can calculate minute by minute the national debt on that thing." Sister admired his toy, as she thought of it.

"If I do that, I won't enjoy the Ball."

As it turned out, none of them enjoyed the Ball for entirely different reasons than the national debt.

A gust of wind sent snow swirling around Sister and Tootie as they walked on a side street toward Madison Avenue.

"I think there have been only about three times in forty years that I've come to this ball and the weather hasn't been filthy. No wonder they stop hunting in New York State early. Genesee Valley stops when the river freezes, which has to be now."

Sister was telling Tootie about a hunt founded in 1876 by hard riding upstate New Yorkers, among them the Wadsworth family, who still led them.

"I'd love to go up there and hunt," said Tootie. "I can take a train up to Rochester and then rent a car to drive down to the Genesee Valley." Turning her head from the wind, the snow on her creamy café au lait skin added to her considerable beauty.

"Next year. I'll come with you. Watching Marion Thorne hunt hounds is always a treat. Then again she has good whippers-in. You know, that's the hardest position to fill."

"That's what you always told us." Tootie listened closely to everything the older woman had ever told her, as the gorgeous young woman loved hounds, horses, foxes, and Sister, herself.

Another gust of wet snow smacked them right in the face.

"Well, who needs skin abrasion up here?" said Sister. "Just go outside. You'll get a few layers peeled right off."

Tootie wrinkled her nose. "Sounds awful."

"Ah!" Sister stepped faster as the shop came into sight.

"Ladies." The owner rose from behind the store's counter when the two swept into the shop. "Welcome."

"We're glad to be here." Sister laughed, brushing off her snow-covered coat.

Adolfo Galdos, balding, pudgy, and sixty-ish, smiled broadly, "One must submit to the weather. That's what my dear Papa always said. He never could fathom how people endured this."

"Cuban?" Sister inquired.

"How did you know?"

"I've never met a proprietor of a tobacco shop from Barcelona." She smiled, but she had recognized the lilt in his voice.

"There you have it." He beamed anew. "For us, tobacco is gold, is art. Someday, and I hope I live to see it, we will return and once again, the finest cigar tobacco in the world will be available to you."

Tootie quietly studied the shop. Cigarette cases with sapphire clasps, lighters of perfect weight and simple design, sparkled alongside impossibly long cigarette holders.

Adolfo noticed the object of Tootie's scrutiny. "A Dunhill. 1938. That lighter will work as good as the day it was made."

Now also studying the display case herself, Sister murmured, "Beautiful. Oh, look at that."

He reached into the case, retrieving a heavy silver cigarette case with handwritten names incised. "This was given to a British officer by his surviving men." He flipped it open where it was gold inside, the officer's name, Cpt. Mitchell Markham, was inscribed therein.

Sister's hand flew to her heart. "What a tribute. My father fought in World War One. He never spoke of it, but I expect it affected him all his life and may be one of the reasons he married so late."

"Do we not ask impossible things of people?" Adolfo's beautiful green eyes met hers. "We left Cuba in 1959. My own father, who owned a tobacco plantation, saw there was no hope and left. Those who grew sugar also fled. Others, thinking the revolutionaries would not come for them, lost everything. Everything."

"This is called progress." Sister grimaced. "No one learns. It didn't work for the French in 1791 and it will never work, period."

Adolfo spoke to Tootie, delighted by her youth and femininity. "I hope, Senorita, that you will never encounter such foolishness."

Shyly, Tootie responded. "I hope so, too."

"Ladies, allow me to show you the humidor. The aroma alone is intoxicating." He stepped out from behind the counter, twirled one hand like a drum major, walked to the rear of the store, opened a glass door and the fragrance of various cigars, cigarettes, long cut pipe tobacco, filled the room. "After you."

The two entered the well-organized room. It was larger than it appeared from outside, looking at the glass door.

Closing the door behind him, Adolfo pulled a wooden box off the shelf. "I regret I cannot sell true Cuban cigars but this is made from seeds taken from Cuba and planted in the Dominican Republic. It's a very good cigar, sophisticated and mild." He handed one Monte-cristo to Tootie.

She held it, in the wrapper, under her nose. "It's al-most like perfume."

"A bit stronger. This one." Adolfo handed her a Plei-das. "Now this is a large cigar, a large gauge but such a cigar draws smoother, easier than the small ones you often see women smoking. Granted those may be more ladylike, but I think in any social gathering it is the women who set the tone. If *you* smoked a Churchill," he cited a monster gauge, "it would become the fashion."

"Well, I—."

"We'll take that," said Sister, "and while I'm here, a box of Tito's, if you have them. They're somewhat hard to find."

"Madam, I have them." Adolfo leaned down and slid a box off the bottom shelf. "Not one of the famous brands, but a cigar for a discerning individual. Yourself, perhaps?"

"No, my gentlemen friend. When he truly wants to relax, he smokes a cigar. When he's nervous, he smokes a cigarette."

Adolfo laughed. "Yes, well." Then he lowered his voice. "So much has changed. Tobacco additives. Well, there was always that, but if you bought a pack of, say, Dunhill regular, you knew they were made with the best leaf from the tobacco plant. Whether it's cigarette to-bacco or cigar, the upper leaves are most prized. The lower you go in price, the lower you go on the plant until you get to those discount brands—those are just chop." He squinted his eyes a moment, shaking his head. "How anyone can put one in their lips, I don't know. Smoking should be a ritual of pleasure."

"We have few true rituals of pleasure in this country. No siestas. No teatime. Other nations have a special part of the day to relax, recharge, give thanks. We do not."

"Well," Adolfo paused a moment. "I cannot criticize a nation which took us in as refugees where we flourished. It took some time but we have made our way, the Galdos family."

"Galdos?" Tootie's eyes opened wider. "Do you know the designer, Sophia Galdos?"

He broke into the biggest smile, "My middle child. My oldest is a vice president at Altria, my youngest is a lawyer."

"Then, painful as your exodus was, I am grateful you are here." Sister reached out and took his hand, squeezing slightly.

Tootie couldn't stop grinning. "I can't believe I've met Sophia Galdos's father."

"She gets her talent from me, of course," Adolfo joked.

Sister plucked two packs of Dunhill Menthols to put with the one Montecristo, one Pleidas, and the box of Tito's. "Ah, I think I must have that World War One cigarette case."

He bowed slightly, handed her the case as well as the small white card, good stock, with the price, $2,800.

Sister noted it. "This is good fortune. And each time I hold it, I'll remember my father and yours, too."

"I believe it will bring you good fortune." He wrote out the ticket for the items, carefully deducting 15% from the cigarette case which he then slid over to Sister for her approval.

"Mr. Galdos, you are very kind." Sister misted up.

She didn't know why she was getting emotional.

"To think of a beautiful woman with this case in her hands pleases me." Then he looked over at Tootie. "Two beautiful women."

Sister rooted around in her purse, pulled out the slender little cell phone, found her small wallet with only the credit cards, and handed over her Platinum American Express.

The transaction completed, the merchandise secure in a plastic bag, Adolfo came around the counter again and gallantly kissed both ladies on the hand.

"Go with God," he said and he meant it.

"And you, too," Sister replied and Tootie echoed her.

Out into the fray they charged. If anything, the storm had worsened.

"I bet Glados Senior nearly died when he suffered through his first New York blizzard," Sister said, head down.

"I got spoiled at Custis Hall." Tootie was born and raised in Chicago. "Princeton reminds me of why I love Virginia. Four seasons of equal length. No long winters. I have good professors but, Sister, I hate it. I want to be an equine vet. I don't need to go to Princeton, but Dad swears he will cut off the money if I don't finish."

"Princeton is one of the best universities in this country, honey. You can go to vet school after your undergraduate work. That gives you three more years, well, three and a half, to work on the parental units. I'm assuming your mother is in league with your father."

"I guess," Tootie responded with no enthusiasm.

After another big blast smacked them, Sister ducked into a doorway. The two women huddled there for a moment as Sister opened her bag, fishing for her cell phone.

"Oh no, I left my phone on the counter." She sighed. "You go on back to the hotel. No point in both of us being out in this."

"How can I ever dream of whipping-in if I can't take a little bad weather on foot? We can sprint."

They did, despite the slippery pavement.

Pushing the door open, they laughed to be out of the storm but they did not see Adolfo behind the counter.

"Maybe he's in the humidor room." Tootie shook the snow off her head, then passed the counter as she walked toward the large climate-controlled room. She turned slightly as Sister triumphantly spotted and retrieved her cell phone: right on the counter where she left it.

"Sister!" Tootie called, before running for the back of the counter.

The older woman followed Tootie, now kneeling down.

"Dear God." Sister exclaimed, for Adolfo Galdos lay on his back, beautiful green eyes staring straight up to Heaven. He'd been shot neatly between the eyes. On his chest lay a pack of American Smokes cigarettes.

Don't miss

A NOSE FOR JUSTICE,
the tail-wagging mystery that introduced
Jeep, Mags, Baxter, and King.

"A hotbed of mystery and suspense . . .
a humor-filled story that is loaded with quirky
but lovable characters."
—WICHITA FALLS *Times Record News*

and

It's Rita Mae Brown &
Sneaky Pie Brown's 20th anniversary!

Mary Minor "Harry" Haristeeen,
along with sleuthing cats Mrs. Murphy
and Pewter, corgi Tucker, and the other residents
of Crozet, Virginia, return in

THE BIG CAT NAP,
a Mrs. Murphy mystery

Available now.